UNSEEN TERROR

The sound rose and fell in an echoing, drawn-out ululation, not like any animal sound she had ever heard. Laura wanted to clap her hands over her ears and blot it out. But she couldn't move.

As the wail died away, Laura realized that the crickets had stopped chirping. In the awful, absolute silence that followed, she could hear the dry thumping of her heart.

She gripped the windowsill, straining her eyes to see out into the darkness, half-afraid of what she might see. The shadows were so close, the darkness so impenetrable, that the woods seemed to be pressing in on her, weaving their thick, twisted branches around the house, closing out the air with their pungent leaves. The stillness was unnatural, intense, as though every living creature had ceased to exist except the two trapped inside this house . . . and one other, out there. Somewhere.

THE BEST IN BONE CHILLING TERROR
FROM PINNACLE BOOKS!

Blood-curdling new blockbusters by horror's premier masters of the macabre! Heart-stopping tales of terror by the most exciting new names in fright fiction! Pinnacle's the place where sensational shivers live!

FEAST (103-7, $4.50)

by Graham Masterton

Le Reposir in the quiet little town of Allen's Corners wasn't interested in restaurant critic Charlie McLean's patronage. But Charlie's son, Martin, with his tender youth, was just what the secluded New England eatery had in mind!
"THE LIVING INHERITOR TO THE REALM OF EDGAR ALLEN POE"
— *SAN FRANCISCO CHRONICLE*

LIFEBLOOD (110-X, $3.95)

by Lee Duigon

The yuppie bedroom community of Millboro, New Jersey is just the place for Dr. Winslow Emerson. For Emerson is no ordinary doctor, but a creature of terrifying legend with a hideous hunger . . . And Millboro is the perfect feeding ground!

GHOULS (119-3, $3.95)

by Edward Lee

The terrified residents of Tylersville, Maryland, have been blaming psychopaths, werewolves and vampires for the tidal wave of horror and death that has deluged their town. But policeman Kurt Morris is about to uncover the truth . . . and the truth is much, much worse!

Available wherever paperbacks are sold, or order direct from the Publisher. Send cover price plus 50¢ per copy for mailing and handling to Pinnacle Books, Dept. 519, 475 Park Avenue South, New York, N.Y. 10016. Residents of New York, New Jersey and Pennsylvania must include sales tax. DO NOT SEND CASH.

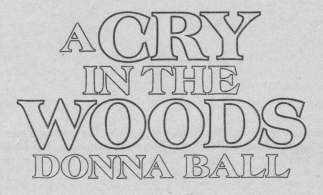

A CRY IN THE WOODS

DONNA BALL

D0002079

PINNACLE BOOKS
WINDSOR PUBLISHING CORP.

PINNACLE BOOKS

are published by

Windsor Publishing Corp.
475 Park Avenue South
New York, NY 10016

First printing: August, 1991

Printed in the United States of America

Chapter One

Laura Kane was dreaming about frogs. It was a silly dream, halfway between a cartoon and a television commercial, and as the morning sun brightened the screen of her eyes and the dream faded into fog, she remembered little about it except the impression of a bunch of comical amphibians splashing around in what appeared to be a child's wading pool. It was a relief to dream, for once, something that could not possibly have a Freudian interpretation.

She turned her head and squinted at the numbers on the travel alarm clock beside the bed. 6:15. She could legitimately sleep another hour, have a leisurely breakfast, and still arrive at the new house before the movers were due. But she was as excited as a child on the first day of school and she couldn't go back to sleep.

She would have driven straight through if it hadn't been for Christy. Her daughter was an exceptionally bright and entertaining five-year-old, but she was a five-year-old nonetheless, and twelve hours in a car listening to the theme song from *The Smurfs* was more than any rational adult should try to put herself through. They had left Philadelphia yesterday morning, picknicked in the Shenandoah Valley, and reached the outskirts of the Great Smoky National Park by

5

dark. They had made frequent stops, and both had been too excited by the adventure to feel the fatigue. Still, Laura knew she had pushed it, and her driving muscles were protesting this morning. Christy hadn't even napped yesterday. She should let her sleep.

But only two and a half hours more would bring them to Calumit Heights.

Laura turned over carefully, trying not to wake Christy, and smiled at her daughter's sleeping face. She had booked a room with two beds, but what child would sleep by herself in a strange motel when her mother's bed was only a few feet away?

Christy slept with her lips parted, her baby-fine blond hair scattered over her cheek, her hand curled around the pillow. Sometimes Laura still marveled at how something so perfect could have come from her. She was a woman who was justifiably proud of her accomplishments and never failed to congratulate herself on what she had achieved, but this was different. This—the fragile miracle of warmth and innocence that slept beside her—was almost more than she deserved, and even after five years of watching her grow and thrive, Laura never ceased to be a little awed by the fact that Christy was hers.

Christy opened her eyes, smiled sleepily, and said, "Weren't the frogs funny, Mommy?"

Laura pushed a strand of pale hair away from her daughter's eyes, smiling back. "What frogs, sweetie?"

"The ones in the swimming pool."

For a moment Laura didn't understand. Then she felt the familiar thrill of wonder and amazement that always accompanied such moments. It was nothing extraordinary, just flashes they sometimes shared, bits of dreams, snatches of thoughts, little more than an extension of the mother-daughter bond that had begun in the womb, yet it always delighted her.

She laughed and rubbed her nose against her daughter's, Eskimo style. "Silly girl, giving your mommy your dreams."

But Christy had little time for such nonsense. She wriggled away and scrambled out of the covers. "Are we going to the house today, Mommy? Are we going to the mountain? Can I have pancakes for breakfast?"

They had pancakes for breakfast in the just-opened restaurant downstairs, and by seven-thirty were on the highway again. It was a crystalline morning that felt more like early September than June, with just enough of a chill in the air to be invigorating. She mentally added another item to her list of advantages the mountains had over city life: a healthier climate.

Christy tried, as she had yesterday, to persuade her mother to let her sit on the floor of the back of the van, where the cartons and suitcases made a perfect playhouse, and once again she met with a firm refusal. After two more attempts to convince her mother to allow her to climb in back "just for a minute," to retrieve a toy well-placed at the bottom of a box or check to make sure she hadn't forgotten to pack her pajamas, she lost interest and settled down, securely belted in the front seat, to watch for cows. The van was packed to capacity with things Laura didn't want to trust to the movers: her P.C., the contents of four file drawers, the Waterford she had bought in a duty-free shop in London, two boxes of Christy's favorite toys, both hers and Christy's entire summer wardrobe, a box of photo albums and personal mementos she considered irreplaceable. She supposed it was a sign of some kind of character flaw that she refused to trust the professionals with the job they were hired to do, but she liked the security of having her things with her.

Her partners, Ben and Hilly, had been appalled when she had traded her BMW for the four-wheel-drive mini-van, but then everything about this move had dismayed them. Laura supposed that the act of exchanging the city car for the country van had been the thing that had finally convinced them of what they had been refusing to accept all these months: that she was serious.

When the architectural firm of Kane, Hildebrand, and Rodgers had been approached about the Calumit Heights development project, Laura had been intrigued. The more she worked on it, the more it began to look like paradise to her. Curving halfway around an almost-forgotten mountain in the heart of the Smoky Mountains near the North Carolina-Tennessee border, Calumit Heights was a planned community that would eventually include upper-, middle-, and lower-middle-income homes, along with shopping centers, restaurants, and other service facilities to support them. An airfield was already in operation which accommodated not only private planes but daily commuter flights to Washington and Atlanta. Barely two years into development, the project was still in its fledgling stage. Only a handful of the homes were ready for occupancy, most of those belonging to people who had had the good fortune to get in on the ground floor and choose the prime lots; the country club was six months away from completion, and the lake was still being filled. But the golf course was green and ready for play, and the private school would open with grades one through three in the fall.

When Laura had bought her Calumit Heights property, Hilly had commented that it was a good investment, and Ben had jokingly suggested that, as much time as she was spending on the site, she might as well put up a tent and save herself the travel time. While she was designing her house the other two offered helpful suggestions, and never for a moment believed she would actually build it. When the house was finished they started to worry, but it wasn't until last week, when she began to pack up her office, that they finally realized she actually intended to leave.

"It's not like you're moving to the suburbs, you know!" Ben exclaimed. "It's not like you have an hour commute to the office! We're talking wilderness here, outback, the goddamn ends of the earth! What do you think you're going to do with yourself out there in the middle of nowhere? And you know something else? I checked. There's not a Pizza Hut or a McDonald's within forty miles! What do you think about that?"

"I think," replied Laura, edging him out of her way with a box half-full of file folders, "that I'll finally be able to do something about my cholesterol."

"It's not like you were just *moving*," Hilly insisted, a worried frown marring a face that was still cherubic at nearly forty years of age. "I mean, moving is one thing, but you've got a business to think of here. You can't just walk out on everything we've built—"

That was one argument with which Laura had no patience. Since Christy's birth she had cut down on the traveling and done most of her work out of her home or with Christy perched on her lap; her partners knew how to adapt. "You know how to use a fax machine, don't you?" she replied, exasperated. "So use it. Even the wilderness has electricity, and telephones too, I wouldn't be surprised. Look, guys," she said, trying to muster up a little sympathy—despite the fact that she had given them the same reassurance speech at least a dozen times over the past six months. "I told you before—we're still partners, I'll still hold up my end of the business. I'll check in with you every day. We'll be in touch over the computer or by fax. I'll come back to town as often as you need me. It won't be all that different than the way we've been working the last few years anyway. The only thing that will change is that you won't be seeing my smiling face every day."

"And we won't be dropping by your place for coffee at midnight," Hilly said glumly, "or making Christy a pallet in the corner of the office while we meet with some out-of-town client."

And Ben muttered, "Maybe we like seeing your smiling face every day."

That was when Laura felt the first sting of tears, and she busied herself scooping things out of her desk drawers, not even bothering to sort them — lint-covered coins, snippets of elastic, old ticket stubs, market receipts, scribbled phone numbers without names — the flotsam and jetsam of ten years of her life were swept unceremoniously into a cardboard box, but the real heart of those years was not so easy to dispose of. Hilly and Ben were more than her partners. They were her family, and she was going to miss them, more than she could think about then . . . more, perhaps, than she would be able to think about for a long time.

Then Hilly said quietly, "You're really going to do this, aren't you? You're determined to do this."

"Come on, guys, we've talked about this all before. Who wants to raise a child in the city? Christy deserves clean air and a good neighborhood and a yard of her own to play in. She deserves to be able to keep a bike for more than two months before it's ripped off, and to walk to school without having her lunch money stolen by some junkie. She needs someplace clean and good and *safe*."

Christy was their weakness. They wouldn't argue with her about Christy. But they both knew this had very little to do with Christy.

The two men looked at her soberly for a moment, and Laura found herself once again searching to stay busier than she needed to be, refusing to meet their eyes.

Then Ben said, "Bad things can happen anywhere, Laurie. Don't think running away is going to make you safe."

Laura removed a thumbtack from the crayon drawing on her bulletin board, placed the paper inside the carton, and calmly closed the lid. "I'm not running away," she said, and she looked at Ben. "Don't you see? I'm running *toward* something—a better life for me and Christy. There's a difference."

After a long moment Ben smiled, though she had a feeling her words had sounded no more convincing to him than they had to her. "Well, then," he said, and hugged her shoulders awkwardly with one arm. "I hope you find it. But I still think you're going to be sorry the first time you pick up the phone and try to order a pizza."

Nodding against the back window of the van was the potted plant Hilly had brought over as a farewell/housewarming gift the morning they left. The remnants of a two-day-old pizza, Ben's parting gift to her, were carefully wrapped and stored in the cooler. Remembering the way they had looked that morning, trying too hard to be cheerful and talking too much, caused something to clutch at Laura's throat and she tightened her hands on the steering wheel. She *was* doing the right thing. People grew up, they moved on; change was a natural part of life and not the end of the world.

But God, she was going to miss them.

Christy spoke up suddenly. "Don't worry, Mommy. Uncle Hilly promised to come see us, and he's going to bring Uncle Ben even if he *is* afraid of airplanes."

Laura's laugh was a little choked as she reached over and tugged her daughter's blond pigtail. "You betcha.

And won't they be surprised when they see the great big guest room we've got for them? With real beds and everything."

"And a swimming pool!"

"And a fish pond!"

"And a gym set!"

For a while they entertained themselves by talking about the house, every detail of which Christy had memorized from her mother's description and the Polaroids Laura had taken on each one of her visits, and the melancholy dispersed into the more familiar, and much more welcome, excitement. She deserved this. She had worked hard for it, she could afford it, and she was going to enjoy it. Sure, changes were hard. It was only natural to feel a few regrets—or a lot—for the life she was leaving behind. But this was a good thing she was doing. She was sure of it.

The highway on which they were traveling gave way to mountainous country roads sparsely dotted by neat clapboard farmhouses and roadside stands. Laura slid the soundtrack to *Cats* in the cassette player, and Christy bounced her head and sang along with the "Jellicle Songs." That, of course, was one advantage to living in the city. Not every child got to see a Broadway show before she had seen *Bambi*.

The road curved higher and the blue haze of the mountains grew nearer. The little towns through which they passed, with names like Heaven and Dogwood and Almost, grew smaller and further apart. Christy counted fifteen cows and four goats. Breathtaking views of mountain gorges caused Laura to slow the car to a mere crawl, and Christy twisted around against her seat belt, exclaiming excitedly over horses grazing on hillsides and sheep bunched beneath chestnut trees.

As they turned onto the even narrower, two-lane road that led to Calumit, Laura's ears began to pop, signaling the change in altitude. She sent Christy searching through the map compartment for chewing gum — a treat that was almost as rare as pancakes for breakfast — and that forestalled the "Are we almost there?" questions for a good ten minutes.

Calumit was a town that owed its birth to the nearby mineral springs which had drawn wealthy travelers in the nineteenth century, and its subsistence to a small but healthy tourist industry and a shoe factory five miles south of town. The town itself boasted three stoplights, a Baptist church, and a string of shops, most of which had been in operation since the 1880's. While Laura was visiting, she had stayed in each of the three charming bed-and-breakfast inns, and she had become inundated with the wholesome, almost exhilarating innocence of the town. Doors went unlocked here, people hailed each other on the streets and stopped to chat. Laura had read about places like this, but had never believed they really existed. It was a good place to raise a child.

Until Calumit Heights established its own fire department and medical center, the residents of the exclusive mountainside community would be greatly dependent on the county — and the painfully inadequate town of Calumit — for those services. That had bothered Laura at first, but Calumit Heights was carefully planned to grow as need demanded. Until then, there were two well-established medical practices in Calumit, and the county supported an emergency services team which, she had been assured, could respond to a call from the Heights in less than twenty minutes. A lot could happen in twenty minutes, of course, but it was still better service than she could expect in the city, where Hilly had once waited three and a half hours for police to respond to a burglary call.

Stopped at the red light just before the left turn that

would take her out of town, Laura drew a deep breath and released it slowly. "Look, Christy," she said, "there's our mountain."

Big and round and green-blue, it sloped sharply upwards and blotted out the horizon directly before them, almost filling up the sky. They were at the only place, Laura knew from experience, where this particular vista could be seen, and she wanted Christy to experience the wonder of it the same way she had the first time she'd seen it.

Christy was impressed into silence for a full five seconds. Then she said in a small, awed voice, "It looks scary. Are we going to fall off?"

Laura laughed and made her turn as the light changed, explaining to Christy why the mountain seemed to disappear as they climbed it. Still, Christy was noticeably subdued as they began the climb up the newly paved road, her eyes wide as they examined the thick shadowed woods that crowded either side of the van.

After two miles the climb became steep enough for Laura to shift into second gear. The tape had played out, and she inserted another. She had forgotten how quiet it was up here, and how isolated. The stillness was something she might have more trouble getting used to than she had expected.

She breathed an almost audible sigh of relief when the road began to widen and the security gate, surrounded by its generous tarmac turnaround, came into view. No sign announced their arrival nor welcomed them to Calumit Heights, nor was one planned; the development was far too tasteful and exclusive for that. The small cedar-shingled building with its card-operated electric gate was enough to insure trespassers they had gone too far, and to let visitors know they had gone far enough. To Laura it meant she was home.

She pulled up close to the gate booth and lowered the window, a little ashamed of the comfort she felt at the sight of a familiar face waving back to her from behind the enclosure. If she wasn't careful, she'd be proving Ben right about her ability to cope with what he called wilderness living.

Joe McCallough, who'd been working security for the project from the first day ground was broken, slid open his own window and smiled broadly. "Good morning, Miss Kane. Moving day, is it?"

"Hi, Joe. Yes, it's finally here."

"Hard trip?" As he spoke, he was gathering up some papers and making a notation on a clipboard. The security program, at this point in the development, was not as elaborate as it would one day be, but it was more than adequate for their needs.

Christy wriggled out of her seat belt and knelt on the seat, craning her neck to peer through her mother's window. "Hi, Joe!" she piped up.

"It's Mr. McCallough," Laura admonished, and Joe laughed.

"Well, aren't you a cute one?" He winked at Christy. "You come see me sometime when your mama says it's okay, you hear? I've got two granddaughters about your age."

He passed the papers through the window to Laura. "Here's your gate card, and some forms the company wants you to fill out about visitors and such. What moving company are you using?"

She told him, and he nodded. "I'll keep an eye out for them. They got your telephone put in last week, so if you need anything when you get up to the house, just give me a call."

Laura was still smiling as she put the car into gear and left the gate. The smile turned into a laugh of pure pleasure, and she impulsively reached across the seat and hugged her daughter with her free arm. "Isn't this great, honey? Aren't we going to love it here?" And then, automatically scolding; "What are you doing with your seat belt off? You know the rules."

"But we're home!"

At a look from her mother, Christy quickly refastened her seat belt and settled down — or at least she settled down as much as an excited five-year-old could be expected to at the end of a long journey — and turned her face to the window, looking for their new house.

The sounds of hammers and bulldozers were familiar sounds of civilization, and even more welcome to Laura because she knew she would not be able to hear them once they reached her house. Construction in that part of the neighborhood had long since been completed.

Laura was certain there was some kind of anthropological or sociological significance to the fact that the most expensive homes, and therefore the first to be built, were toward the top of the project, and the first five miles of the winding, laboriously climbing road that led away from the security gate were deserted. Even after she reached the developed area, the houses were so well-designed to blend into the environment that few, if any, signs of population were evident. Each home was located on a lot of no less than two acres, and none was visible from the street or from its neighbors. She made a game out of having Christy count mailboxes, but even those were few and far between.

At last she turned off the feeder street and onto a blacktop drive that curved around a long, steep hill. At the top of that hill, screened by giant mountain laurel and towering oaks, was her house.

Laura repeatedly congratulated herself on the fact that, while her house might not be the largest or the most ostentatious in the project — that honor had gone to Hugh Bullard, one of the developers—she had certainly chosen the best lot. From the front of the house, all along the winding drive to the street, the natural integrity of the wooded area had been maintained; when it had been necessary to remove a tree, a wild azalea or domesticated shrub had been planted in its stead. The undergrowth had been cleared out and a brook had been diverted to form a small waterfall, but for the most part the environment was as pure and as untouched as nature had intended it. The back of the house faced a natural glade that was almost half an acre, and there Laura had designed a swimming pool whose flagstone terraces, boulders, and cascading plants made it look like a mountain lake. The lot backed up against a national forest, and on three sides was surrounded by several thousand acres of heavily forested mountainside, guaranteeing that, no matter what the fate of the rest of the community, her lot would remain unmolested and her privacy insured in perpetuity.

The house itself, conforming to the standards set forth by the project, blended into the environment so naturally that it almost seemed a part of it. Its three-storied, glass- and wood-siding facade took its inspiration from the rolling mountains that surrounded it and made use of curves, rather than angles, so that from the outside it appeared almost perfectly round. It wasn't, of course; it climbed the slope of the hillside in terraces and gentle abutments, taking full advantage of the view from every room with floor-to-ceiling windows. There were three bedrooms and four baths, an office on the lower level, an attached garage, and three curving decks. There were no indoor pools, high-tech exercise rooms, gourmet kitchens, or whirlpool baths lined with imported Italian marble. Those amenities Laura had been more than happy to include in her other clients' designs, but for herself she wanted function, simplicity, and elegance. This was her dream house, and for a long time after she had parked the van and turned off the engine she simply sat there, smiling, looking at it.

Not so with Christy, however. She was out of the van almost before the engine had stopped running, scrambling up the front steps, peering through the stained-glass double front doors, down the steps again, around the side of the house, exclaiming over the swimming pool and the custom-built wooden gym set with its swings and climbing ropes and tunnels, back to the front of the house to ask why there were no goldfish in the ponds, and up the front steps again. By that time Laura had her keys out and, laughing, she followed her daughter up the steps and unlocked the door.

Christy raced back and forth, squealing with delight at the footprints her Keds left in the plush carpet, while Laura, grinning like a kid on Christmas morning, inhaled the aroma of fresh paint and new carpeting and absorbed the spacious beauty of vaulted ceilings and muted sunlight drifting through high windows. Home. It was beautiful. It was perfect. It was hers.

She caught Christy's hand and took her on a tour of the house, from the ground-floor office, through the first-floor living, dining, and play areas, to the third-floor bedrooms, making a mental note that one of the first new rules would have to be no running on the stairs. Christy heartily approved of the Care-Bear wallpaper in her room — as well she should, as she had picked it out herself after only three days of searching every wallpaper, paint, and decorating store in Philadelphia — and was particularly taken with the sunken tub in her mother's bathroom. They ended up on the deck outside Laura's bedroom, looking out over the backyard and the swimming pool.

Laura picked Christy up and rested her on her hip, for although the deck was only four feet off the ground

18

on this side of the house, Christy was too short to see over the rail. "Now," Laura said seriously, "I want you to promise me two things."

"Two things," Christy repeated, listening intently.

Laura smiled. "First, that you'll never go in the swimming pool unless somebody is with you." Christy was a good swimmer—she had been taking lessons at the Y since baby classes at six months of age—but there was no parent alive who did not have nightmares about children and swimming pools.

"Oh, Mommy," Christy said disdainfully, "I learned that at swimming class!"

"Good for you. And number two—don't go into the woods. There are no trails or roads up there, nothing but miles and miles of trees, and it would be real easy for a little girl to get lost. It would be easy for a grown person to get lost. So always stay where you can see the house."

Christy turned her head toward the woods and regarded them soberly for a long moment. Then she said, in a very subdued tone, "I don't like the woods. There's bad things in the woods."

Laura hadn't intended to frighten the girl, and she didn't like the way her small brow puckered with a frown. She gave Christy a little squeeze. "What kind of bad things, honey? Who told you that?"

She shrugged. "The big bad wolf lives there. And trolls. And monsters."

One corner of Laura's lips turned down wryly. "I see Uncle Ben has been at Grimm's fairy tales again," she murmured. "Listen, sweetie. Those are just fairy tales. No bad things live in the woods—just God's creatures, like you and me. There's nothing to be scared of."

"I don't like the woods," Christy repeated firmly, and wrapped her arms around her mother's neck.

Concerned, Laura opened her mouth to explain fur-

19

ther, but was interrupted by the blast of a horn from the front of the house. Christy, her anxiety completely forgotten, wriggled down and ran to the front door, shouting excitedly, "They're here! They're here!"

For perhaps the first time in the history of moves everywhere, the movers were early.

Chapter Two

At six o'clock that evening Laura sat in the middle of the living room floor, surrounded by half-emptied cartons and piles of crumpled newsprint, tired, sweaty, and a great deal less enthusiastic than she had been when the day began. She had followed the suggestions in the mover's manual: the kitchen first, then the bedrooms. She had put Christy to work unpacking her own room, though she suspected there was a great deal more playing than unpacking going on. She was just trying to decide whether to finish unpacking the books, start carrying out some of the trash, or go into town and try to find something for dinner, when the doorbell rang.

Christy came clattering down the stairs, shouting, "Uncle Hilly! Uncle Hilly!"

"No running on the stairs!" Laura called, wading through newsprint and making a futile effort to smooth back her hair as she made her way toward the door.

It was not Uncle Hilly. The man standing at the door was tall, silver-haired, and fairly good-looking in an overly polished way. He grinned and held up a bottle of wine decorated with a big red bow.

"Why — Mr. Bullard." Laura pushed at her straying hair again and left another smudge of newsprint across her cheek. "What a surprise."

"We came to welcome you to the neighborhood," he announced. "And now that we're neighbors I think we can be on a first-name basis, don't you? You remember my wife, Isabel?"

Isabel Bullard was a trim woman with a no-nonsense manner and a firm handshake that was every bit as efficient as the short, utilitarian cut of her salt-and-pepper hair. But her voice was warm and her eyes twinkling with good humor. "Hi, Laura. And don't let that business about welcome to the neighborhood fool you. You've got to know we've all been champing at the bit to see what kind of house the head architect designed for herself."

Isabel stepped inside, her husband thrust the bottle of wine into Laura's hand, and Christy said, disappointed, "You're not Uncle Hilly!"

"No, darling, this is Mr. and Mrs. Bullard. Say hello, and then run out to the kitchen and see if you can find where Mommy put the glasses."

"Isn't she sweet?" Isabel gave Christy a cursory smile and turned back to Laura. "But no, that wine is for later, and from the looks of this place you're going to need it. We came with an invitation for dinner, but first you've got to show me around."

"I told her you'd be too busy for company," Hugh complained, following his wife inside and casting a critical, appreciative eye over the interior.

"But not too busy for dinner," Laura said, "if you're serious about that invitation. I haven't had a chance to go to the store and the cupboards are bare."

"Everyone forgets food on moving day," Isabel said. "That's what neighbors are for. I bet you forgot paper towels and soap too. . . . Goodness, you're not doing this all by yourself, are you?"

"I told you she wasn't married," Hugh pointed out.

"But I thought you'd have someone helping you out."

22

"I helped," Christy piped up.

"You sure did, honey." Laura rested a hand affectionately on her daughter's head. "To tell the truth, she added to Isabel, "I've found that people who try to help on moving day only get in the way."

"My sentiments exactly," Isabel agreed briskly. "Find your own system and stick to it. But we are going to feed you — a few of the neighbors are coming over for a barbecue and you'll want to meet all of them. Now, show us around so we can all gossip about your house over hamburgers."

Laura laughed and gestured the way through the rubble toward the stairs. She had never cared much for Hugh Bullard, but she thought she could come to like his wife.

Isabel was appropriately appreciative of the use of light and space, and Hugh was silently smug that his house remained the showplace of the neighborhood, but Laura received her own gratification as Hugh looked enviously over her back lot. "Damn good investment, this one," he commented. "Makes me wish now I'd kept it for myself. Of course, you'll want to fence it all in."

"Fence it in? Why would I want to ruin this great view?"

Hugh shrugged. "Oh, we've had some trouble with bears this summer. Seems like the drought is pushing them down out of the mountains right through those woods."

"Bears!" Laura cast a quick, alarmed glance around for Christy, but the child had long since grown bored with grown-up talk and had gone back to her new room.

"Bears, my ass." Isabel Bullard gave her husband a dry look. "This man wouldn't know a bear from a raccoon, and if you ask me, the only things that are alive

23

in those woods are a few scrawny squirrels and hedge-hogs anyway. At least that's all *I've* ever seen."

"Well, Sam Keller says—"

"When Sam Keller comes home with a bear strapped to the front of his pickup truck, then I'll believe it. Sam is the local sheriff," Isabel explained to Laura, "and I have a feeling he gets his kicks out of teasing us city slickers." Isabel slipped her arm companionably through Laura's, tactfully turning her away from the deck and just as deftly changing the subject. "He's nice, though. All the locals go out of their way to be friendly—as well they should, considering what we're doing for the economy of this godforsaken little back-water."

With only one last uneasy look toward the shadowy woods that surrounded the house, Laura followed Isa-bel's lead. "So how do you like living here so far? Aside from the bears, of course."

"Oh, we're turning into real country squires. Plant-ing begonias, laying up firewood . . . if you don't think about how far away from civilization you are it's really kind of nice. Of course, if I don't get into Lord and Tay-lor's pretty soon I'm going to start going through seri-ous withdrawal, not to mention what a person's supposed to do for a hairdresser around here." She shrugged. "Trade-offs, I suppose. Of course, Hugh is on the road all the time, and I try to take the plane into Washington once or twice a month, just to keep in touch with real life. But it's a great place to raise a fam-ily."

"Speaking of which," Hugh interjected, "Scott should have that barbecue fired up by now. We'd better get back before he tries to cook something."

"Scott's our son," Isabel explained. "Fortunately, he's already raised. But there are already several families with children your little girl's age, and more moving in before school starts. You'll meet some of them tonight."

"It'll just take me a minute to change," Laura said.

Isabel waved a dismissing hand. "Don't be silly, nobody changes for dinner around here. Besides, if you're anything like I was on moving day, it'll take you a half hour to find your closet."

Laura glanced at Isabel's spotless tennis whites, then down at her own cut-off shorts and T-shirt. "Are you sure?"

"Just wash your face and hands and you'll be fine. Where's that little Christy? I'll bet she could use some help tying her shoes. It's been a while, but I think I could manage that."

Laura willingly allowed Isabel to take charge while she hurried to run a comb through her hair and scrubbed the newsprint off her face. Bears notwithstanding, she had a feeling she was going to like it here. A lot.

Scott Bullard was seventeen years old—or at least he would be, in two months—and as far as he was concerned he was far too old to be spending the summer with his parents. It wasn't that they were bad folks, for parents; mostly they stayed out of his way, and there was something to be said for having carte blanche with his dad's Porsche for the summer. But what good was a Porsche when there was no place to drive it? And who wanted to spend the summer in the back hills of Tennessee when he could have been in Switzerland, cycling through the Alps with his roommate and two of his best buddies? Or at least, part of the time they would have been cycling. Scott's visions for most of the trip had centered around Swiss wine, Swiss girls, free-wheeling hostels, and more Swiss girls.

In the fall he would return to the New England Preparatory School for Boys. In the meantime he was stuck here, looking for something to do, being polite to people he didn't know, and mostly just letting his parents show off what a fine young man they'd raised the same way they showed off their new house. It was boredom, more than anything else, that had turned his attention to Cathy Sykes.

Cathy worked part-time at the dime store in town, went to the local high school, and thought watching year-old movies on his VCR was a big deal. But she crimped her shoulder-length blond hair and looked good in a halter top, and she didn't whine too much about what she was going to do when he went back to school, so he supposed he could have done worse. The best thing about Cathy Sykes, of course, was that she was very easy to impress.

She liked coming to his house, so he invited her as often as he could. At least she was someone to talk to when his folks were having a party, and having her there always gave him an excuse to cut out early. So, as dusk deepened over the mountain and the sound of adult laughter and adult voices grew freer, and his dad started flipping the second round of hamburgers on the grill—clowning around, as he always did after the third martini—Scott pocketed the keys to the Porsche and called, "Hey, Dad, I'm going to take Cathy home."

His father acknowledged with a half wave, and his mother looked up from demonstrating her hold on an imaginary golf club. "Be careful on these mountain roads." She always said that. And she always added, with casual insincerity, "Good night, Cathy. Come again soon."

Cathy looked a little hurt as they walked down the steps of the deck and around the side of the house to the garage. "Are you mad at me?"

"Hell, no." He slipped his arm around her waist. She

26

was wearing a cotton sundress with no back, and he liked the feel of her smooth bare skin against his forearm. "I just thought you'd like to take a ride. Maybe go somewhere and talk."

She cast him a flirtatious look. "About what?"

He ran his fingers up her side, grinning, and she giggled and broke away when his fingers started to creep inside the curve of her dress near her breast. He let her beat him to the car.

He took the long way around toward the main road, liking the way Cathy leaned toward him in the bucket seat and rested her hand on his thigh when he drove. On impulse, he switched back and took the little street that wound behind his house, up the mountain, and dead-ended where construction had ceased near the beginning of the national forest. Even though he didn't think any of the houses were occupied in this part of the neighborhood, there were streetlights and the security guards were always patrolling around, so he pulled off the shoulder and onto the narrow dirt road the construction crew cut for access through the woods.

"I've never been back here," Cathy said, and her hand left his thigh as she turned to look out the window. "Where does it go?"

"We'll find out."

As it turned out, the dirt road didn't go very far. Banked by deadfalls and bulldozed undergrowth, the rutted road traveled about ten feet into the woods, then faded out into a trail that disappeared beyond the highbeam of the headlights. Scott killed the engine and switched off the lights, pleased with himself.

Cathy looked around uneasily. "Are you going to be able to get the car back out?"

"Sure. This baby'll go anywhere I want her to." Scott had no idea whether or not he could turn the car around without hitting something; at that point it

27

didn't seem important. He started to reach for her, then realized the front console would make what he had in mind difficult, if not impossible.

"Let's go for a walk," he suggested.

"Out there?" She peered out into the shadows again and shook her head. "I don't know, Scott. It looks kind of spooky to me."

He took her hand, grinning. "I'll protect you."

One thing about Cathy Sykes: She liked to make out as much as, or more than, any girl he had ever known. After a few more moments of pretended reluctance, he coaxed her out of the car.

He made a big show of holding her close, and she slipped her fingers inside the back of his belt as they stumbled through the woods, smiling at each other in the dark and whispering even though there was no one around to hear. There was enough moonlight to cast a grayish tint on the ground and keep them from tripping over the most obvious fallen logs and slippery rocks, but Cathy gave a muffled squeal every time a vine wound around her ankles or a bramble snagged her dress, and Scott got slapped in the face by a leafy branch more than once. After a while, blazing a trail through the forest became more of a nuisance than an adventure, and he gave up looking for a cozy spot to settle down. He stopped when a heavy screen of mountain laurel made further exploration impractical, and turning Cathy into his arms, kissed her expertly.

She responded with her usual passion, French-kissing him until his jaw muscles ached trying to keep up with her, but when he tried to urge her to the ground she protested, "No, Scott, I'll get pine sap all over my dress."

He didn't argue. He edged his thigh between her legs and caressed the rounded slope of her buttocks, nibbling at her ear the way she liked. She moaned a little, and slipped her hands beneath his T-shirt, teasing the flesh around his waist. He moved his hands up her bare back, and was just beginning to get his fingers inside the opening of her dress when suddenly she stiffened and started to push away.

"Ah, come on, Cath," he muttered breathlessly, pulling her even closer.

"Listen!" There was a sharp edge to her whisper and she braced her hands against his shoulders. "There's something out here."

"I don't hear anything." Scott couldn't hear anything except his own uneven breathing and the distant roar of blood through his head. Because she acted like she wanted to struggle, he temporarily abandoned the effort to get his fingers inside the front of her dress and started caressing her bare back again, fastening his lips on her neck. "You taste good."

"Scott!"

He heard it this time; the sharp crack of a branch and the slow scuffle of movement through the leaves. It startled him enough to penetrate the heated fog that muffled his brain and make him forget, momentarily, how good Cathy tasted.

He looked up. "It's just an old squirrel or raccoon, knocking a branch out of a tree," he said. But he realized for the first time how dark it was back in those shadows; as hard as he looked he couldn't make out one tree from another, and what he could see suddenly seemed to be formed of ragged, menacing shapes. Anything could be lurking around in there.

Cathy shivered. He could feel her skin prickle underneath his hands. "I don't like it out here," she said anxiously. "Let's go back to the car."

On the other hand, how often did a guy get a girl alone in a place like this—quiet, uninterrupted, and so far from civilization that nobody could find them if they looked? Was he going to let a squirrel blow his chance at what could very well be the highlight of his summer?

"Hey," he teased, and tried to snuggle up to her again. "I thought you were a country girl. Loosen up, will you?"

"No." She twisted away with some vehemence this time. Her face, in the moonlight, was overly white and she wasn't faking the fear in her eyes. "This is crazy. I'm going back to the car." It wasn't a suggestion, and she took two hurried steps in that direction before she looked back at him. "Are you coming?"

"Damn," Scott thought, and for a moment was almost tempted to let her find her way back to the car by herself. A few more minutes and he knew he could have gotten as far as he wanted with Cathy, and what kind of guy ran away from the dark? But she was only a few steps away and already he was feeling nervous; he didn't know what he would do if he looked over his shoulder and saw a pair of beady eyes staring back at him.

With a muffled curse he kicked a broken stick out of his way and muttered, "Yeah, I'm coming." But he pushed in front of her as soon as he could, and took grim satisfaction in the way she had to scramble, occasionally clutching at his T-shirt, to keep up with his long strides.

His minor irritation had turned into a full-blown temper tantrum by the time he reached the car, though he wasn't sure who he was madder at: Cathy or himself. He only knew that the closer he got to the car, the faster he walked and the harder it was to keep from looking over his shoulder to see that nothing was following besides Cathy, and the more times he resisted the urge to do that, the harder it was to keep from running. His heart was beating fast and he was breathing hard as he flung himself into the car, and he didn't even wait for Cathy to fasten her seat belt before he gunned the engine and slammed it into reverse.

The car lurched back a foot or two, the back tires caught and spun, and he floored the accelerator. The tires whined furiously, flinging up rocks and shredded leaves, but the car did not move. Scott punched the clutch and slammed it into first gear; the car rocked forward a few inches and the tires began to spin again.

"Shit!" He banged his fist against the steering wheel and flung open the door. He stalked around the car, but returned in less than a minute for the flashlight his dad kept stored in the console. Cathy rolled down her window and leaned out, watching as he played the beam of the light over marshy humus soil.

"Are we stuck?" she asked in a small voice, and Scott glared at her.

He played the flashlight over the tires again, then walked around the car and examined the area in front. There was no place to go even if he could pull forward. He was going to have to back out all the way to the paved road, but first he had to get the tires out of the trench. He waved the beam around the surrounding ground, looking for something he could prop under the tires to get traction. Any other place in the world he would have been able to find a plank, a broken cardboard box, enough gravel to rake under the tires and cushion the mud. There was nothing here but dead leaves.

"Shit," he said again.

He spent about ten minutes stripping off branches from some kind of vine and stuffing them under the tires, only to find the energy wasted when he tried, once again, to back out. Cathy sat with her hands folded in her lap, meekly silent, and watched his efforts until he gave up.

"I've got to go find tree limbs to put under the tires," he told her shortly. She did not volunteer to come with him as he grabbed the flashlight and set off into the woods again.

For the first ten yards or so Scott was so mad he barely bothered to even watch where he was going. But the first time he looked over his shoulder and couldn't see the car, a shadow of uneasiness crept down his spine and he guided the flashlight beam more carefully, examining his surroundings. The ground cover was still thick here, and he wasn't about to go poking his hands down into that mess, looking for broken sticks and branches. He felt his neck muscles tense as he moved further into the woods.

It was quiet. Somehow the silence bothered him more than a whole circus of unexplained noises would have done, emphasizing the report of each twig his footsteps cracked and every stone he sent rolling. The darkness too seemed even more pronounced contrasted with the beam of the flashlight, and he never let the light linger too long on any one place for fear of what he might find staring back at him.

At last his erratic beam picked up a good-sized branch poking out from beneath the dead leaves on the ground before him. He bent to pick it up, and it didn't crumble in his hands; it was sturdy enough not to break under the weight of the car, but not so wide that the tires couldn't get over it. A few more like that one and he would be in business.

He tucked the branch under his arm and spread the flashlight beam forward, planning his next step. Then he heard it. The sharp crack of a stick his own weight had not broken, the rustle of the undergrowth somewhere off the left. Something was moving out there.

The blood seemed to freeze in his veins, just for an instant, and he stood stock still. *Raccoon,* he told him-

32

self. *Squirrel*. The hair on the back of his arms prickled and he didn't even breathe, listening intently over the erratic pounding of his heart. No squirrel chattered, no raccoon scurried away. Nothing moved. But something was out there. He could feel it, hunkered down in the bushes just out of the range of his flashlight, watching him.

Pussy, he derided himself with a great deal more bravado than he felt. *Nothing's out there*. He was as bad as the girl.

He looked down at the branch in his hand. He thought about how far away the car was. But if he went back now he'd only have to come back for more wood. And how would he explain it to Cathy if he went running back without bringing what he'd come out here for? She'd have a ball laughing that one up with her hick friends in town.

He took a deliberate step forward, and then another. The round beam of light in front of him jerked a little with each step. He kept it pointed straight at the ground ahead, looking for wood.

The damp woodsy air had a faint unpleasant odor to it, something he hadn't noticed before, but the deeper he moved into the woods the stronger it seemed to get. Dead meat . . . old, dead meat, like an animal carcass rotting in the undergrowth. The thought of unwarily putting his foot down on something squishy and pustulant made him recoil, and he slowed considerably, examining the ground very carefully with the flashlight before each step. But it wasn't just something dead; it was something dirty — a bad-breath odor, an open-sewer odor, an egg rotting in the sun. It was a thick and pervasive *presence*. It was alive.

He could hear it breathing.

The wind. The rustle of a small animal. His own breath, rasping harshly through his teeth. But it was none of those things. The sound was low and thick, a hissing rattle, in and out, punctuated by soft rumbling grunts. Not a human sound. Not an animal sound. But breathing.

A cold sweat broke out on the back of Scott's neck. His throat closed up. He wanted to run. But he didn't know which way to run. He couldn't make his feet work. Something was out there, and what if he turned and ran right into it?

The piece of wood he'd been carrying slipped from his numb fingers and hit the ground with a muffled thump. There was a sharp, guttural sound and a violent crashing in the bushes as something began to rise, to charge. . . . Wildly, uncontrollably, Scott swung the beam of his flashlight toward it.

He had just a glimpse, an impression of hugeness, bigger than a bear, more powerful than a cougar; slick skin shining white in the moonlight and the head, the enormous head, and a flash of eyes trapped in the light, and then it moved.

He didn't know if he screamed. He didn't even remember running. All he knew was the branches that tore at his face and the screeching of his breath in his ears and the crashing, tearing sound of undergrowth. He tripped over a root and went sprawling; the flashlight rolled into the bushes, but he wasn't on the ground long enough to even feel the impact of the fall. He plunged blindly through the woods, and he could feel it pounding the earth behind him; the smell of it was locked in his nostrils, its heat was pushing against its neck. Something grabbed the back of his shirt and for an instant, a deadly instant, he was sure it was a claw, but he flung himself forward and the material ripped away from the thorny branch and he kept on running, slipping and sliding down a small incline, splashing through a marshy puddle until he saw—he thought he saw—he was sure he saw the dim outline of the car parked just ahead.

Dragging in breaths that sounded like sobs, he pushed himself toward it. His lungs were bursting, the separate beats of his heart were no longer distinguishable. It was the car. He could see it now. Twenty yards, thirty . . . safety. He tried to call out to Cathy, but couldn't make the sound. He almost lost his balance and scraped his arm on a tree trunk. He righted himself again and pushed forward, scrambling for traction on the slippery leaves.

And then something grabbed his shoulder and whirled him around.

Every ten minutes or so Laura would remind herself that she should go home. There were boxes and litter all over the house, at last report Christy had not been able to find her pajamas, and she wasn't even sure there was coffee for breakfast. Laura was not the kind of person who left a job half-finished. But each attack of conscience grew easier to ignore, and she kept promising herself she would leave in a few minutes. Meanwhile, the padded deck chair was luxurious beneath her weary muscles, the screwdriver she sipped was just heavy enough on the vodka to produce a mild lethargy, and the reflection of the torch lamps on the rippled surface of the lake below was lazily fascinating.

The Bullards' three-tiered deck wrapped around the entire back of the house, providing a magnificent view from any vantage point and more than enough room for entertaining. Eight couples had been invited tonight, with children ranging from age four to twelve; Laura had already found several playmates for Christy as well as two prospective baby-sitters. She liked her neighbors.

Mary Beth Jennings would be Christy's teacher in the fall. She and her husband Mike had a five-year-old boy and a seven-year-old girl, both of whom Christy had already declared to be her best friends. The children had persuaded Mike, who was as genial and out-going as his wife—and who, Laura thought she had heard someone say, was Bullard's lawyer, which explained what had convinced him to move his family out here—to take them up the street to their house, so that Christy could see their new puppies. In a moment of weakness, Laura had agreed to let Christy go, but had spent most of the time since planning the exact tone of firm refusal she would use when Christy came back wanting a puppy of her own.

Mary Beth sat down on the floor of the deck beside Laura, a petite woman whose bouncy dark ponytail and freckled nose made her look barely older than some of her students. She was also the only woman who, in cotton shorts and a rumpled *Phantom of the Opera* T-shirt, was dressed as casually as Laura. She encircled her bare knees with her arms and, noticing the direction of Laura's gaze over the lake, commented, "It kind of grows on you, doesn't it?"

"It's beautiful," Laura agreed. "Especially at night, when you can't tell the lake isn't even half-filled yet."

Mary Beth chuckled. "You should see it in the daylight. It's nothing but a mosquito-infested swamp. It makes me glad we picked the forest view."

"That's what I thought too, until Hugh told me there were bears in the woods."

Mary Beth lifted an eyebrow. "So it's bears now, is it? Great. Something else to worry about."

Laura shrugged and sipped her drink. "I don't know. I think Hugh is just jealous because he ended up looking out over a swamp instead of a forest. Bears don't come this close to civilization, at any rate."

"That's not necessarily so, you know," said a male voice behind her.

Laura twisted around to see Ted Jacobs standing over her shoulder. Except for a perfunctory "hello," those were the only words he had spoken to her all evening—or to anyone, as far as Laura had observed—and she was surprised.

She had known Ted Jacobs, of course, without a formal introduction, or she had known *of* him. Ted Jacobs was an M.D. who had given up gall bladders and kidney stones for the fictional world of technological intrigue and the *New York Times* best-seller list. He was the darling of the talk-show circuit, and his face adorned the back covers of a million suspense-thrillers, but like most celebrities Laura had met he was somewhat disappointing in person.

He was a tall lean man with aquiline features and a New York pallor. His blond hair was severely parted on the left and fell in a straight wedge over his right ear, reminding Laura of an early Andy Warhol or a more recent punk-rocker. The wire-rimmed glasses he wore seemed a little pretentious, and he had spent the evening silently stalking, watching the crowd, making everyone feel as though he were cataloging them for inclusion in his next book—a prospect which most people found flattering, but Laura found merely annoying. She had spent too many evenings at too many upscale cocktail parties not to recognize the role of the bored intellectual when she saw it being played out before her eyes, and her tolerance for self-important snobs was limited. She had not expected to have to put up with it at a neighborhood barbecue.

Still, she made a polite little inquiring sound, and he surprised her by pulling a deck chair and sitting down. "Most animals are territorial," he explained, "occupying the same few square miles their whole lifetime—or if

37

their survival requirements are met, for generations. When their territory is destroyed, where are they supposed to go?" He lifted his shoulders in an elaborate comment on the perils of modern life and took a sip of his drink. "I imagine a lot of wildlife have been looking for new homes over the past year or so."

Mary Beth shared a covert look with Laura that expressed her amused appreciation over being singled out for such attention, and Laura smothered a smile by lifting her own glass. Mary Beth said, "It seems to me a smart bear would just move on up the mountain. There's plenty of room."

"There may not be plenty of food, though," Ted pointed out. "A big construction project like this can upset the ecology in ways we don't even know about."

Laura tried to ignore the prickle of conscience for her own part in the development. "This isn't the first time a few trees were cut down for the sake of progress," she pointed out. "But I've still never heard of the disenfranchised wildlife mounting a revenge."

Ted Jacobs's thin lips formed a smile that transformed his face from saturnine to almost pleasant. "On the other hand," he countered, "it's not every day that suburbia moves into virgin forest. We're the interlopers here, not the bears."

"Excuse me?" Mary Beth looked confused. "You can't mean *really* virgin. These woods aren't that old!"

He nodded, sipping his drink. "Older than the first settlers, we know that much for certain. And as far back as anyone can tell, no one has ever disturbed this forest."

"I didn't think there was any really untouched land left anymore," Laura said. "Not in this part of the country, at least."

"Oh, sure. You'd be surprised at how much of the country has never been adequately explored. I admit, you're more likely to find virgin areas out West, but it's not all that rare in this part of the Smokies. Our little piece of paradise is the site of the first human habitation in untold centuries."

Laura groaned softly. "Now I do feel guilty."

"Well, I don't," Mary Beth said cheerfully. "I feel like a pioneer. Not that I didn't before. Wait until you hear the wild turkeys calling at night, Laura; makes you want to grab your shotgun and hang the old roasting spit over the fire."

Laura laughed. "Thank you, but I prefer my turkeys wrapped in plastic and stamped Grade A."

Ted Jacobs smiled. "A convenient social conscience."

"Absolutely," agreed Laura. She took another sip of her drink. "Who am I to argue with the Department of Agriculture? As long as they approve of the mass slaughter of feathered fowl, so do I."

"Mommy, Mommy! Look what I've got!"

"Oh, no," Laura moaned under her breath as Christy appeared, holding a fuzzy tan puppy under her arm.

"His name is Corky and Mr. Mike says I can have him for my very own," Christy announced happily, bouncing to a stop before her mother. "Can we take him home now, Mommy, please?"

"Now, Christy." Mike Jennings laid a calming hand on the little girl's head. "I didn't say you could have him. I said you could ask your mother."

Mary Beth gave Laura an apologetic look. "We're trying to get rid of a litter," she explained. "We only have two left. Males," she added hopefully. "Cocker spaniels, sweet temperaments, and really good with children."

Laura looked in dismay from Mary Beth to her daughter. "Oh, Christy, honey, a puppy is a lot of responsibility."

"You'll say yes, Mommy, I know you will. You said I could have a puppy—"

"I said someday," she corrected firmly. "When you're older. We just moved into our new house and we have so much to do, I'm afraid we just won't have time to take care of a puppy."

"Maybe," Mike Jennings added helpfully — and belatedly, as far as Laura was concerned, "you should wait awhile. A little fellow like this takes a lot of looking after. And he really should have a fenced yard to play in."

The fence again. But at least this time there was a valid reason. "We've already lost three pups," Mary Beth explained. "We think there's a pack of wild dogs living up on the mountain and dogs this age — well, what do they know? They hear the call of the wild and off they go."

"But we have a *big* yard," Christy insisted. "He won't get lost. I'll watch him every minute. He can sleep in my room and play in my swimming pool and —"

"I don't think so, honey."

The puppy chose that moment to wiggle around and lick Christy's face. Then, panting happily, it turned its liquid brown eyes on Laura. Christy looked at her with equally liquid blue eyes. Laura thought of her new carpeting and the finish on the legs of her Queen Anne furniture. She thought about the flower beds she intended to plant and the fence she did *not* intend to erect.

"He won't make a mess, Mommy," Christy said in a quavering voice. "I promise."

Laura knew when she was beaten. "All right. You can take him home. But," she added firmly over Christy's squeal of delight, "not tonight. You give him back to Mr. Jennings tonight and we'll pick him up in the morning, after we buy a collar and leash and some dog food."

"I'll just play with him a little more," Christy said by

way of compromise, and ran off with the Jennings children toward the lawn.

"Stay right there," Laura called, "under the light!"

"Okay!" Christy gave her a bouncy wave and set the puppy down in the middle of a circle of children.

"Kids and dogs," commented Mary Beth wryly. "The master manipulators. With the help, of course, of well-meaning husbands," she added with an apologetic shake of her head. "Laura, I'm sorry. If you don't want—"

"No, that's all right." Laura returned a resigned smile. "I did promise her a puppy, and I guess this is as good a time as any."

Ted Jacobs looked up, a preoccupied frown on his face. "Did you say it was wild dogs that got your pups?"

Mary Beth looked surprised. "Nothing *got* them. They just ran off, and they warned us about wild dogs when we first moved here. Why?"

Ted drew a breath as though to reply, then seemed to change his mind. His frown deepened as he glanced down at his glass. "Nothing. I was thinking about something else."

Mary Beth gave Laura a questioning look, but Laura shrugged it off. She had heard enough about bears and primal forests, and the last thing she wanted to do was encourage more of Ted Jacobs's maudlin speculations. She would have enough trouble sleeping tonight as it was.

Sam Keller had to duck quickly to avoid a sock in the jaw. As it was, the Bullard boy's flailing fist caught him square on the shoulder, knocking the flashlight out of his hand. He tightened his grip on the boy's shoulder and shouted, "What the hell's the matter with you, boy?"

41

Scott Bullard swung again, and Sam's first instinct was violence. He caught the kid's wrists, and was about to throw him to the ground when he got his first good look at his face. His skin was white and wet with perspiration, scarred with the red welts of branches and streaks of mud. His eyes were wild and he was breathing like a freight train. Sam could feel the shaking of the kid's arms beneath the grip of his hand. This kid wasn't drunk, drugged out, or acting like an ass just for the hell of it. He was scared to death.

Sam gave him a quick shake and said sharply, "Whoa there! Get a grip, kid." And as Scott Bullard's eyes seemed to focus on him and some of the fight went out of his wire-tight muscles, Sam added more conversationally, "You got any idea what the penalty is for striking a police officer? What the hell was chasing you out there anyway?"

Scott stared at him, continuing to gasp lung-rattling breaths, and as the raw terror in his eyes faded to mere panic Sam thought he would speak. Then Cathy Sykes came stumbling through the undergrowth, making enough noise to cause even Sam to jump.

"Scott! Is that you? Oh, thank goodness! I was so worried, I thought you'd gotten lost, and then the sheriff came and—what happened to you? Are you okay?"

She stopped a few feet away, staring in concern at the marks on Scott's face and his torn and dirty clothes. Sam left the kid to compose himself as he retrieved his flashlight. He couldn't resist turning the beam back toward the woods from which Scott had come, and out of the corner of his eye he saw Scott stiffen and jerk his head around, as though expecting something to leap out at them when disturbed by the light.

The flashlight beam made an eerie trail through misshapen deadfalls and tangled undergrowth, bouncing off the heavy trunks of distant trees before being swallowed up by the darkness beyond. The narrow swatch of light played briefly to the right and left, and it was easy to see how a kid could get spooked in those woods. No matter which way Sam moved the light the darkness was never completely dispersed, and it was only natural to imagine that something was hiding just outside the range of the beam. He turned the flashlight away sooner than he probably should have, but he didn't expect to find anything.

Cathy insisted, taking a step forward. "What happened?"

Scott cast a brief, desperate look toward Sam and his nerves quickened in alertness for what the boy was about to say. Then Scott looked at Cathy, hesitated, then swiped a hand over his face, pushing at his rather-too-long hair.

"Nothing," he muttered.

Though Sam knew it was useless, he prompted "Did you run into something out there? What were you running from?"

Cathy's eyes went wide with interest, but Scott Bullard replied angrily, "Nothing! Nothing, okay? I—I thought I heard Cathy scream, that's all. The car was stuck and I left her out here by herself and I thought she was in trouble."

"Oh." Cathy seemed disappointed. "I wasn't in trouble. The sheriff was here and we were just calling for you, that's all."

Sam knew Scott was lying, and there was a part of him—a surprising and not very noble part—that was almost relieved. Kids were always letting their imaginations run away with them. It wouldn't be hard for a grown man to get spooked in those woods at night. He had probably seen a snake or a possum and was too embarrassed to tell his girl he'd been scared by it.

Sam had enough to worry about without chasing

around in the dark after a city boy's case of nerves. Still, he could not prevent a prickle of disquiet when he remembered the look on the boy's face, and he kept thinking about Brett Howard.

But it was clear he was going to get nothing else out of Scott Bullard.

Sam said, "It's too dark to do anything about your car tonight. Why don't I give you kids a ride home?" He laid a light hand on the boy's shoulder, but Scott jerked away as though stung. He was still trembling.

Sam waved the flashlight beam forward, lighting the path to the car. And because his conscience wouldn't entirely let it go at that, he added, "There are safer places around here for you kids to hang out, you know. I don't want to have to round up a search party to comb these woods, so next time pick another spot, okay?"

Cathy replied meekly, "Yes, sir." But Scott Bullard didn't say a word. He hurried toward the car with uneven steps, and didn't look back.

Chapter Three

Sam took Cathy home first. It was out of his way, but he thought he might be able to get something more out of Scott once they were alone. He didn't know what more there could possibly be, and he still wasn't entirely sure he wanted to hear it if there was anything to hear, but he was curious. He supposed he never would have gotten into law enforcement if there wasn't a part of him that was, despite his better judgment, always a little curious.

But on the trip home Sam got first-hand evidence of where the expression "clam up" had come from. He didn't press; he tried to make conversation in an easy, man-to-man way, about the way he'd been treed by a wild boar when he was a kid, and about the time an eight-point buck, charging through the predawn woods like a hell-breathing demon, had scared him so badly he'd fallen out of the deer stand and broken his wrist. Those were probably exactly the wrong things to say, because Scott sat beside him so stiff and silent that his lips were white with the effort of pressing them together.

Sam pulled the car up in front of the Bullards' house. "Looks like your folks are having a party," he commented.

Scott fumbled with the door handle, and got it opened. He looked back, and in the courtesy light from the open door his face was still ghastly white, hollow-eyed. "It wasn't a deer," he said. His voice was low and hoarse. "And it wasn't a wild boar either."

But that was all he was going to say. He got out and slammed the door.

After a moment's thought, Sam killed the engine and followed him up the walk.

Sam Keller hadn't been any more pleased than any of the other locals when the bulldozers and cement mixers had started crawling up the mountain, but he had realized sooner than most of the others that there wasn't a hell of a lot he could do about it. He had resigned himself to making the best of a bad situation for the sake of the eighteen months of his unexpired term, and so far his efforts had paid off. Most of the newcomers knew him by his first name and respected his way of doing things; he was always welcome in Hugh Bullard's house.

Scott plunged up the stairs without a word, and Sam followed him through the open front door, feeling it was only courteous to seek out his daddy and explain what had happened to his car. Hugh Bullard mumbled something about damned irresponsible kids, and then cheerfully pushed a drink into Sam's hand. Since he was technically on duty for another fifteen minutes, Sam discreetly put the drink aside, but didn't mind helping himself to some of the chips and dip that were set out. Maybe it was in sympathy for the boy, who would have enough explaining to do when morning came, or maybe it was his own uneasiness. But he didn't say anything to Hugh Bullard about the rest of the episode in the woods.

If the truth were told, Sam didn't particularly like his routine patrols of the Heights, and he would be glad when the community's private security force was effi-cient enough to make them unnecessary. He had noth-ing against the people, particularly, and so far they'd given him no trouble, but things were always busy up here, something was always going on. The party to-night was a perfect example: too many people with too much to say, trying to outttalk and outdrink one an-other. In town the quiet wasn't just a figure of speech, it was a state of mind, easy, relaxed, comfortable. The normal, everyday pace of the Heights seemed frenetic to Sam, and it was never more than a few minutes be-fore the strange faces, strange accents, and constant movement started to get on his nerves.

He was just about to thank Hugh for the chips and take his leave when Mike Jennings called him over. He liked Mike, but for a moment he considered pretending he hadn't heard. Then he saw Mike and Mary Beth were with a woman he hadn't met yet, and because he felt it was his duty to become familiar with all the new faces on the Heights, he went over to say hello.

Laura was ready to go home. Christy was asleep in her arms, the puppy was curled up on her feet, and Laura was starting to have trouble keeping her own eyes open. She'd noticed the man in the tan uniform, and idly wondered out loud if there was any trouble. She had never intended for Mike to make an introduc-tion.

Cliché though it might be, Laura had a stereotypical image of Southern sheriffs in her head — mid-to-late fif-ties, balding, a little wide in the girth — and she was somewhat disappointed that this one did not conform. He might have been forty, and though he wasn't partic-ularly athletic-looking, he was far from pot-bellied. His hair was more red than brown, and his complexion had the evenly weathered look of someone who spent more time out of doors than he should. He had alert, friendly eyes of a nondescript hazel, and when he smiled, his essentially unremarkable features were transformed into a countenance that was intensely interesting.

He smiled now, and extended his hand as Mike made the introductions. Somewhat awkwardly, Laura reached over Christy's head to accept his handshake. She said, "So you're the bear man."

"Pardon me?"

"Hugh Bullard was telling me about the bears in the woods," she explained. "He said he got the idea from you."

"Oh." His eyes twinkled, but his voice was sober as he replied, "I wouldn't worry too much, ma'am. We haven't had a man-eating bear around these parts for, oh, five or six months now."

Mary Beth chuckled, and Laura replied, "In that case I'll feel safe sleeping with my windows open."

Mike said, "I used to hunt bear with my dad when I was a kid, up in Maine. We'd go every winter and never spotted any bear. I'll bet there's good hunting around here."

"Not really," Sam replied. "At least not on this mountain. Most of the good hunting is found in second-growth forests; you have to work too hard to find anything up here."

"Is it true then?" Mary Beth said. "That this is original forest?"

"I don't know how original it is, but it's old. I think it used to be some kind of Indian holy ground. At any rate, nobody ever thought it was worth clearing out and building on before, not with so many fertile acres of valley around."

Laura said, "Great. So now we've desecrated Indian holy ground."

Sam chuckled. "You'd be hard put to find a thousand acres of land in this country that wasn't holy ground at some time or another. And there aren't too many Indians around left to complain about it are there?"

"That's one way of looking at it, I guess."

Mike asked him a question about the construction that was going on on Highway 20, and Sam answered it as best he could. But most of his attention was on Laura. He had a weakness for the mother-child picture she presented, it was true, and the little girl sleeping in her arms was enough to melt the coldest man's heart, but he had to be honest with himself. Laura Kane was an attractive woman. She had long, slim legs that looked good in shorts, and small, squarely shaped knees. Pretty knees. Her straight honey-brown hair was pulled back from her face and fastened at the nape of her neck with a barrette, fanning midway between her shoulder blades. Her skin was a delicate, almost translucent covering for finely etched features, and there was a small mole or birthmark just above her upper lip which on another woman, might have been viewed as a flaw. On Laura it looked sexy. The pale blue circles under her eyes, which she did not try to hide with makeup, gave her a fragile look, but that was only an illusion. Sam could see the outline of lean feminine biceps where her arm curved to cradle her daughter's head; Laura Kane was obviously a woman who took care of herself.

No one had said anything about her husband, and any one of the four gold bands she wore on the fingers of a left hand could have been a wedding ring. He knew, of course, that she had to be married; no woman with a child would move way up here by herself. But when he scanned the crowd for unfamiliar faces, he didn't see anyone who could be married to Laura Kane, and that puzzled him.

Not that it mattered, of course. She was way out of his league.

But when she smothered a yawn with the back of her hand and murmured something about going home, Sam was quick to volunteer, "I've got to be getting back too. I'll walk out with you."

Laura gently eased her feet out from under the puppy's sleeping form. She glanced at Mike. "You don't mind keeping him tonight? I'll pick him out as soon as I get a chance tomorrow, I promise."

Mike grinned. "What's one more night?"

But Christy stirred and looked up at her mother with sleepy, disturbed eyes. "Don't leave Corky, Mommy. The monsters'll get him."

"Honey, I told you—"

Christy's arms tightened around her neck and her voice became querulous. "No, Mommy, the monsters!"

Laura looked at Mary Beth helplessly. "I wish I knew what this thing with monsters was, all of a sudden."

"It's probably just the move," Mary Beth assured her.

"Mommy, don't leave Corky!"

Laura could sense a crying fit coming on, and she did not want to repay her hosts' hospitality by leaving with a screaming child. That was a poor excuse for giving in to her daughter's demands, she knew, but Laura had always been too easily manipulated when it came to Christy—perhaps because Christy used her weakness against her so seldom.

She looked down at the sleeping puppy. "Well," she admitted reluctantly, "I suppose I could make him a bed in the garage."

"My bed," Christy said contentedly, "he can sleep in my bed." She snuggled down into her mother's arms again.

"We'll see about that," Laura replied, but Christy was already asleep.

"Oh, to be a child again," Laura murmured with a rueful shake of her head, and groaned a little with the burden of Christy's weight as she stood up.

"Why don't you let me carry her to the car?" Sam offered. "You can take the puppy."

Laura looked at him blankly for a moment, and Sam thought he'd been too pushy. Some women were touchy about turning their kids over to strangers, and you couldn't blame them, all things considered. He started to apologize, then Laura said, "Oh. I just realized—I don't have a car. I walked down with the Bullards."

Sam could see Mike getting ready to offer to drive her home, so he said, "No problem. My car's right in front. I'll drive you."

She laughed a little. "I don't think we need a police escort. Isn't that a waste of the taxpayers' money?"

He glanced at his watch. "I'm off duty."

"Well in that case, and if you're sure you don't mind . . ." She surprised him by shifting Christy's weight into his arms. "Thank you."

She scooped up the dog, and it took them nearly five minutes to say their good-byes and get out of the house. In all that time, Christy didn't stir. Laura couldn't help but admire the ease with which Sam Keller handled the child; most men were awkward around children, especially those they didn't know well. He seemed to have an instinct that was hard to find.

She couldn't help asking, as they reached the car, "Do you have children, Sheriff?"

"No. And it's Sam, if you don't mind. Everybody calls me that. You want to put the pup in the back seat?"

The back seat was screened from the front, and it seemed as safe a way as any to transport the wriggling little animal that, once roused, did not have Christy's capacity for immediate slumber again. Laura secured the dog in the back, then got in the front passenger seat. Sam slid Christy into her arms.

Because he was afraid his answer to her earlier question had seemed a little abrupt, Sam volunteered, "I was married once, back in Atlanta. It only lasted a couple of years."

"What happened?"

That was the kind of question only a city girl would ask, with absolute ingenuousness and insincerity: at cocktail parties, to strangers on the bus, just as casually as you might say, "Where're you from?" Out here, a man's personal business was a little more sacred.

But strangely, Sam felt no resentment as he started the engine with a shrug. "She didn't like living on a cop's pay."

He hesitated before putting the car in gear, then added, "That's not fair. She didn't like going to bed every night wondering whether she'd be a widow by morning. I didn't much like that either. That's how come I ended up back here."

Laura said, "My house is the last one at the top of the hill." He put the car in gear and pulled out into the street, and she added, "You said 'back here.' Did you grow up around here?"

"Born and bred. It hasn't changed much either."

"Until recently."

He said nothing.

"I guess you locals must think we're all crazy, trying to build paradise out of the wilderness."

He seemed to think about that for a moment before replying. "Not crazy. After all, we've always thought there was something pretty special about this place. But I worry about you-all sometimes."

She looked at him, surprised. "Why?"

He smiled, a friendly, reassuring smile. "I just think it might take you a little longer to get used to paradise than you think, that's all. It's kind of lonely up here. Cabin fever and all that."

"Oh, good." Laura leaned back against the seat. "I thought you were going to tell me more bear stories."

He laughed.

Laura pointed out the driveway to him, and he switched his headlights on high. She had forgotten to turn on the lampposts that lined the drive. "This is really nice," he commented, surprised. "You hardly cut down anything."

"You must be an ecologist at heart."

"If that's another way of saying I don't like to see things change, I guess so."

He pulled up in front of the house, leaving the headlights on to light their path as he came around to her door. He took Christy from her so that she could find her key and collect the puppy, and Laura commented ruefully as she opened the door, "Habit, I guess. I came up here to find a place where I wouldn't have to lock my doors, but I don't seem to be able to stop doing it."

Sam noticed the elaborate security system by the front door as she switched on the lights and observed, with a lawman's sagacity, "It's not such a bad idea. You're pretty far out in the middle of nowhere."

Laura turned to him with a smile, reaching for Christy. "Well, thank you . . ."

"I'll carry her up for you," he offered.

"Thanks." She seemed genuinely relieved. "To tell the truth, I'm so tired I'm not even sure I can carry myself up the stairs." She picked up the puppy again, who was already beginning to sniff suspiciously around the crumpled newspapers, and explained, "We just moved in today, so be careful of the clutter. I guess it shows you what kind of person I am that I chose to go to a party instead of finishing the unpacking."

"A sensible one," Sam commented, and she flashed him a smile that was full of infectious warmth.

"I guess it won't kill her to go to sleep dirty one

night," Laura murmured worriedly as Sam laid Christy on the bed and tugged off her tennis shoes. "I hate to wake her up for a bath."

"I'll bet it won't even kill her to sleep in her play clothes."

The puppy wriggled in Laura's arms and yipped, and Christy opened her eyes sleepily, extending her arms. "Corky."

"No, baby, Corky's got his own bed in the garage. You can see him in the morning." Laura decided Sam was probably right about the play clothes, and she bent down to draw the covers over Christy. "Good night." She kissed her forehead.

But as she bent over, Corky somehow managed to squirm out of her arms and into Christy's. Christy smiled and closed her eyes. "Corky says good night too, Mommy."

The puppy huffed out a sigh and laid its head on Christy's shoulder. Christy's breathing was deep and even.

Laura looked at them for a long helpless moment and then muttered, "Well, maybe for just one night." She glanced at Sam, and shrugged. "So I'm a rotten mother."

He grinned. "Rotten disciplinarian. Good mother."

They left the room together, and conversation had been flowing so easily between them that Sam felt no restraint about asking, "Where is Christy's father?"

"In England."

He decided to be more direct. "Are you still married?"

Laura's smile was tight, but her voice was perfectly casual as she answered, "He is. But not to me."

Sam was sure there was more to the story than that, and he would have liked to have known it. He would have liked to have known a lot of things—like why a woman as young and attractive and smart as she was was alone, and why she would bring a little girl all the way out here to live in the middle of nowhere, and what she was doing for dinner tomorrow night.

As they reached the foyer and stood for an awkward moment, each of them wondering what to say now, Sam realized that he was actually seriously considering asking her out. She would think he was crazy, of course. He had barely known her half an hour. And even if she accepted, where would he take her? Laura Kane was hardly the type of woman to be interested in the amusements of a town like Calumit.

Still, he had almost worked up the courage to do it when she said, with an apologetic little gesture, "I'd offer to make coffee, but I'm not sure I could find the pot."

"That's okay." He reached for the doorknob. "Maybe another time." It was a stupid idea. What would a classy lady like her want with a man like him anyway?

She went forward to turn on the porch light. "Well, thanks for your help."

"Sure thing. Good night, now."

Laura went back upstairs, almost too tired to undress herself. Her bedroom, which would one day be a soothing oasis of peach and cream, was piled high with empty cartons and a disarray of items she had not decided where to put yet. At least the bed was made with fresh linen, and the towels and toiletries had been unpacked. Maybe she could find the energy to take a shower.

The bedroom still smelled vaguely like fresh paint, and she opened a window, leaning on the sill as she looked out. The one thing she had not anticipated about the country was how dark the nights would be. Even with the moon she couldn't separate the shadows of the back lawn from the deeper shadows of the woods beyond. Another thing she had not expected was the *loudness* of the country. The crickets weren't just chirping; they were screaming, a rhythmic in-and-out pulse that seemed to get louder with every beat. That would definitely take some getting used to.

She supposed that she should open Christy's window too, to air out the room. And spread newspapers on the floor for the dog if she expected to have a salvageable carpet by morning. Wearily, she started to turn away from the window, and then she froze, every nerve in her body prickling at the sound that cut across the night.

Wild turkeys, she thought. Hadn't Mary Beth said something about wild turkeys? But then it came again; not a warble, not a screech, but a long wailing keen. It gripped the back of her neck and traveled down her spine like a shudder.

It rose and fell in an echoing, drawn-out ululation, like a howl but not a howl, not like any animal sound she had ever heard or imagined to hear. It was primitive, fierce, anguished, and triumphant; it was the sound of a creature of the jungle or the darkest, most ancient forest, and yet . . . it was not. It was a sound so alien, so unacceptable to the rational, civilized mind that Laura wanted to clap her hands over her ears and blot it out. But she couldn't move.

As the wail died away Laura realized that the crickets had stopped chirping. In the awful, absolute silence that followed she could hear the dry thumping of her heart.

She gripped the windowsill, straining her eyes to see out into the darkness, half-afraid of what she might see. The shadows were so close the darkness so impenetrable, that the woods seemed to be pressing in on her, weaving their thick, twisted branches around the house, closing out the air with their pungent leaves. The stillness was unnatural, intense, as though every iving creature had ceased to exist except the two trapped inside this house . . . and one other, out there. Somewhere.

A sudden crashing sound jarred her frozen nerves, and Laura's cry was choked in her throat as she whirled around. Something was downstairs. Wildly, unthinkingly, she rushed out onto the landing and caught the rail in a white-knuckled grip, staring down.

Sam Keller stood in the foyer, his body half shielded by the partially open door, peering up at her. "You forgot to lock the door," he pointed out unnecessarily. And when she continued to gape down at him, he seemed embarrassed and added, "Sorry. I knocked. I guess you didn't hear."

She felt foolish, light-headed with relief. All her elaborate concerns about security, and the first night she was here she had forgotten to lock the door. It hadn't been a crash she'd heard. Just the sound of the heavy front door opening. And the other sound . . .

Had he heard it too? Was that why had had come back?

Her heart started pounding again, so badly that she couldn't even ask.

Her continued silence seemed to unnerve him, and he cleared his throat a little. He said, "Um, I don't mean to bother you, but I was wondering . . . would you like to have dinner with me sometime?"

For a moment she didn't react. When the shock wore off her first sensation was of laughter bubbling up in her throat, and she had to choke it back determinedly. But there he stood, looking anxious and uneasy, still half-hidden by the door, and all he wanted was a date. Strange noises in the night, wild things prowling in the woods, and men remained the same everywhere.

He hadn't heard anything out of the ordinary outside. Her nerves just hadn't adjusted to country life yet.

And she was so relieved, so grateful for the absurdity of it all, that she almost blurted out an unthinking acceptance to his invitation. She caught herself just in time.

"Thank you," she said. Her regretful smile was genuine. "But I don't think so."

"Okay, no problem." He was already backing out the door. "Good night again."

For some undiscernible reason she called, "But maybe . . ."

He stopped.

"Maybe we could have lunch sometime," she finished inanely.

He grinned. He stood there grinning at her and making her feel as silly as she probably looked, and then he gave a rueful shake of his head. "Okay," he said. "Lunch it is."

Laura locked the door after him, and set the alarm. She was still smiling as she went back to her bedroom. After only a moment's hesitation, she closed her window too, and then locked it.

She didn't hear the sound again that night, and she slept the deep and dreamless sleep of the exhausted.

Chapter Four

The one thing Laura knew she would never grow to like about living in the country was the amount of time it took to get anything done. One didn't dash around the corner for a quart of ice cream or a package of dinner rolls, or call up the drugstore to have a few toiletries delivered, or stop in at the department store on the way home from work for some pantyhose and a paperback book. Going to the store was a major production requiring half a day or more, and Laura had learned, in the week she had been in her new home, to make lists and consolidate all her shopping into one trip.

She had also learned that one did not go into town wearing ragged shorts and a tank top with no bra, so on that Thursday morning she changed into a pair of knee-length culottes and a crisp white shirt, then washed Christy's face and hands and locked Corky in the garage. He protested vociferously, but remembering the stains he had already left on her new carpet, Laura felt no remorse. She mentally added carpet cleaner to her list of purchases.

She braked a little on the downhill curve, and then she saw something unusual outside the Jennings house. A Calumit Heights security jeep—looking exactly like a mail truck except that it was painted blue with white stripes—was parked at the curb next to the drive, its dome light flashing. A little alarmed, Laura slowed and then on impulse turned into the driveway.

From the outside, the house looked undisturbed. Still, she hesitated a moment before agreeing to allow Christy, who was already wriggling out of her seat belt at the prospect of seeing her friends Carrie and Sean, to get out with her. Probably one of the kids had accidentally set off the burglar alarm. Or Joe was making a social call and had unintentionally left his dome light on. What other explanation could there be for his presence in an area that, to this point, had an absolutely zero crime rate? Still, it was eerie to see that dome light flashing, and there was a hollow feeling in the pit of Laura's stomach that she had hoped to never feel again.

No one answered her knock, so she took Christy's hand and started toward the back of the house, calling. After a moment, to her enormous relief, Mary Beth's voice answered, "Back here!"

Laura met Mary Beth coming around the side of the house. "Are you okay?" she asked. "I saw the security truck and—"

"Yes, we're okay," Mary Beth assured her quickly. But her usually ebullient air was subdued and there was the faint trace of a distracted frown between her brows. "It's just the weirdest thing. Come on, I'll show you."

Laura released Christy's hand, but Christy did not run off to find Carrie and Sean as she had been so anxious to do only a few moments ago. She stayed close to her mother as Mary Beth led the way around an elaborate rock garden and down a set of terrace steps to the backyard.

"After we had that trouble with the pups I told you about," she explained, "we decided to fence in a run for Lulu—she's the mama—and put in a little dog door so

60

he could go in and out. Well, the puppy never did earn to use the door, so he stays in at night, but Lulu ook to it right away and spends half the night wandering in and out. But last night—God, it must have been n the *dead* of the night, because I barely woke up—Lulu came scrambling inside and ducked under the bed and there she's been ever since. Wouldn't even come out for breakfast. And when I went outside this morning—well, this is what I found."

She stopped where one of the back doors opened onto the yard, and gestured.

The kitchen was on the bottom level of this house, Laura remembered, so the dog door must have been installed in the kitchen door. The run was an enclosed affair that joined the house at the back of the garage, about six feet wide, twelve feet long, and seven feet high where it met the low overhang of the garage. It was constructed of a medium weight chain-link fencing material—somewhat overstated, in Laura's opinion, for the restraint of two small cocker spaniels, but apparently Mike Jennings had gone to some trouble to follow the lines of the house and make the run as esthetically unobtrusive as possible. All this hard work and expense, however, had not withstood whatever had happened last night.

The top of the run had been peeled away at one corner like the lid of a tin can. There was a ragged, gaping hole torn in the far end of the enclosure and the whole thing was canted at an angle, as though it had begun to buckle under a heavy blow.

Joe McCallough shook his head slowly. "I don't know what to tell you, Mr. Jennings. The ground's too dry to hold footprints, and I don't see signs of anything else being disturbed. You say you didn't hear anything last night?"

Mike frowned, staring at the wrecked dog run. "I

might have heard something, but I thought it was just the dog."

"Our bedroom is on the other side of the house," Mary Beth added. "It's hard to hear anything back here when the windows are closed."

"And that dog of yours—it didn't bark or anything?"

"No," Mary Beth admitted, puzzled. "And that's strange. She's no Lassie, but she's pretty protective, especially since we moved out here. She barks at everything. But whatever it was must've scared her pretty badly. She's still curled up under the bed. You ever hear of a dog being too scared to bark?"

"No'm, I can't say that I have." Joe McCallough went back to examining the evidence, but his expression was not very encouraging.

"What I'd like to know," Mike said, a little stiffly, "is how anybody could get through that famed security force of yours to do something like this."

"What I'd like to know is why," Mary Beth added.

Laura thought those were both very good questions, but she only had an answer for one. Joe, predictably, took it personally and replied far more adamantly than she would have.

"You know damn good and well I can't guard every inch of this perimeter. I can only be responsible for them that come through the gate, and there are probably trails up through those woods we'll never know about."

Laura added, in what she hoped was a reassuring tone, "The size of the security team will grow with the community. But right now, Joe is right—we can't guard the woods and back roads and forget about the houses, can we?"

"This came pretty close to the house if you ask me," Mike replied, unpacified.

Laura had no answer for that. The Jennings house,

ke hers, bordered on the national forest. But unlike
ers, it only faced the woods on one side, and was set
much further away from them. She knew that the only
oad that led to the Heights was the one that termi-
ated at the gate, but surely there must be other points
f access she did not know about. One thing was cer-
ain. No one would traverse that forest at night just to
ear up the Jennings dog pen. So whatever it was had
ot come through the woods.

She could not resist touching the metal wire, testing
ts strength. It was fairly heavy, almost like cyclone
encing. And she could see from where she was stand-
ng that the wire had not been cut or sawed, but ran-
lomly bent back and twisted apart. What had they
used to tear that hole in the end—pliers? She glanced
up at the corner where the roof had been torn off the
sides, a good twelve inches above her head. Had the
burglar brought a ladder?

Joe stood up from his examination of the hole in the
fence and dusted off his hands. "Vandals is all I can say.
Bunch of kids, looking for excitement."

Mary Beth stared at him. "Vandals? Why would *vandals* want to sneak into our backyard and tear up our
dog run?"

Joe hesitated, then shrugged. "Why do they want to
drive down the road with a baseball bat, knocking
down mailboxes? To make you mad, to get their kicks,
just to get away with it. I don't know."

Mike drew a sharp breath, and Laura knew what he
was going to say. The wire had not been cut, but torn
and bent, both at the top and the sides. It would take an
ordinary man with ordinary tools half the night to do a
job like that. And for what? To scare a dog? And what
about Lulu? Why hadn't she barked? It made no sense.

Laura looked at Mary Beth and saw the same denial
in her eyes that was in Mike's. Yet none of them—most

63

especially not Laura—were willing to put their thoughts into words.

And then Mary Beth gave a little shrug, and a very faint smile, and said, "What other answer is there? Space aliens?"

They all smiled self-consciously, and turned to go into the house. Laura almost tripped over Christy, who was holding on to her leg, staring at the dog run with round frightened eyes. She said, "They didn't get Lulu, did they, Mommy?"

"Oh, honey." Laura bent to stroke Christy's hair. "You heard Mrs. Jennings say Lulu is just fine. So is the puppy."

Christy seemed somewhat relieved, but she still didn't let go of her mother's leg.

Mary Beth said, "I'm sorry, Christy. Sean and Carrie are watching TV in the family room. Do you want to go say hello, and see the dogs?"

Christy looked up at her mother. "They don't mean to be bad, Mommy. They're just hungry."

Laura extracted Christy's arms from around her leg and knelt beside her. "Who, honey?"

Carrie looked back at the dog pen. "This is their place. And they're hungry."

Laura met Mary Beth's puzzled look helplessly. "Who's hungry?" she repeated. "The dogs?"

Christy shook her head, but would say nothing else.

Laura picked Christy up, lifting her eyebrows at Mary Beth in a resigned mother-to-mother look. The men had already rounded the corner of the house, and Mary Beth gestured toward the sliding door that opened into the breakfast area. "Would you like some coffee? And there are probably some blueberry muffins left, if the kids didn't get them all."

"No, thanks. I was just on my way to town. Is there

64

anything I can do for you? Anything you want me to pick up while I'm in town?"

Mary Beth's lips turned down ruefully. "How about an electric fence?"

Mary Beth walked her to the van, and Laura noticed that Mike was still talking to Joe, leaning on the window of the jeep while Joe sat behind the wheel, obviously anxious to be on his way. Laura tried to think of something reassuring to say to Mary Beth, but she couldn't — anymore than Joe, apparently, could placate Mike. Laura was having enough trouble trying to reassure herself.

It was probably just a prank. No harm had really been done; nothing stolen, no one hurt. If it had been a serious attempt at burglary, the criminals certainly wouldn't have been stopped by a dog run and a cowardly cocker spaniel. But as she drove the winding road down the mountain, her hands tightened on the steering wheel until they ached and it was anger, not fear, that tautened her muscles and clenched her jaw. Damn it all, she had come here to get away from the crazed druggies and their senseless crimes. She had gone, as a matter of fact, practically to the ends of the earth. She wouldn't have thought a criminal could even *find* this place. And what about that elaborate security system Bullard had touted so loudly? Wasn't any place safe anymore?

She glanced over at Christy, and realized her mood was affecting her daughter's. Christy sat glumly hunched against the shoulder strap of the seat belt, picking at a loose thread from the embroidered Big Bird on her cotton overalls. Laura forced her shoulders to relax and flexed her hands, briefly, on the steering wheel.

She reached over and tapped Christy's knee, distracting her from the damage she was doing to Big Bird.

"Do you want me to buy some hot dogs for lunch? We haven't had hot dogs in a long time."

Christy looked up at her anxiously. "Maybe we could give some to the monsters. Then they wouldn't come around anymore."

Laura took a deep breath and tried again. "Hey," she said brightly, launching into their favorite game. "Do you know what I wish? I wish I was a cat. Not just any cat, but a big fluffy white cat. Then I'd never have to go to the grocery store or answer the telephone or work at my job. I'd just sit in the sun and sleep on velvet cushions and whenever I got hungry someone would bring me food and I'd never have to take a bath."

After a moment Christy giggled, then sat up straighter, bouncing against the restraints of her seat belt. "I wish I was a . . . fish!"

"What kind of fish?"

"A stripy one. Orange and red stripes, and all the other fish would be jealous because they don't have any stripes at all. And I could swim all day long and go to bed whenever I wanted."

"And you'd never have to take a bath!"

"And no one would ever have me for dinner!"

They played the game the rest of the way into town, where Christy quickly became distracted by a display of wind socks at the gas station, and then by a woman pushing a twin stroller on Main Street. Laura was constantly grateful for the notoriously short attention span of children.

Her first stop was the hardware store, a rambling, musty-smelling structure with floors that sloped where additions had been made and walls that were, in the oldest parts, age-stained pine. There one could purchase everything from soup pots to weaponry, and she spent half an hour lost in a maze of merchandise that was arranged in no particular order at all before finally

66

leaving with a rake, a shovel, a package of cup hooks, and several miscellaneous items that she didn't really want but couldn't resist.

At the local supermarket, she stocked up on groceries to last a week or more. Then mindful of the perishables she had stored in the car, she warned Christy not to dawdle at the toy counter while they rushed into the dime store for tracing paper, thumbtacks, and household glue. Laura wasn't usually an impulse buyer, but neither was she very organized at the business of moving from a five-room apartment to a twelve-room house. She kept seeing more things that she needed or had forgotten: soap for the guest bath, extra coat hangers, paper cups for the kitchen—not to mention flea shampoo and a coloring book and crayons for Christy. Her bill totaled $20.52, and when she handed the clerk her MasterCard the woman just stared at her.

"We don't take that."

"Oh." Laura put the card back and took out her checkbook. "I'll just write you a check then."

"We don't take checks either."

Despite what Isabel had said about "friendly locals," Laura sensed a definite hostility in this woman's manner. She was middle-aged, the way women used to look when they reached forty-five or fifty—sagging, tired, lumpy. She had a bad dye job and rod perm; perfumed face powder, several shades brighter than her skin tone, cracked in the wrinkles on her face. She looked at Laura as though she were a bad debt, and that embarrassed and confused Laura.

Quickly, she checked the cash in her wallet. Seven dollars and change. She said, "Look, the grocery store took my check, and so did the hardware store—"

"Maybe they can afford to."

There were other people in line behind her, and Laura's embarrassment began to turn to anger. Christy

67

tugged at her sleeve. "Don't you have enough money, Mommy?"

"Yes, honey, I have enough money." She looked back at the clerk and said stiffly, "I'm going to write you a check. You can call the bank and find out for yourself that it's good."

"Can't. Today's Wednesday. The bank's closed."

"Take the lady's check, Jessie," said a quiet, amused voice behind her. "There are public officials waiting to go back to work here."

Laura twisted around to see Sam Keller standing behind her.

The clerk started to protest, "Now, Sam, you know I can't —"

"You're not going to have any trouble," he assured her. "That's a personal promise."

Laura scrawled out the check, tore it from the book, and pushed it across the counter with what she considered an admirable restraint of temper. She handed the smaller bag to Christy, took the larger one for herself, and said politely, "Have a nice day."

Out of the corner of her eye she saw Sam Keller lay a dollar on the counter for the package of razor blades he pocketed, and he followed her out the door.

"I suppose I should thank you for being a character witness," she said.

He rubbed a knuckle against the side of his chin, hiding a rueful grin. "Sorry about that. Some folks are still a little suspicious of strangers. It'll be different once they get to know you."

She shrugged it off lightly, trying to be a good sport. "I'm used to dealing with pickpockets and cutthroats. A little rudeness won't hurt me."

"How's the new house?"

"The shower leaks, there's a crack in the kitchen tile,

68

and the guest room closet door won't close. Otherwise, it's great."

He chuckled. "It's nice to know even architects have trouble with new houses."

"I don't build them, I just design them."

Christy looked up at Sam. "Are you a policeman?"

"The closest thing we've got around here," he replied agreeably.

She gazed at him with interest. "Do you have a gun?"

"I do. I just don't carry it very often. How come? You got somebody you want me to shoot?"

Laura was not at all sure she liked the way he'd put that. She liked it even less when Christy met his smile soberly and replied, "I have to think about it."

She walked a little faster toward the van and said in a mild undertone, "I don't like to encourage talk of violence around Christy."

"Kids don't think about it as violence," he replied, completely unaffected. "To them it's just the natural way of things."

They had reached the van, and Laura shot him a skeptical look as she bent to unlatch the rear door. "I'm really not sure I want to know what you mean by that."

"I mean," he answered anyway, "that children are all little savages at heart — just like we all were once upon a time. Kids are just closer to their roots, you might say."

"I think you have a rather warped perspective on things," Laura murmured.

He caught the edge of the rear door as it swung open and guided it upward. "I'll have you know I have a reputation around here as quite a philosopher, but this probably isn't the place to get into that. How about that lunch you promised me?"

Laura couldn't quite hide her surprise, and while she was searching for a reply Christy said eagerly, "Can we go to McDonald's?"

Laura turned to her with a quick smile, "No, honey, there's no McDonald's around here." She looked back at Sam and made a gesture toward the groceries in the back of the car. "I really can't. I've got to get these things in the refrigerator."

"What, these two bags?" He looked inside the van and immediately picked out the bags that contained the perishables—which, with an attention to detail one rarely found in larger supermarkets, had considerately been packed together. He lifted them out of the van and called to the bag boy, who was pushing a cart toward the front door. "Hey, Ken! Come put these back in the cooler for me, will you? We'll pick them up after lunch."

"Sure thing, Sheriff." The young man took the bags, and was back inside the store before Laura could do more than utter a few inarticulate words of protest.

She stared at Sam, half amused, half exasperated. "You are persistent, aren't you?"

He lifted one shoulder with a half grin. "That's another thing I have a reputation for."

Christy said, "I want a hamburger."

Sam bent down and informed her confidentially, "Well, it just so happens I know the cook personally, and I don't doubt that she'd fix you the best hamburger you ever had if I asked her real nice."

"Better than Mommy's?"

Sam glanced at Laura, his eyes twinkling. "Well, that depends. How good is your mama's hamburger?"

Christy screwed up her face and declared loudly, "Awful!"

Sam laughed and Laura pretended to be insulted, and though she knew Sam Keller was using unfair persuasion tactics concerning lunch, she was so relieved to see Christy's good humor restored after the grim mood in which they had begun the trip to town that she didn't mind. Sam caught Christy's hand and cheerfully allowed her to monopolize the conversation as they walked the block and a half to the cafe called Bob and Mary's. Laura watched with what she hoped was not too obvious a display of motherly indulgence.

"I thought you had to go back to work," Laura said as they entered the cafe. It was little more than a storefront, with six or eight formica tables in mismatched shades of yellow, green, and gray flanked by equally mismatched captain's chairs without cushions. An open counter separated the kitchen from the eating area, and the aroma was a pungent mixture of sweet and sour, frying and baking.

"I keep what you might call flexible hours."

Sam paused to nod at several of the customers, and on the way to their table introduced Laura to them—the president of the bank, a local preacher, a mechanic at the gas station. Laura decided that, despite the unimposing decor, the food there must be good.

Sam ordered a hamburger for Christy, and included her seriously in the discussion of exactly how she would like it prepared. Though Laura had always been suspicious of men who were *too* nice to children with unmarried mothers, there was something so artlesss about Sam Keller's interaction with Christy that she found herself liking him despite herself. He ordered countryfried steak for himself, and Laura, using the same philosophy she did while visiting foreign countries, followed suit.

When Christy opened the bag that contained her coloring book and crayons Laura admonished, "No, honey, it's not polite to color at the table."

Sam gave Christy a sympathetic look. "With my mother it was always, 'It's not polite to read at the table.'"

"Ah," Laura said. "So you were an intellectual child."

71

He lifted two crossed fingers. "Me and Batman. Just like that."

Laura chuckled.

"Do you have a puppy?" Christy wanted to know. "I have a puppy. His name is Corky."

"I know," Sam replied. "I've met him, though you probably don't remember. How's he getting along?"

Laura leaned back and let Sam and Christy monopolize the conversation. She felt a little sorry for Sam, but he had known what he was getting into, and she had too few mealtimes in which she was free from the responsibility of entertaining Christy to intervene. And Christy, for her part, missed her Uncles Ben and Hilly, and it wouldn't hurt to let Sam take over the role for a short while.

When the food arrived Christy turned her attention to her hamburger, and Laura looked in a mixture of dismay and admiration at the platter of country-fried steak smothered in gravy, served with mashed potatoes, green beans, macaroni and cheese, and corn muffins. "My goodness," she murmured. "Guess who won't be having dinner tonight."

"I figured it was something like that," Sam said, buttering a muffin. "You weren't actually turning me down the other night. You just don't eat dinner."

Laura laughed a little. "Something like that," she agreed. "And also," she had to add honestly as she cut into her steak, "because it sounded a little bit like a date."

He lifted his eyebrows a little. "I see. My mistake." He looked as though he wanted to pursue that subject further, but then glanced at Christy and said instead, "How's that hamburger, high-pocket?"

Christy, with her mouth full, nodded enthusiastically and murmured something intelligible.

The food was so good, and the atmosphere so comortable, that Laura almost forgot her host. Midway through the meal she looked up with an apologetic smile and said, "Sorry, I'm not being a very good conversationalist. This is really good. Thanks for asking us."

He smiled. "Cooking is one thing mountain folks can still do better than anybody else in the country."

Laura took a paper napkin from the dispenser on the counter and wiped a smear of mustard from Christy's chin. "How did you get into law enforcement?"

"That sounds like one of those polite questions you really don't care about the answer to. But I'll answer it anyway. When I got out of the Army I needed a job, and the police department was the only place that was hiring."

"So much for my illusions about our gallant men in blue. But obviously you decided you like it."

"As a matter of fact, I hated it." He speared a couple of green beans with his fork and shrugged a little. "I guess I could tell you some hair-raising stories about life on the streets, but the fact is I was pretty lucky. I never had to shoot anybody, and I never got shot at— though I had some close calls there, a couple of times." He hesitated, and his brow furrowed a little with thought. "It was just that you never knew what to expect. What was waiting around the next corner, behind the next door. And after a while I started to feel like maybe it was time for my luck to start running out."

He took a bite of the green beans and finished. "That's what I like about being back here. You always know what to expect. A few traffic tickets, a drunk driver now and then, and when husbands and wives fight they don't use guns. I'm not saying we don't have our problems, but I know who's likely to abuse his kids, or take a notion to shoot out his neighbor's porch light, and I can kind of watch out for it. No surprises."

Laura said, "I wouldn't think there was enough happening in a little place like this to keep a good lawman busy."

He smiled. "That's another thing I like. Plenty of free time."

It was on the tip of her tongue to mention the incident at the Jennings house, but then Christy said, "I'm finished, Mommy. Is it polite to color on the floor?"

Sam glanced around. "I'll tell you what. The lunch rush looks like it's about over. I bet Mary wouldn't mind if you spread your crayons and coloring book on one of those empty tables over there while your mom and I finish eating." Then he looked at Laura. "If that's okay with you?"

Laura took another napkin and cleaned Christy's face and hands. "I guess that would be all right. But you pick a table and stay at it. Don't go wandering around bothering the other customers."

When Christy was happily settled down at a table across the room, garnering indulgent looks from a couple of men who were finishing their lunch, Sam said casually, "How long have you been divorced?"

Laura swallowed, took a sip of tea, and met Sam's eyes calmly. "Who said I was married?"

He answered, "I see."

There was nothing judgmental or condescending about the way he said that, and there was nothing in his eyes at all except polite interest. Still, Laura felt a little defensive.

She wasn't embarrassed about the circumstances of Christy's birth; it had happened at far too late a stage in her life and with far too much love and certainty to be tainted by anxiety at what others would think. But there was still enough insecurity inside her to make her uncomfortable when explaining the situation to people she didn't know very well. Usually, she handled such

74

moments with a blasé, offhand comment or a politely frozen smile, but for some reason she felt Sam Keller deserved more than that.

So she found herself explaining. "I was working on a project in England, and I became involved with a very prominent, very charming journalist. I knew he had been separated from his wife for several years, and I don't want this to sound like an excuse, but I didn't know he had no intention of ever divorcing her. I'm not sure I would have married him if he had been free. I was almost thirty years old, and I knew it might be my last chance . . . so you see, when I found out I was pregnant there wasn't even a moment's choice. I wanted her, I could afford to give her a good life, and whether or not I had a husband just didn't matter."

He nodded. She couldn't tell whether it was in sympathy or understanding. "Do you ever wish it had been different?"

Laura felt a faint trace of amusement. What was it about men that simply would not allow them to accept the fact that women and children could manage very well, and sometimes better, without them?

She answered, "I won't say it's always been easy, juggling my schedule, just the millions of little details that go along with raising a child, trying to be everywhere at once. But I do the best I can, and no, I don't really wish anything were different. Christy and I have something very special. I wouldn't change it."

He looked thoughtful. "I've got to know one more thing. What made you decide to move way up here by yourself?"

Laura looked down at her plate, peeling back a sliver of cheese from the macaroni with her fork. She tried to keep her voice pleasant as she replied, "You certainly do ask a lot of questions, don't you?"

He was unrebuked. "Comes with the job, I guess."

Laura was relieved when the bell over the door jangled and a man said, "There you are, Sheriff. Somebody said they thought they saw you come in here."

He was a wiry, ageless man in a plaid cotton shirt, straw hat, and pants that were so ill-fitting they puckered at the belt. He stalked over to the table before Sam could even form a greeting and said, "Now listen here, Sam, you've got to do something about them kids. This is the third time this month they've turned over that dumpster, and this time they kicked a great big hole through the rust in the side. Now you know damn good and well when folks come up to dump their trash they're not going to drive way back into town with it — they're going to pour it out right on my land and what am I supposed to do, sit out there twenty-four hours a day with a shotgun? I tell you, you gotta do something!"

Sam said politely, "Hoyt, this is Laura Kane. Laura, Hoyt Kramer."

Hoyt gave her a perfunctory glance, and lifted his hat, revealing a round bald head speckled with liver spots. "Sorry, ma'am. Didn't mean to interrupt your meal." He turned back to Sam. "Well?"

Sam rubbed his chin. "How about if I call the county and see about getting a new dumpster with a fence around it?"

Hoyt nodded, only partially mollified. "And I'll tell you something else. Ever since they started digging out the side of that mountain it's sending the animals down in herds, rooting around in that trash, dragging it back into the woods. Some of those rats must be the size of yearlings from the mess they're making. You going to do anything about that?"

"I'll send a couple of deputies up this afternoon to check it out."

"Well, they better do more than check it out, is all I

76

can say," Hoyt muttered. "Somebody's got to clean up that mess and it sure ain't gonna be me." He nodded at Laura. "Afternoon, ma'am."

When he was gone, Sam said, "There's not a chance in hell the county will spring for a new dumpster, much less a fence. Hoyt lives way out on the other side of tarnation, and nobody ever uses that dump except him and a couple of other farmers back in the hills." He smiled. "Now you see why everybody calls this a glamor job."

But something about the interchange had disturbed Laura, and she said hesitantly, "That dump—is it anywhere near the woods?"

"Almost everything is in the woods once you get out of town. But if you mean up near the national forest— well, yeah, kind of. Why?"

The little chill that prickled at Laura's neck made her feel foolish, and she said, "Nothing. It's stupid. It's just that something happened in the Heights this morning last night actually—and when he said something about a hole being torn in the dumpster it reminded me of it."

As succinctly as possible she told him about the Jennings dog run. She expected him to smile at the connection she'd made, and when he didn't she was far from reassured.

"That's odd," he murmured. A frown knotted his sandy brows.

"I thought so too."

"No, I mean odder than you think. It sounds like something somebody zonked out on PCP would try, and I've got to tell you we don't see a lot of that around here. Unless old Joe was asleep at his post, there's no way anybody could have gotten up there to do something like that. So it had to be somebody in the Heights."

"Oh, great. So I've got a drug-crazed maniac for a neighbor."

He looked at her quickly. "Sorry. Sometimes I think out loud. Bad habit. It's probably—"

"Nothing to worry about," Laura mimicked in an exasperated tone. "Typical male condescension."

He smiled. "Actually, I was going to say it's probably something I should look into. You can worry as much as you like; it doesn't make my job any harder. Do you want some dessert? It's peach cobbler today."

For a moment Laura just stared at him. Then she murmured, "You are—very unusual."

His eyes twinkled. "That's a start."

She did not ask what it was a start for; she already knew. What she didn't know was how she felt about it, and she didn't think it was a subject she wanted to pursue just then. She said, "But you don't think there's any connection between what happened to the Jennings and the dumpster."

"There might be." He refilled her glass, then his own, from the plastic pitcher of sweet tea that had been left on the table. "In a roundabout way. There are always going to be troublemakers around, and since the Heights project got under way we've had more than our share of incidents, as the press would call it. I just don't want it to get out of hand."

"What? Do you mean vandalism?"

"Some of it. And then there was—" He seemed to debate for a moment, then said, "I don't guess you heard about Brett Howard."

She shook her head.

"He was one of the first surveyors your people sent out here."

"They're not my people," she felt compelled to point out.

"Right." Absentmindedly he tore open a packet of

78

sugar and stirred it into his tea. "Anyway, that first summer he was working up on the mountain and just disappeared. We beat the woods for him for a good three weeks, never found a trace. You've got to understand that mountain was a maze before the bulldozers went in, so thick a coon dog couldn't even get through, so we knew from the start if he was up there we didn't have much chance of finding him. I had to just leave the file open . . . till the next winter, when they started blasting, clearing things out. One of the workmen found him — what was left of him."

Laura, who had been about to indulge herself in one more corn muffin, lowered her butter knife back to the plate, her appetite completely gone. "Not — murdered?"

"No," he said quickly, though the troubled, thoughtful look that shadowed his eyes lingered. "At least that doesn't seem likely. The carnivores had pretty much done their job so the coroner didn't have much to go on, but our best guess was some kind of animal attack." His smile was a weak imitation of the ones Laura had seen before. "I guess that's how the bear stories got started."

That was enough to ruin her afternoon, and she was sure she didn't want to hear any more. But she was equally sure she hadn't heard it all. She said, "And?"

He looked at her as though trying to gauge her reaction to what he had not even said yet. "This isn't very good mealtime conversation."

"I have a strong stomach."

His gaze was steady and unevasive, which she appreciated. But a moment later she wished she hadn't asked.

"He had been more or less torn apart," Sam said. "His spine was crushed, and his rib cage peeled open, his arms and legs ripped out of their sockets. A messy way to die."

Laura swallowed hard. "Bears—do that?"

He hesitated. "Bears sometimes crush their victims to death. I don't know about the rest."

"Maybe those carnivores you talked about—"

"Maybe."

But the reply was too brief, and the answer too pat, to be entirely satisfactory. If Laura had asked more questions he might have answered them, but she had heard enough, and Sam said, "Anyway, that was a long time ago and doesn't have anything to do with what's going on now. It's just that some folks took it as a kind of sign that the mountain should be left alone, and you know how these things can get blown up out of proportion."

Laura smiled weakly. "Right. The fancy city folks move in with their air pollution, their littering, their broken bodies cluttering up the place. . . ."

"One," he corrected. "One broken body."

That was hardly reassuring, and Laura was remembering something else. Something she had read somewhere. She said uneasily, "Bears—don't get very big around here, do they? Three or four feet?"

His lack of an answer, his muddied, disturbed gaze, was worse than anything he could have said.

"Mommy, look!"

Laura jumped at the sound of Christy's voice, and had to pretend much more enthusiasm than she felt as she admired her daughter's crayola work. Sam joined in as an amateur art critic, and they did not speak of bodies or bears or vandals again.

But that night Laura had feverish nightmares about running through the woods, and was awakened in the still hours of the morning by the puppy, who was standing at her window and whining furiously. She scooped up the dog, who was trembling with agitation, and ran to check on Christy, who was murmuring fitfully in her

80

sleep as though in the throes of a bad dream, but otherwise seemed undisturbed. As soon as Laura released the puppy he ran back to her window and started crying again.

She checked all the doors and windows, and finally went back to her bedroom, where Corky was whimpering and pawing at the window. She looked out, and saw nothing.

She took the dog downstairs, curled up in an armchair, and tried to watch television. But she couldn't concentrate. Long after Corky had fallen asleep in her lap she sat up, tense and watching, listening and waiting, and she did not sleep again that night.

Chapter Five

Sometimes, when the land was filled with sadness, it was necessary for good people to do bad things. The good Queen Laura had made a rule that no one was to go into the woods, and the Warrior Princess Cristilina was breaking that rule. But it wasn't a bad thing. Only the brave Cristilina could save the land, and how could she save it unless she could see the enemy?

In the heart of the woods lived the monstrous snowmen. They ravaged the land, terrified small children, and made puppies cry in the night. Everyone was scared of them. Everyone, of course, except the Warrior Princess.

With her faithful lucky dragon Corky at her side, Cristilina left the castle fortress and began the long and dangerous journey toward the Dark Forest. In a silken pouch she carried priceless treasures from the Castle Strong: glittering jewels, magic potions, sweet elixirs. These were gifts with which to persuade the snowmen to stop ravaging the land, terrifying small children, and making puppies cry in the night — just as the Pilgrims had once made friends with the Indians by giving them shiny beads and red cloth. But just in case the snowmen didn't want to be friends, Cristilina also carried a magic sword which would slay the beasts at her command, and the land would be safe again.

The priceless treasures were chocolate-chip cookies in a paper bag, the magic sword a bright orange Nerf baseball bat. Corky, with his tail in the air and his nose to the ground, looked more like a cocker spaniel than a lucky dragon, and the Warrior Princess was only a five-year-old girl in cotton shorts and a Smurf T-shirt. But the monstrous snowmen were real, and it was still up to her to save the land.

Laura glared at the telephone she had just hung up, pushed her hand through her hair, and muttered, "I don't believe this."

She didn't believe that Ben had pushed the meeting with Simmons up ten days; she didn't believe that he had forgotten she had told him specifically she wouldn't have the plans ready until the twentieth; she didn't believe that he'd had the gall to ask her to fax him those very plans by noon tomorrow when he knew perfectly well she hadn't even hooked up her machine yet, and it would take her that long to find the Simmons file. What she *did* believe was that he had done this deliberately, as some diabolical way of punishing her for moving.

Or at least that was what she wanted to believe. The truth was that things like this happened all the time. Simmons had scheduled an unexpected trip to Europe, and had made it clear that either the plans had to be ready before he left or they would lose the job. Ben had tried to reach another agreement. He had even offered to finish the plans himself, which turned out to be an empty gesture when he realized that Laura had taken the files on all her current projects with her. It was nobody's fault. But it was a hell of a mess.

Laura glanced at the clock on the microwave, which

was the only one in this part of the house which was currently plugged in. It was twelve-fifteen. She had been in the middle of fixing Christy's lunch when the phone rang. If she got right to work it was possible — just possible — she could finish the plans tonight. She had worked on shorter deadlines. But where in the thriving metropolis of Calumit, Tennessee, was she going to find a fax machine?

First things first. She looked out the kitchen window, which overlooked the front of the house, and then opened the door, calling for Christy. She was probably still playing on the gym set and couldn't hear the call, because there was no response. Laura picked up the community directory which Joe had given her on the first day she arrived, thumbing through for Mary Beth Jennings's number. She dialed quickly.

When Mary Beth answered, she said, "What was the name of that baby-sitter you recommended — the one I met at the Bullards' party?"

When she explained the situation, Mary Beth was quick to volunteer to take Christy for the afternoon, and Laura was tempted. But she wanted to save the services of friends and neighbors for emergencies, and she wasn't at all sure when she'd be able to reciprocate on Mary Beth's behalf.

So she answered, "Thanks, but I need to start trying out baby-sitters, and this is as good a time as any — while I can keep an eye on both of them."

Mary Beth gave her Cathy Sykes's phone number, and the subsequent phone call proved Cathy to be not only available, but delighted at the prospect of spending the afternoon in the Heights, swimming in a private pool and playing video games with a five-year-old. After copying down the somewhat convoluted directions to Cathy's house, Laura promised she would pick her up in half an hour.

Then she went to find Christy.

The brave warrior Cristilina waded through the Swamp of Horrors, waged war against the Bee People in the Dreadful Fields, and at last reached the outskirts of the awesomely big Dark Forest. The great lucky dragon, far braver than even the bravest warrior princess, forged ahead to check for danger. When he saw his mortal companion was not following, however, he stopped, looked back with an inquiring wave of his tail, and yipped softly.

"Ssh, lucky dragon," Christy commanded. The great dark bigness of the forest seemed to swallow up her voice, making it tiny and unsure. "The snowmen are sleeping. They're gonna be awful mad if you wake them up."

She stood in a patch of sunlight with the green expanse of clipped lawn spreading out behind her, the windows of her very own house winking like merry eyes in the distance. She took one step forward and the sunlight disappeared. The forest had cold breath, scented with pine and crunchy dry leaves. She tilted her head back as far as she could, but still couldn't see the tops of the trees, just trunks that splayed like the legs of giants all around her and twisted arms that drooped with broken fingers. She felt very small. And it was past her lunchtime.

But warrior princesses did not get hungry, and they did not run away just because the woods were dark. Besides, the snowmen were sleeping. She was sure of it.

She shouldered her magic sword and moved bravely forward.

Christy was not playing on the gym set. Neither was

she beneath the shadows of the spreading oak tree, nor throwing sticks for Corky across the open green lawn, and she didn't answer when Laura called. Laura's first reaction was impatience, which quickly became mitigated by a prickle of alarm. She raced around to the pool, but the wooden gate that guarded the pool area was firmly closed and the water was still and undisturbed. She called again. There was no answer but her echo.

Laura shaded her eyes and searched the backyard slowly, inch by inch. It was a big yard, but not big enough to hide a girl and a dog from this vantage point. Not unless . . . Her eyes stopped moving as they met the shadows of the woods. And she knew she did not have to look any further.

Her heart was tight in her chest as she called out Christy's name one more time, then started running toward the woods.

Damn it, damn it . . . The words were beating out the rhythm of her steps. *I should have been watching her. I should have known something was wrong the first time she didn't answer.* Christy knew better than to go near the woods. She had *told* her . . . but Laura's anger was only a thin membrane that separated reason from blind, stupid terror and she thought, *Damn it, Christy, you know better!*

Leaving the grassy glade for the abrupt entrance into the woods was like stepping into another world. Here it was dark and cool and dank-smelling. She could hear the rasping of her breath, and her eyes actually hurt as they adjusted from the bright sunlight to the dimness within.

She stopped, and shouted, "Christy!"

A bird screeched back a reply and something scratched its way up a tree.

"Christine Louisa Kane, you come here this minute!"

Near the edge of the woods there were quite a few

pines and saplings struggling for scraps of sunlight beneath the limbs of much taller, much older trees. But as she moved further in she tripped over the roots of corpses that had given up the effort, and even the thick foliage of stubborn rhododendron seemed sparser, dwarfed by the giant oaks and elms that had proven themselves kings of the mountain. Boulders jutted from the earth, hiding small mossy holes that were the homes of foxes or raccoons or wharf rats or whatever it was that lived in this dark miserable place. Laura thought about snakes. And wild dogs. Had she followed Corky up here? Was that what had happened? And which way had they gone? The forest was so big, with a million places to hide. . . .

"Christy!" she shouted again, trying to keep the edge of panic out of her voice. "Christy, Mommy's not kidding! Come back here now!"

She pushed aside a branch, ducked low to avoid another one, and tried not to think about how big this mountain was, how deep and endless the woods, how she might easily be looking in the wrong place, and how the Sheriff's Department had searched for Brett Howard's body for three weeks. . . .

Something rustled up ahead and she stood still, her heart pounding, listening hard. "Christy?"

The rustling grew closer, more frantic, and Laura sank to her knees as something small and furry burst into sight and flung itself toward her. "Corky!"

The puppy bounded into her arms, nipping at her hair, licking her face, scratching her legs as it wiggled in her lap. "Corky, you great dog! What a good puppy! I'm so glad to see you!" She hugged the dog, dodging its wet tongue without much success, breathless with relief. "What a good puppy! Where's Christy, Cork? Where's Christy?"

What the dog did next was hardly enough to earn

him a medal of honor, nor even honorable mention in a Christmas column devoted to canine heroes — considering the fact that all he had to do was turn back the way he had come and run into the bushes, it was not actually a display of more than ordinary intelligence — but for Laura, it was more than enough to warrant an extra helping of Puppy Chow for dinner. Corky bounded forward about ten yards, Laura plunged after him, and there was Christy, sliding down a small granite outcropping and coming toward them.

"Hi, Mommy," she said.

Laura wanted to grab her and shake her hard, screaming invectives and promises of dire punishment. What she did was scoop the child into her arms and hug her until she wriggled to be set free.

"Thank goodness," she breathed, more than once. "Thank goodness you're all right."

She held Christy's shoulders and looked at her sternly. "Don't you know you scared your mommy to death? Didn't I tell you never to go into the woods? Didn't you promise me?"

"I'm sorry, Mommy. But I was going to save you. I was going to save everybody from the snowmen."

"The what?"

"The snowmen monsters."

Laura took a deep breath and released it slowly. Although what she really wanted was to get out of these woods and back into the light, she slipped an arm around Christy's shoulders and sat down on the damp, humus earth, bringing Christy with her.

"Listen to me," she said quietly, looking into her daughter's eyes. "Make-believe is a good thing. Remember we talked about that?"

Christy nodded slowly.

"Do you also remember we decided it was important to know when to stop playing make-believe?"

Again the nod.

"Monsters are just make-believe, Christy. And the time to stop playing make-believe is when the pretending makes you do things you're not supposed to do—like going into the woods. I don't want you to ever do that again, honey. Do you understand?"

"I understand."

"It's very, very important."

"I won't do it again, Mommy. I don't like it out here. I'm glad you came."

"Good." Laura gave her an affectionate slap on the bottom and got to her feet. "Now, let's go back to the house. We've got to go pick up your new baby-sitter because Mommy has to work this afternoon. She's going to take you swimming. You'll like that won't you?"

"Yeah!"

"And Christy." Laura bent down once more and looked into her daughter's eyes intently. "You see for yourself that there aren't any monsters out here, don't you? So no more bad dreams?"

Christy looked around slowly, thoroughly. Laura let her take her time. And then Christy said solemnly, "They're sleeping. They only come at nighttime. In the day they sleep."

Laura felt a shiver prickle her skin which was more than helplessness. "Christy . . ."

"Don't worry, Mommy," Christy said earnestly. "I left some cookies for them. Maybe they won't be mad if they find the cookies."

Laura looked at her daughter's small, upturned face, the absolute sincerity in her eyes, and knew she had reached one of those points at which it became abundantly clear that parenting was not a learned art. She wanted to tell herself it was a phase which should be allowed to run its course. She tried to remember the text of one of those cozy mother-child "talks" advocated by popular parenting magazines for just such occasions. She wondered whether it was time to overrea and seek child counseling. But instinctively she kne none of those measures would provide a solution merely a stopgap.

From the beginning of time children had cowere from imaginary monsters, parents had tried to convince them the monsters were not real, and childre had gone on crying in the dark . . . and the reason wa not very surprising. The monsters *were* real. Only in th adult world they had names like Cancer, and Nuclea Accident, and Street Crime. It was a hard truth, but truth nonetheless. The monsters did not go away whe one grew older, they just changed faces.

And standing there in the shadow of the woods wit the hint of a damp breeze breathing down her neck Laura had nothing whatsoever to say to her child.

So she smiled a little, and took Christy's hand, an led her out of the woods.

Almost from the moment of Christy's birth Laur had made a silent bargain with herself: She would b there for Christy, day in and day out, always available no matter what it took. But at the same time she woul not feel guilty for those times when the full focus of he attention had to be directed somewhere else and sh turned the responsibility for Christy's minute-to minute supervision over to someone else. For the firs three years of Christy's life she had had a live-in house keeper; after that she had relied on dailies. She ha hoped to spend this last year before Christy started school without outside help, but the episode that morn ing had convinced her otherwise. An idle child ha little choice but to get into mischief, and even the mos diligent mother could not be on active duty twenty-fou

90

hours a day. She expected to rely on the services of Cathy Sykes a great deal in the future.

The directions Cathy had given Laura took her halfway down the mountain, along an unmarked country road, and left on a dirt track marked by a deserted trailer and a sagging split-rail fence, and Laura was quite convinced she was lost until she saw the rusty mailbox painted with the black letters SYKES exactly where Cathy had predicted it would be.

Behind that mailbox was a gray shack propped up on cinder blocks. The porch sagged on one end, and soiled pieces of cloth hung limply over unscreened windows. The dirt yard was littered with rusted-out scraps of metal, threadbare tires, an old mattress, and an armchair whose stuffing and several springs had spilled out through its faded flower-print upholstery.

A couple of rangy barn cats roamed the yard, and a hound of some sort was tied to a tree. The dog heaved itself to its feet when Laura turned into the yard, let out a baleful half-moan, half-bark, and flopped down in the shade again. Laura sat in the car for a moment, half hoping she had the wrong place.

A woman wearing men's jeans and a flannel shirt sat on the porch, shelling peas and staring at her. After a moment Laura felt so uncomfortable under that stare that she opened the car door and got out. "Stay here, baby," she warned Christy, and started toward the porch. At that moment the screen door opened and Cathy Sykes came out.

In plaid walking shorts and modest white shirt, she was totally out of place in the midst of what Laura could only call squalor. She lifted her hand to Laura cheerfully and called, "Hi, Mrs. Kane!" Then she quickly bent and kissed the woman on the porch, and hurried down the steps, as though anxious to be away. Laura couldn't blame her, but she could hardly call herself a responsible parent if she let it go at that. She met Cathy halfway up the steps and said pleasantly, "Is this your mother?"

Cathy looked uncomfortable. "My grandmother."

Fixing a smile on her face, Laura went the rest of the way up the steps and extended her hand. "Hi. I'm Laura Kane. Cathy's going to be doing some baby-sitting for me this afternoon. I thought you might like the phone number where she'll be."

The woman was old, Laura could see that now, but she was a broad-shouldered, firmly kept old. Her gray hair was pulled back in a ponytail high off her neck, and her face was weathered brown and heavy. There was a cigarette burning in a cracked saucer on the plant stand next to her, and instead of taking Laura's hand she lifted the cigarette and took a slow drag, her dark eyes assessing Laura narrowly.

She said, "You live up there in one of them fancy new houses on the hill, don't you?"

"That's right." Laura retrieved her hand a little self-consciously.

"Bunch o' damn fools," the woman said contemptuously. "Gonna get yerselves killed, every one of you."

Laura said, "Excuse me?" and Cathy, at the same moment, pleaded, "Granny . . ."

But the old woman ignored her granddaughter and looked straight at Laura. "Them woods is the summer hunting ground of the Nighteaters, everybody knows that. Even ignorant white folks know that. Has been as long as anybody can remember. Before the first white man set foot here, that's for damn sure. Probably the first Indian too. You think that's gonna change just because you city folks take a notion to slap up your million-dollar houses? Hell, no. They're just gonna start huntin' *you* is all." Her chuckle was almost a cackle, full of nasty delight.

Laura stared at her. *Monsters in the woods, Mommy. Bad things.*

Cathy said uncomfortably, "Granny is part Cherokee. She's full of all kind of wild stories." As she spoke she edged down one step, as though hoping Laura would follow suit and she could make her escape.

The woman said sharply, "Ain't nothing wild about it, gal, and you mind your elders! I seen one of 'em with my own eyes, I did, when I wasn't no older than that young'un sittin' in the car, and so did my granddaddy and his granddaddy before him, so don't you give me no sass about wild stories!"

Cathy cast an anxious apologetic glance toward Laura, but Laura didn't see. She couldn't stop staring at the grandmother. *Monsters in the woods . . .*

She cleared her throat and said, "I, um, heard that the mountain used to be Indian holy ground."

The other woman gave a snort of what might have been laughter. "Yeah, you could call it that, I reckon. What happened is they was scared out of their heads, is what. Cherokee and Chickasaw too, and Shawnee before them. Made a treaty that none of them would ever hunt there—right smart move, that—and dedicated it to the spirit that lived there. Nobody ever broke it either. Oh, I reckon the first settlers tried, seems to me I remember a tale or two, but in the end it was easier to kill off the Indians than to kill off what lived on the mountaintop. Still it took 'em two hundred years to forget, didn't it? Two hundred years to move right up in there amongst 'em." She probed a back tooth with her tongue—as though searching for a particle of food or a stray shred of tobacco—found it, and spat it out. "Damn fools."

Cathy said a little urgently, "We've got to go, Granny." Clearly she was afraid Laura would change her mind at any moment, and she would be out an afternoon's work and the rare opportunity to swim in a private pool. "Scott will bring me home tonight when I'm finished. Don't wait supper for me."

The grandmother held Laura with narrowed, speculative black eyes. "Dihi," she said flatly.

Laura blinked. "What's that?"

"The Cherokee word for 'em. What you-all call Nighteaters."

"What does it mean?"

The old woman brought the cigarette to her mouth and pursed her lips around it. She took her time drawing in and exhaling a cloud of gray smoke. Then she answered, "Killer."

It would be illogical to say that Laura went home that afternoon and put the disturbing conversation with the old Indian woman out of her mind, but that for the most part was exactly what she did. Adults defend the sanctity of their worlds with weapons children cannot even begin to imagine, and one of the most effective of these is Work. A sense of purpose, the absolute conviction that nothing bad can happen as long as one is busy, productive, important: *No, Doctor, I can't be rushed into surgery this afternoon, I have a presentation to make tomorrow morning. No, this plane can't crash, I've got to be in Geneva in two hours. No, you can't kill me now, my boss is expecting me for dinner.* Laura couldn't think about monsters that afternoon; she had a set of plans to finish before morning.

Nonetheless, the memory would strike her when she was least expecting it — listening to the sound of Christy squealing and splashing in the pool, pausing to rub the back of her neck after hours of hunching over the drafting board, looking up when Cathy asked if it was all right to fix Christy a snack — it would sneak up on her,

94

take her by surprise, and leave her wary and disturbed.

There's bad things in the woods, Mommy.

What monsters, honey?

Dihi. Killer.

It was rational to assume that Christy had heard those stories before. The old woman had said everybody knew about the Nighteaters, hadn't she? And Cathy had been at the party the first night they arrived. She, or someone, must have said something to Christy that set her off.

But that did not explain why Christy had looked out over the forest within twenty minutes of their arrival at their new home and declared there were monsters in the woods.

And Laura could not think about it today.

Her first-floor office had a southern exposure and was surrounded almost completely by glass, affording her a one-hundred-eighty-degree view of the backyard and the forest beyond. In theory, it was perfect: an abundance of light, a serene view beyond, and the added advantage of being able to keep an eye on Christy at all times. But as soon as Laura had started to unpack, she had begun to wonder if she'd made a mistake.

At first she wasn't sure what it was. She tried to blame it on the sense of disorientation some people feel in multi-windowed high-rises: too much air, too much space. She was too easily distracted; there was always something much more interesting going on outside the windows than inside the office. She would find it impossible to concentrate. The sunlight was too intense, the shadows too sharp, she couldn't make her furniture look right. But the simple truth was that she felt exposed, like a fish in a bowl with nothing to protect her from the outside world but a thin layer of glass. She couldn't get over the feeling of being watched. And there was nothing serene about the view of the forest at all; it only served to remind her of how far away she was from all that was familiar. Several times an hour she would stop whatever it was she was doing and go to the window just to check . . . for what, she wasn't sure. She didn't feel comfortable here. She didn't feel safe.

Perhaps that was why her eyes kept drifting toward the woods, and she couldn't seem to get the sound of that old woman's laugh out of her head.

On the positive side, Cathy turned out to be marvelous with Christy, despite her unlikely background. She was bright and energetic, and whenever Laura checked on the two of them Christy seemed to be having a great time. Cathy brought Laura glasses of iced tea without being asked, made Christy's dinner, and even cleaned up the kitchen afterwards. At eight o'clock, she gave Christy her bath, and read her a bedtime story. When Christy was asleep, Cathy asked if it was all right to call her boyfriend to pick her up, and Laura added a generous tip to the amount they had agreed upon earlier. While Cathy waited for Scott, Laura took a break from the work that was almost, but not quite finished, and went into the kitchen to make herself an omelet.

A few minutes later the doorbell rang, and Laura left the beaten eggs in the bowl and went out to say good night to Cathy. She was surprised to see Sam Keller standing at the open front door.

Cathy looked a little frightened as she said, unnecessarily, "Mrs. Kane—it's the sheriff."

Sam smiled and came inside. "Relax, Cathy. I didn't come to arrest anybody. Just being neighborly."

Cathy's look of trepidation turned to curiosity as she closed the door behind him.

"Hi," Laura said. "What brings you up here?"

"Nothing in particular. Just doing my rounds, and I thought I'd stop by."

Laura gestured toward the kitchen. "Excuse me a minute. I've got butter melting in a pan, and I—"

"Don't let me interrupt your supper."

"There's Scott," Cathy said, as headlights flashed on the glass-paneled door. She grabbed up her purse and the bundle that contained her towel and wet swimsuit. "Good night, Mrs. Kane!"

"Good night, Cathy. And thanks again."

When the door had closed behind Cathy, Sam stood there a minute, feeling a little awkward and wishing he had not given in quite so readily to the urge to turn into Laura's driveway. He had no legitimate business here, and it was plain he was intruding. But she had been heavily on his mind since he left the Jennings place, she and the little girl way up here in the woods by themselves, and he hadn't thought it would hurt just to check and see that they were okay. Now she stood before him, with her hair bundled up in a knot on top of her head, wearing a cotton skirt and a big shirt with the sleeves rolled up over her elbows; even in bare feet and with a pencil stuck behind her ear, she looked more competent than a lot of policewomen he had known, and the protective impulse embarrassed him.

Laura said again, "Excuse me a minute while I turn off the stove."

"Don't stop your cooking, I don't mean to stay."

"Come on back to the kitchen with me then. As a matter of fact, this is the first chance I've had to eat all day, and I'm starved."

The first time Sam had been here he hadn't paid much attention to the house; the furniture had been covered with boxes and the floor littered with the clutter of moving day, and it had looked like just another house to him. Now, walking through the living room with its low-slung, jewel-toned sofas and chairs, and the vibrant artwork on the walls that didn't look like reproductions, he could not help feeling a little intimidated. This was unmistakably the home of a woman with class and style: not too big, not too flashy, but unmistakably elegant. It made the two-bedroom clapboard house on Walnut Street that he called home look like an outhouse, and he felt as out of place as — well, as this house was in the middle of the wilderness.

After he got over being impressed by the recessed lighting and the curving half-walls that served as room dividers, the sleek polished lines of low tables, and the striking display of collectibles arranged just out of a child's reach, the first thing he noticed was that there was a great deal of glass. There were floor-to-ceiling windows in the living room and two skylights over the spiral staircase, a dining area that was almost all bay window, and sliding glass doors in the kitchen. The lawman in him reacted instinctively to the security risk, and he wondered if she was remembering to set her alarm at night. Then the boy who was raised by a woman who considered leaving fingerprints on the windows akin to swearing on Sunday wondered how in the world she expected to keep all that glass clean.

In the kitchen, with its black Jen-Aire appliances and bright yellow lacquered eating area, he felt a little more comfortable. True, the room still had a little of the city-yuppie touch, with its glass-fronted cabinets and neat displays of pasta in art-deco containers, but there were crayon drawings attached to the refrigerator with butterfly magnets, and newspapers spread beneath two yellow dog dishes, one filled with water and the other with kibble. The air was scented with the smell of brewing coffee and scorched margarine.

Laura went forward quickly to lift the omelet pan off the range, examined the contents, and apparently decided they were not beyond salvage. She put the pan down on the countertop and picked up the wire whisk

98

and the bowl of eggs. "Are you sure you don't mind if I go on cooking? Would you like a cup of coffee?"

"I'll get it, you just go on with what you're doing." He found a mug tree beside the percolator and poured himself a cup of coffee, black. Two years of marriage had instilled in him a few good habits, so he poured a second cup for her and took both to the little yellow table. "Cathy Sykes is a nice kid, isn't she?"

Laura agreed, pouring the omelet mixture into the pan. "Her grandmother's a little weird, though."

Sam chuckled, pulling out one of the spindly-legged chairs from the table and examining it critically before testing it with his weight. It was surprisingly comfortable. "She's one of our local characters. Did she tell you she was descended from royalty?"

Laura cast him a surprised look over her shoulder. "No."

"Some kind of Cherokee chief or medicine man—I forget." He sipped his coffee. "Matter of fact, she's a little bit of living history—her ancestors were among the few Indians around these parts to hold on to the same land for over two hundred years. She'd be quite a legend if she weren't such a nut."

Laura said, carefully lifting the edges of the omelet, "She told me about the Nighteaters."

Again he chuckled. "Our local version of old Sasquatch."

Laura was in the midst of the delicate process of folding over the omelet; her hand jerked and the omelet split in half. She turned as the gooey cheese mixture began to spread from the broken center and sizzle in the pan. She said, "Sasquatch. Isn't that the same thing as—the Abominable Snowman?"

He nodded. "Bigfoot, Abominable Snowman—different names for different parts of the country, I guess." And then he seemed to notice something odd on her face, for he inquired, "Why?"

Laura turned back to the stove, rescuing the omelet just before it became inedible. But her hands were clumsy, and it broke into four pieces as she slid it onto the plate.

"Nothing," she said, but her voice sounded tight and her denial unconvincing. "It's just that . . ." She turned with the plate in her hands, knowing she should feel foolish for even mentioning the coincidence, but not feeling foolish at all. She felt, in fact, completely off-guard and more than a little disturbed. "Christy has been having nightmares ever since we moved here, about monsters in the woods. She calls them snowmen."

Sam nodded sympathetically. "Kids have been scaring each other with stories like that for generations. I'm sorry if they upset Christy."

It was a facile explanation, and not one Laura had not considered before, but somehow hearing him say it out loud was enormously reassuring. In fact, merely having him here was reassuring in a way she couldn't analyze and did not particularly want to understand.

She set the plate on the table, and noticed the cup of coffee he had poured for her. She smiled. "Listen, I feel silly eating in front of you. Let me make another one."

He was not shy about accepting. "To tell the truth, I haven't had anything since lunch and it does smell good."

"Go ahead and start on that one then. It's kind of messy, but everything I cook is."

She slid the plate over to him and went back to the stove, melting more margarine in the pan, taking out eggs and cheese. At that point there was the pattering of tiny claws on the linoleum and Corky came in, a rubber bone clenched between his teeth, which he immediately dropped in his excitement over greeting the visitor.

"Well, hello there, young fella." The puppy danced on his hind legs, pawing Sam's knee with his front ones, panting and begging to be petted. Obligingly, Sam scratched him behind the ears.

"Christy must be asleep. He always comes down to make sure everything's all right with the rest of the world once he's sure she's sound asleep. For a little pup, he's pretty responsible." And, his heroism in the woods that morning not forgotten, Laura reached into a canister and took out a dog biscuit. She smiled affectionately as Corky left Sam immediately and came to snatch the biscuit from her hand. "Actually," she said, "he's a pain in the butt. But I like him anyway."

Sam hesitated, then said, "You know, I did come up here for something more than supper."

"Oh?" Laura poured the omelet mixture into the pan. "What was that?"

He said, "I stopped by the Jennings place earlier."

Laura glanced at him. "And?"

He chose his words carefully, toying with the omelet. "It was just like you described."

She folded the omelet over. It broke into two pieces, which was an improvement on the last one. "Joe said it looked like vandals."

"Could be."

She patted the broken pieces of the omelet with the spatula and said, without turning, "Did you figure out how they got the ladder up there to tear open the top of the pen?"

Sam was startled, and he tried not to show it. Clearly, little got past this woman, and he'd have to be careful not to underestimate her in the future. "No," he admitted. "It was damn odd. Sometimes a burglar will try to get in a house through a dog door, knowing that's one door that won't be wired, but any fool could see the Jennings dog door is too small for even a child to get through. And besides . . ."

"Besides," she finished for him, sliding the omelet onto her plate, "why would they tear the run apart like that if all they wanted to do was get in? Why not cut a nice neat hole?"

"Right," he agreed. He was frowning at his plate in a way that Laura, even on such brief acquaintance, had already learned to mean he was baffled and did not like it.

"So, did you come here to tell me you don't have a clue in the case?"

He looked up at her. The minute he said it he knew he shouldn't have, but something about her at that moment struck him as fragile — standing by the stove in a shirt that was too big for her, balancing a plate in one hand while she pushed a strand of hair away from her face with the back of the other — and he said, too soberly, "Laura — do you own a gun?"

She set the plate on the table, staring at him.

"Forget it," he said quickly. "I'm sorry. Seems like every time I see you I say something to worry you. I tell you what. Why don't we forget about police business for a while and talk about something else. Normal things."

She sat down slowly, still looking uneasy, and he took a bite of the omelet. He smiled, and said conversationally, "So. Where did you go to high school?"

For a moment she didn't respond. Then she gave a surprised little laugh of concession, and she told him.

They were putting the dishes in the dishwasher when Christy began to scream. Dinner had stretched out into several cups of coffee served with microwave brownies; they lingered at the table and talked about unimportant things; they drank more coffee and talked about not-so-unimportant things, like how Laura had built a business from a dream and how Sam had raised three little sisters after the death of his father when Sam was twelve.

They were laughing softly over something one or the other of them had said when Christy screamed, and the sound was so unexpected, so out of place in the atmosphere of comfortable warmth that had grown between them, that at first it didn't register. For a moment they simply stared at each other, and then the scream came again.

Laura dropped the dish and ran from the room; Sam was right beside her. She took the stairs two at a time, tripping over the puppy who scrambled between her feet, and met Christy at the top of them, standing in her pink pajamas with her fists pressed to her eyes and her face violet red, screaming, "Mommy! Mommy! Mommy! Mommy!" over and over again.

Laura swept her up. "Baby, it's okay, it's okay, Mommy's here. Hush, now, it's okay, just a bad dream. . . ."

Christy wound her thin arms around Laura's neck so tightly that it hurt. Her shoulders hitched with each choking breath, and her words, muffled and blurred with broken sobs, were incoherent. Laura sat on the top step, holding Christy in her lap, kissing her hot, wet face, and stroking her hair, and all she could make out was, "Make them stop . . . make them stop. . . ."

Corky tried to wiggle into Laura's lap, nuzzling Christy anxiously, and Sam picked him up and sat on the step below Laura. Sam reached out a big, masculine hand and laid it lightly atop Christy's head. "Hey there, high-pocket," he said softly. "What kind of bogey man is after you? You want me to go check under your bed, scare him away?"

The sound of a man's voice seemed to have a calming effect on Christy, and Laura was surprised at the small prickle of resentment she felt for that. Christy lifted her blotchy, swollen face, and after a couple of hiccuping breaths, managed, "The chick—chickens. Feathers—and blood. Blood, Mommy, and they were screaming! The chickens were screaming!"

Christy buried her head in her mother's neck again and Laura made soothing noises. Over Christy's head she met Sam's questioning look, and had nothing but absolute bafflement for a reply.

"Honey, there aren't any chickens around here," she said. "The last chickens you saw were in the petting zoo. Are those the ones you mean? Why are you dreaming about chickens?"

"K-killed them," Christy said, burrowing deeper into the protection of her mother's shoulder. "Killed all of them. Pulled off their heads and tore off their wings and—and tore out their insides!"

"Good God," Laura said softly, hugging Christy more tightly. She was not one of those parents who liked to blame all the evils of the childhood world on television, but she could think of no other explanation. Cathy had let Christy watch TV this afternoon, and what would a country girl know about programs that were suitable for children? If she could at that moment have gotten her hands on the television producer who had inspired such gruesome visions for a five-year-old to take to bed, she would have cheerfully strangled him.

"Hush now, sweetie." She kissed Christy's forehead and shifted her weight so that she could see her face. "It was only a dream. A bad dream. Stop crying now, honey. It was just a mean old dream."

Christy shook her head, shuddering. "The green one. The pretty green one. They tore off its feet, Mommy, and its head too and it *kept moving*. It kept trying to fly away but—"

"That's enough," Laura said sharply. The rage and

104

helplessness that filled her were overwhelming, and she realized that her hands had tightened on Christy's shoulders sufficiently to replace the horror in the child's eyes with surprise. Forcefully, she relaxed her grip, and said, deliberately softening her voice, "It's over now, honey. All gone. Don't think about it anymore. Mommy's here, and nothing's going to hurt you."

Sam reached out again and ruffled Christy's already tangled hair. "Say, you know what the best cure for bad dreams is I know? A nice big cup of hot chocolate. How's that idea strike you?"

Christy looked at him, and after a moment she sniffled, and nodded. When Laura, with a grateful look at Sam, started to pick her up, Christy mumbled thickly, "I can walk by my own self." She reached for the puppy, who was more than happy to be freed from Sam's restraining arms, and by the time she had accepted a couple of wet licks on the face, she was almost smiling.

But she held on very tightly to her mother's hand as they went down the stairs.

Scott and Cathy would have been home a lot later if they hadn't had a fight at the Burger Barn. As it was, the digital clock on the dashboard glowed a mere 10:29 when Scott jerked the car to a stop in front of Cathy's house. The old hound was baying with more energy than he had ever been known to use, and every light in the house was ablaze, but Scott did not notice either of those things immediately, or if he did he didn't think they were important.

Cathy said, "I wish you wouldn't get so mad."

"And I wish you wouldn't go blabbing everything you know, especially when you don't know anything." Scott cut the engine and popped the door locks. "There wasn't anything out there except some old hermit

105

maybe, and you've got to go spreading it all over town that he chased me out of the woods—"

"I never told anybody except Jimmy Crow, and that's only because . . ."

Scott got out of the car and slammed the door. And then he heard the commotion. A woman yelling, a muffled explosion, some kind of screeching in the distance. He would have heard it all sooner if the hound hadn't been barking and lunging against its chain like something gone wild. The disturbance wasn't close, but it was loud, and carried easily through the woods the way sounds in the country tend to do. Another explosion, and then another, and he realized dimly that what he was hearing was gunfire.

"Jesus, what—"

Cathy was already out of the car, clutching the open door and staring toward the dark tangle of woods that climbed the mountain behind the house, just as he was. "Granny!" she gasped. "Oh, Scott, she's got the shotgun!"

More shouting, another cracking shot. And what was that screaming?

He pushed away from the door. "I'll call the police."

Cathy clutched at his arm. "Scott, don't—"

"Are you crazy? That old woman's got a gun! Don't you hear that noise? Who knows what's going on out there?"

"She's probably just drunk and—"

"And she's got a gun!"

"But—"

There were two more shots in rapid succession, and Cathy fell silent. Scott gave her one last I-don't-believe-you're-for-real look, and hurried toward the house.

Sam sat at the kitchen table across from Christy, do-

106

ing little magic tricks with coins, while Christy sipped her hot chocolate and munched a brownie and Laura scrubbed spilled chocolate and milk off the stove and countertop. Over and over she berated herself for not being more careful of Cathy. The whole point of having her over this afternoon had been to supervise her, hadn't it? Who knows what kind of gruesome stories the teenager might have told Christy—probably not even realizing how gruesome they were. Christy knew nothing about chickens; there was no reason for her to dream about them. It *had* to have been Cathy.

Christy said, "No, Mommy, don't be mad at Cathy. She didn't tell me any bad stories."

Sam stopped in the middle of his magic trick and raised an eyebrow at Laura. "Where did that come from?" he murmured.

But Laura was not up to explaining that just then. She knelt beside Christy and wiped a chocolate mustache from her upper lip, smiling gently. "I'm not mad at Cathy, sweetheart. It's just sometimes girls Cathy's age don't realize that the things they say, or the things they see on television, can give little girls nightmares."

Christy shook her head adamantly. "It was the snowmen," she said, and her voice trembled a little on the word. Her eyes started to film with tears. "The snowmen did it."

Laura closed her eyes slowly and tried to think of something to say. Something that would *work* this time. Nothing came.

As though sensing her mother's defeat, Christy slid down from the chair and went over to put her cup in the sink. Corky followed, hoping, no doubt, for more spilled chocolate.

There was a sudden shriek and Laura jumped. The cup clattered in the sink. Sam smiled apologetically and reached down to a small device on his belt, pushing a button that ended the noise. "Sorry. The Sheriff's Department's version of the beeper. Looks like duty calls."

Laura stood up when he did. "Do you need to call in?"

"No, I'll catch it on the car radio."

He went over and knelt beside Christy. "Say there, how would you like to be guardian of this magic quarter here?"

Christy looked at the coin he held out solemnly.

"It's a magic quarter now, so be careful not to spend it or you'll give the magic away."

Christy took the coin from him carefully. "Will it keep away the snowmen?"

Sam smiled, and tugged at a strand of her hair affectionately. "I wouldn't be a bit surprised."

Laura walked him to the door, more reluctant to see him go than she wanted to admit.

His expression was gentle and touched with sympathetic concern. "Are you going to be okay?" he asked.

She nodded. "Thanks, Sam. For everything."

He smiled. "Sure thing." He looked as though he wanted to say something more, then seemed to remember the call waiting for him in the car. He opened the door, then looked back.

"Laura—"

She waited.

He said, "Be sure to lock up after me, okay?"

She waited until his headlights flashed on the window on his way out, then locked all the doors and windows and set the alarm. Strangely, that did not make her feel any safer.

When Sam checked in with the dispatcher, he was glad he had not taken the call on Laura's phone. With everything else on her mind, this little bit of news was

108

all she needed. As a matter of fact, it wasn't exactly his favorite way to end the day either.

If one envisioned the mountain as a cone (which of course it wasn't—more like an irregular N-shaped hump) with the Heights on the upper eastern face, the Sykes place, which marked the beginning of a small smattering of outlying farms, was on the western lower slope. With his knowledge of the back roads and the police car pushed to a speed he would have jailed anybody else for using, it took Sam exactly twelve and a half minutes from Laura's driveway to the front of the Sykes house. All the while he was turning over possibilities of what he might find when he got there.

He knew that Minnie Sykes kept a still somewhere on that junkyard she called a farm, but as far as he could tell she'd never tried to sell the stuff and he had never seen any reason to bust her for it. In this part of the country the making of moonshine was something of a dying art, and as long as the stuff was clean and no federal excise laws were being broken, he tried to maintain a tolerant attitude toward what was, after all, an endemic but basically victimless crime. His first thought was that she had had a drop too much and started shooting at things just for the hell of it.

And if those kids had walked into a drunken shooting spree, this could be very serious indeed.

The heaviness in his stomach dispersed immediately when he pulled up and saw both of the kids, apparently unharmed, and Minnie too. Scott Bullard was standing by his car with his hands bunched in his pockets, looking nervous and uncomfortable. Cathy was standing with her grandmother in a patch of yellow light from the house windows, shouting and gesticulating angrily. Minnie was still clutching her shotgun and shouting back.

Sam took it all in at a glance as he got out of the car

and slammed the door. He walked over to Scott. "What's going on?"

Scott shot him an uneasy look. Sam suspected he was remembering the last time they had met. "The woman's crazy," he muttered. "She's flipped her freaking lid. Can I go now?"

"Just hang on for a minute." Sam walked over to the two women.

"Will you just stop it with that crazy talk?" Cathy was crying. "Do you see what you've done, do you just see? Now you've got the police out here and—"

"Don't you tell me what to do, girl! I got a right to defend my own property, ain't I? I'll kill 'em, I tell you, I'll kill ever damn one of them—"

"Who are you going to kill, Miz Minnie?" Sam inquired mildly.

She turned on him with a curl of her lip which was as explicit as a spit in the face. "Well, if it ain't the almighty law! A damn sight too little and a hell of a lot too late!"

Sam reached out his hand. "You want to let me see that fowling piece you got there?"

She glared at him, and for a moment he was certain he was going to have to wrestle it from her hands. Then, abruptly she thrust the shotgun toward him. "It's empty. Ran out of shot. Came back to the house to get some more. Not that it would do any good. They was gone."

Sam checked the chamber and found it empty. But he did not return the gun. "Who?"

Cathy turned away, looking miserable and embarrassed, and started back over toward Scott. Minnie replied shortly, "The goddamn Nighteaters, that's who! Who the hell did you think?"

Sam nodded, careful to keep his expression blank. "Did you get any of them?"

110

"Hell, no, nary a one! By the time I'd got there the damage was done and they was fleeing for hell, but the sound of my buckshot ought to put the fear o' God into 'em for a good long time—" She broke off suddenly and narrowed her eyes at him. "You don't believe me, do you? You don't believe a goddamn word I'm saying."

Sam said patiently, "Now, Miz Minnie—"

"Don't you puff out your chest at me, young man! I was sitting up here guarding this mountain when you was still shitting your diapers, so don't you stand there and tell *me* what's what! Come on, then." She jerked her head angrily toward the back of the house. "Come on, big lawman. You come on up in the woods and you see for yourself what they done to my babies."

The last thing Sam wanted to do was to go hiking up a mountainside in the middle of the night with a half-drunk old woman, but he didn't have much of a choice. In the light from the windows he could see drops of something dark splattered all over the front of Minnie Sykes's clothes. It looked like blood.

He said, "Be right with you." And went back to the car.

"Ain't no need to worry about your gun!" she jeered after him. "Too late for that now! They won't be back tonight—I seen to that!"

Sam told the kids to wait there until he got back, then he returned to Minnie with a torch. "Okay," he said, flipping the beam on. "Lead the way."

Disdaining the light that he waved in front of her, Minnie turned and plunged ahead.

The path she took was so well-concealed that a man with good eyes would have had trouble finding it in the daylight. Sam couldn't help wondering what it was she was hiding back here in the woods that she would go to so much trouble to keep secret. Whatever it was, it was apparently of no importance

111

any longer, because she was leading him right to it.

After about two hundred yards his calves began to feel the strain of the uphill climb and his lungs were hot with the unaccustomed exercise. He said, "Tell me something, Miz Minnie. If you're so all-fired worried with these Nighteaters you keep talking about, why don't you just move? Go somewhere where they won't bother you."

She stopped in her tracks and turned on him, her dark eyes flaring. "Because this is my *place*," she said. And if she had raised her fist to the sky and declared, "As God is my witness, I'll never go hungry again!" the effect could not have been more dramatic.

Sam had no answer for that, and she turned to lead the way again. She wasn't even winded.

Sam had not been out in the woods at night since he was a kid, coon hunting with his dad. He hadn't liked it then, and he didn't like it now. He had never liked what he couldn't see. Dark doorways, cluttered alleys with a dozen places for a gunman to hide, empty warehouses that ticked with the sound of his own breath . . . His skin prickled now, as it had done then, and he wished he had just hauled Minnie in for questioning and let it go at that.

All told, he estimated they went about a quarter of a mile into the woods. He could smell the carnage before he reached it, and his heart began to pound and his throat tightened up. Then Minnie stopped, and he played the flashlight over the ground about ten feet in front of her.

His blood went cold at what he saw.

"Jesus Christ," he whispered.

Chapter Six

At six o'clock in the morning, Ted Jacobs sat before his computer. The blank amber screen cast eerie shadows over his face; the cursor winked at him like a knowing eye. There was nothing written on the screen, absolutely nothing. But he saw volumes.

He saw a busy street corner; he heard the squeal of brakes, a sickening thud. Screams and shouts of shock rising and falling like the sighing of the wind. Craig grabbing his arm, pulling him forward through the crowd. Ted tried to walk away, of course. But Craig was one who never turned his back. He always had to be in the thick of things.

And that little girl, lying in the gutter. She was wearing a blue knit cap, and a pink parka. The left side of the cap was black with blood, the left side of her face was caved in. Death rose from her in steamy waves, like something he could smell. There was blood splattered on the lamppost where Ted put his hand, he remembered that very well. He had spent days after that washing his hands, over and over again.

The look on Craig's face as Ted turned away. Shocked, disbelieving. Pleading. Finally disgusted. Then merely empty. Ted had never seen such emptiness on another human being's face. He hoped never to see it again.

Abruptly, Ted pushed away from the desk, out of the chair, and walked over to the window. Fog pressed against the windowpanes, a thick soupy barrier between night and day, refusing to let the one depart and the other arrive. He put his palm against the glass, as though testing its strength. He thought about the things that could be hiding out there.

His office was lined with books: fiction, non-fiction, classics travelogues, first editions, and paperbacks. Most of them were the result of a lifetime's collecting, but one entire shelf was devoted to a relatively new subject of interest. He went over to it now and picked up a volume at random. It was *Monsters of the Deep or Legends from Beneath the Sea*. He flipped through pages replete with sea serpents and giant-tentacled squids, then replaced it. There were others. *Werewolves and Vampires. Phantoms That Kill. Alien Invaders. Beyond Human Understanding.*

An idle hobby. But not so idle. Because whenever the memories became too much, whenever the panic that gathered in his chest threatened to crush him, these were the volumes to which he turned for comfort. Dark tales of beasts and ghouls and terrified screams in the night. Because nothing was quite as frightening as what he carried around with him day after day, inside his own mind.

He supposed, in a way, that was what had attracted him to this place. Because it had frightened him. Because there were snakes and bobcats and sharp-toothed foxes in the woods, and because the woods themselves were evil, one could tell just by looking at them. And because of the sounds he heard in the night. And because of the things they said lived there, in the darkness.

He was no stranger to fear. He had lived with it all his life, in ways he was only now beginning to understand. But being afraid of what you could see, or even imagine, was infinitely easier than being afraid of the things you could never change.

Today the fear was a big thing, as thick as the fog and just as insidious. The books did not help. The blinking, accusing eye of the cursor on the computer screen was no escape. Today the fear had the sour taste of emptiness, the chill of loneliness, the permanency of winter.

He left the office, and changed his clothes. Then he went out into the fog, and ran.

Laura stayed up until two o'clock, partly to finish the plans, partly because she was too wired from all the coffee she had drunk to even think about sleeping, and partly because every time Laura tried to carry Christy to bed she would wake up and cry to stay with her mother. At two A.M. her eyes were burning, and Christy was sleeping soundly enough to be transferred from the sofa to her own bed without waking. But Laura had barely closed her eyes before she was awakened again—by that awful, night-piercing wail that cut across the darkness of the forest, pierced the sanctuary of her tightly locked home, and stabbed coldness into the pit of Laura's stomach. Christy, sleeping peacefully at last, did not hear it, but Corky did. He peeked his nose out from under the foot of Christy's bed and whined plaintively, and when the sound came again he scurried into a far corner and would not show himself again. Laura did not sleep well at all after that.

She was awake at seven o'clock in the morning, trying to untangle the coils of cable and electrical wire that were the life's blood of her computer and her fax machine. She even got as far as locating and attaching a modem to the telephone, but when she attempted to attach the telephone to the fax machine the plugs did not match. The problem was that half her equipment had come from her home, the other half had been scavenged from the office, and there was a distinct possibility the two were not compatible. If she had had a full night's sleep and half a day to waste, no doubt she could have sorted it all out, but at the present time the entire enterprise looked hopeless.

By the time she had fixed breakfast for Christy, who had recovered with a child's resiliency from the events of the night before, and taken Corky out, who also seemed to have forgotten his night terrors, it dawned on her that the solution to her problem might be closer than she thought. Hugh Bullard struck her as the kind of man who wouldn't even go to the golf course without a fax machine at hand; surely he, like Laura, had realized the necessity of having one in his home.

Sure enough, Bullard had a completely operative home office. He was out of town, but Isabel was more than happy to make the equipment available to Laura. At nine o'clock, Laura bundled Christy into the van and drove the short distance to the Bullard house.

She would have preferred to walk, but it was a damp, miserable morning that swathed the mountain in fog as thick as cotton candy and wept out a constant drizzle that clung to the windshield of the van and swallowed up the headlights when the road dipped. Christy was awed by the fact that they were

116

actually driving through clouds; Laura was fervently glad she did not have to drive all the way to town in this mess.

Isabel greeted her with coffee and warm cinnamon rolls—straight from a can, she confessed wryly, then added, "I've got to get some help up here, but Hugh is so damn paranoid about the locals he won't have anybody in. I keep thinking a few more months of my cooking will change his mind about *that*, but so far no luck." She gave a philosophical shrug. "Come to think of it, he's probably right. There's nothing else to do around here *but* take care of the house, and I'm already so bored I'm seriously considering taking up knitting." Then she cheered. "I'm going to New York next week, though. With Hugh out west doing his wheeling and dealing, I decided I deserved a little treat too. Would you like to come along?"

Laura laughed, helping Christy out of her sweater. "Good heavens, no. I've still got boxes to be unpacked."

Isabel waved that away. "You'll still have boxes to unpack this time next year, believe me. But I can sympathize—the charm of this little burg hasn't worn off for you yet. Don't worry, it won't take long."

Laura helped Christy into a chair, warily eying Isabel's glass-topped table and immaculate ivory place mats. "Whatever you do," she murmured to Christy under her breath, "don't spill anything."

Christy gave her mother one of those I'm-not-a-*baby* looks, and picked up her glass of milk.

Laura accepted a china cup of coffee from Isabel, and followed her into the adjacent family room. "Why is Hugh paranoid about the locals?" she asked, although, remembering her experience with Cathy Sykes, she could understand how a

117

little paranoia would be justified.

"Oh, you know how it is. The environmentalists gave him some trouble at first. Then it took forever to work things out with the county services—although if you ask me, that wasn't resistance so much as it was plain inefficiency, and what can you expect from a bunch of hicks? Then there was that surveyor we lost—you heard about that?—and we had some trouble getting a construction crew together for a good long time after that. And there's been a little vandalism—nothing serious, but enough to get Hugh's back up. He thinks everyone's plotting against him. Now come on." She set the platter of cinnamon rolls on a low Chinese lacquer coffee table. "Eat some of these things before I'm forced to finish them all myself."

They chatted for a while about inconsequentials, and it occurred to Laura to ask Isabel what she thought of Cathy Sykes. But she knew that would have been a waste of time. Isabel did not strike Laura as the type of woman who would take much of an interest in her son's personal life, and even if she did, what could she tell Laura that Laura had not observed for herself yesterday?

She faxed the material to her Philadelphia office at 10:20, and asked Isabel for suggestions as to where she might find a computer technician who would hook up the machinery that would link her to the outside world. Isabel promised to think about it and get back to her. It was with no small relief that Laura got Christy, with her sticky fingers and uncontrollable curiosity about breakable objects, out of Isabel's house and back into the van.

The sheriff's car was waiting for her when she pulled into her driveway.

Sam had been sitting there for about ten minutes,

118

absently dropping magnetic pins onto the metal-backed county map that was a miniature version of the one he kept in his office. One of his deputies had suggested the map would be a good thing to have for roadblocks and such, but it was really no more than a toy. Any man who did not know the county roads better than this map did didn't last long on Sam's force.

He had seen Laura's van in front of the Bullards' house, but hadn't wanted to bother her there. While he waited he dropped those star-shaped magnetic pins on the map and went over in his head what he was going to say to her, but after a while the pins stopped making random patterns. Minnie Sykes's place. The dumpster at the end of old County Road 12. Mike Jennings's house. The three stars — red, green, and yellow — formed an irregular line no more than two miles long as the crow flies. Did he want to count whatever it was Scott Bullard had seen in the woods? Another pin. What about if he went back a bit, to where Brett Howard's body had been found? Slowly, reluctantly, he placed another star. And he looked at the map for a long time. That last star, a blue one, had landed not more than five hundred yards from where he sat now. Right behind Laura Kane's house. And the line was unbroken.

Impatiently, he swept the magnets back into their little container on the side of the map and tossed the whole thing back into the glove box, where it belonged. It was a stupid exercise, meaning nothing. He got out of the car to meet Laura.

Christy came running up first, as fresh as spring-time and looking like she didn't have a care in the world — which, in the case of a five-year-old, was as it should be. "Hi, Sheriff Sam!" she said happily, and held out her open fist to him. "Look, I've still got my

119

magic quarter! I thought I losted it when I woke up, but it was under my pillow and boy, was I glad!"

"Good for you, high-pocket." He lifted her on to his hip and appreciatively examined the evidence she offered.

Laura moved close and murmured, "Sheriff, really. We've got to stop meeting like this."

She seemed to be in good spirits this morning too, except for a slight trace of deepening shadow underneath her eyes, and he hated to ruin her mood. So he smiled back. "Next time I'll wear a plain brown suit and knock three times on your back door."

But his smile must not have been as convincing as he thought, because a flicker of curiosity crossed her eyes as she turned to lead the way up the steps.

"Lousy morning," she commented as she turned on the lights inside. The subtle lighting, which had seemed so artsy and restful last night, cast an uneasy glow over the fog-shrouded room this morning.

Christy wriggled out of his arms and he answered, "It'll burn off. Probably turn hot by this afternoon."

Laura said, "Christy, honey, go take Corky out on his leash, but don't stay outside—it's too nasty. You can take him up to play in your room if you'll promise not to let him chew up anything."

"Okay," Christy agreed cheerfully, and scampered off.

Laura turned to him. "Why do I get the feeling you didn't come up here for another one of my great cups of coffee?"

"No," he admitted. "I didn't." He saw the smile in her eyes grow shadowed with disturbance but he couldn't help it. He said, "I need to ask you some things."

She gestured him toward the sofa, and she sat in

one of the amethyst club chairs opposite it, pulling her feet up under her. She waited for him to begin, and he didn't know *where* to begin.

He sat on the edge of the sofa, which was too plush and too deep for a big man's comfort, and linked his hands between his knees. He said, "You know that call I got when I left here last night? It turned out to be from the Sykes place. Seems Cathy and Scott had come home to find the old woman shooting up the woods and the boy, at least, had sense enough to call the police."

He thought he detected a faint tensing in her shoulders, but her expression did not change. He went on. "It turns out the old woman had been keeping a flock of gamecocks out in the woods behind her house — she called them 'show chickens,' but they were fighting cocks, all right. Naturally, she had to keep them way back there or somebody would've caught wind of what she was up to and we would've shut her down in a heartbeat. That kind of thing is about as illegal as it gets." He was digressing — postponing was more like it. He took a breath.

"She said she had fifty. When I got there there were maybe a dozen left. And it was a slaughterhouse." If he closed his eyes, which he had barely done all night, he could still see it — the woods gleaming with blood and entrails, cages reduced to twisted balls of wire and splinters, feathers dancing grotesquely in the trees. And the stench. He had showered for thirty minutes when he got home, and still imagined he could smell it.

He said flatly, "Something got to those chickens, all right. And whatever it was was pretty particular about what he ate. Tore off the heads and feet and gutted them, and carried off the rest."

Still no visible reaction.

He said, "When I walked up, the first thing my light picked up was a green cock. It had been decapitated like the rest, but I remember that one in particular. Laura," he inquired quietly, "how did Christy know about all that, every detail just right, before it even happened?"

At last she moved. She took a deep, unsteady breath, like one emerging from an underwater swim or waking from a long sleep, and she stood. She walked over to the free-standing fireplace, a sleek brass model that yawned like an open mouth in the middle of the room. She touched the polished exterior, then moved over to the window, facing away from him.

He said, "Nobody else knew what was going on. The kids have each other for alibis, and just to make sure, I checked with some people who saw them down at the Burger Barn while all this was going on. Nobody could have told Christy. She was asleep upstairs. We both know that. So how come she had a nightmare, and twenty minutes later I'm walking right into the middle of what she dreamed about?"

Laura cleared her throat softly. It made a whispery sound across the empty room. "I don't know." She turned, and her face seemed paler than usual, and her eyes stunned. "I don't know," she repeated more clearly. Her hand wandered nervously to her throat, fluttered there a moment, then dropped. "She's never—I've never known her to be precognitive before. I don't understand."

Sam frowned a little. "Precognitive? Doesn't that mean seeing into the future, and such as that?"

She nodded, but her attention wasn't really on him. He could see she was as shocked by all of this as he had been, and he didn't know why he had expected anything else.

"Well, it doesn't matter," he mumbled, mostly to himself. "The way I figure it, whatever got at those chickens did it at about the same time Christy had her dream. So she wasn't seeing the future; she was seeing what happened."

Laura looked up sharply, and he seized on that immediately. "Something?" he demanded. "What?"

She shook her head. "No. Nothing, really. It's just that—well, all kids are a little telepathic, don't you think? I never thought much about it, it only seems natural, especially between a mother and child. I mean, you carry that child *inside* you all those months, she's formed from your cells, she's part of you and birth doesn't really sever that bond—nothing can. I never thought there was anything particularly . . . unusual about it."

Sam said carefully, "Are you telling me your little girl is some kind of—psychic?"

Again she shook her head, more insistently. "Nothing like that. It's just that . . . sometimes we know what the other one is thinking. Nothing dramatic; just sometimes. Haven't you ever been so close to somebody that you could read each other's thoughts?"

Sam admitted slowly, "No. I can't say that I have. But I don't see what that has to do with—"

"Nothing," she said quickly. "It doesn't have anything to do with anything. Are you sure I can't get you some coffee?"

She started toward the kitchen, reminding Sam of a startled bird about to take flight. He stood up. "Laura, look," he said gently. "This is not an interrogation. Nothing you can tell me is likely to shed any light on the case, and that's not why I'm asking. I don't mean to badger you, but the truth is I was up half the night trying to figure this thing out, and anything you can say to help me clear it up in my own head would surely be appreciated. That green chicken," he said, and was filled with a dreadful sort of wonder all over again as he thought about it. "How the hell did she know about the green chicken?"

Laura looked at him, helpless and confused and yet — wary. She was telling the truth, but not all of it. "I don't know," she repeated. "Usually it's just us. She's never known about things that were happening outside before."

He watched her carefully. "And you're sure nothing like this has ever happened before?"

She released a small breath, and her shoulders seemed to sag a little. "Not . . . exactly. But it reminded me of — something that happened once. I was in an accident, and Christy was at home with one of my partners baby-sitting her, and she woke up screaming and seemed to know exactly what was happening to me . . . while it was happening."

The tightness of her voice indicated a painful memory, and Sam said sympathetically, "A car accident?"

Laura intended to let it go at that. She drew in a breath to say, "Yes," but the words that came out were, "I was attacked. In a parking garage."

Laura knew the expression on his face. She had seen it on the faces of each of the half-dozen or so officials to whom she had been required to tell the story. It was a professional look. Quiet, calm, and in control. But most of all professional. She wondered vaguely whether they went to school to learn that look.

His voice sounded tight, as though he were forcing gentleness into it, as he said, "Rape?"

Rape. A simple, concise, all-purpose word. He had heard it before, had seen it before, had no doubt dealt with it dozens of times before. He could understand that. But how could he understand the senseless horror, the sick, black boiling pit of evil that was the reality of what she had been through?

It would have been simple to just nod her head and say no more. He would not have pressed her. She did not have to relive it. It was over, a subject closed that never had to be opened again, she did not have to say anything. And yet she did. For she had learned, finally she had learned, that monsters who hid in the dark were always much larger than those viewed in the full light of day. And she had run just about as far as she could go.

She said, "I had a business dinner. My partners, Ben and Hilly, they were kind of surrogate fathers for Christy, and we always arranged these things so that one of us would be able to stay with her. That night it was Hilly who was baby-sitting while I took the client out to dinner."

Her hands were pressed together in front of her, palm to palm, so tightly that her shoulders hurt. Deliberately, she separated them. The next sentences were spoken in a detached, almost rote manner, the same speech she had given to all of those polite, competent, calm people who were in control. It was getting easier. And it was not.

"I got home about twelve-thirty. I parked in a garage about two blocks from my building—it was just an empty garage, no attendant at night, and he was waiting for me. He put his arm around my throat . . ." Unconsciously, her hand touched her throat, and then dropped. "And he had a knife. He kept saying, 'You don't scream, baby, and I won't hurt you.' He kept saying that." She took a breath. But still her voice was calm.

"He tied my hands with my stockings and stuffed my underwear in my mouth and he cut me. The insides of my thighs. And he rubbed his fingers in the blood and wrote things—on my face, and my breasts. I don't know what. But no, he didn't rape me.

"I wasn't hurt badly. The scars are almost gone. But Hilly said . . ." There, for the first time, her voice caught, and she rubbed her arms to forestall a shiver. "That about the time it was happening, Christy woke up—she wasn't even four at the time—and started screaming about the bad man who was cutting Mommy. That's . . . that's what reminded me."

She could have said more. She could have told him about the smells, motor oil and exhaust and strong perspiration; the sounds of distant traffic and the rhythmic, manic panting in her ear, the breath of the man who was going to kill her, the last sound she would ever hear. The terror. The helplessness. The *humiliation* of helplessness. Those desperate, cowardly, whimpering moments of promising a criminal anything, offering him any favor, bargaining away your soul if only he wouldn't hurt you anymore . . .

But she said nothing. And neither did he, for a long time.

And then she looked at him. She didn't know what she expected to find there—the professional detachment of a man who has heard it all before, the quiet sympathy of a friend, the polite awkwardness of someone who doesn't know what to say. She didn't expect the anger that tightened his lips or the hurt that narrowed his eyes—more than sympathy. Empathy, deep and unfeigned. Frustration. The look of a good cop. Or a good friend.

She took a breath, tried to manage a reassuring smile, and failed. She hugged her elbows tighter and she said, "You always think it won't happen to you. I live in a safe neighborhood. I'm alert. I know what to do in an emergency. I can protect myself. I had built a *business,* for God's sake. I was raising a child and outdoing men in a man's world and I'd never met a situation I couldn't handle. I was smart, I was quick, I was strong. I was safe. But when he came at me with that knife I couldn't even scream, I was so scared. And I never . . . felt safe again."

Her voice tremored on the last words, and Sam came over to her. He put his arm around her shoulders because he didn't know what else to do, and it felt like an awkward gesture. But then, after a moment, some of the tension left her shoulders, and she didn't move away. So neither did he.

Then Christy came clattering through the back door, and self-consciousness overtook them as they stepped apart. Laura called, "No running on the stairs!"

Christy replied, "Okay!" and slowed to a skip as she took the stairs, Corky scrambling after her.

Laura looked back at Sam. She seemed a little embarrassed, and her smile was weak and fleeting. "Anyway, I know that doesn't have anything to do with last night. Even then, she was just—picking up on what I was feeling. Last night—the chickens—had nothing to do with me. I can't explain it."

Sam said, "I'm glad you told me." He wasn't being a police officer now.

Laura gave a little turn of her wrist that rang as false as her words did. "I didn't mean to make a big deal out of it."

127

But it was a big deal. And he wished he had more to offer her than comfort.

At last he said, quietly, "Do you know what Calumit means?"

Her glance was hesitant and questioning, and she shook her head.

"It's an Indian word. It means 'peaceful resting place.' Sanctuary."

Some of the haunted look faded from her eyes, and she smiled. "That's nice. I like that."

Sam smiled back, and turned to go. And he made a silent vow to himself that from that moment on he would do everything in his power to make this place live up to its name for her sake, and her child's.

Chapter Seven

The fog did not burn off by midday; it merely thickened and grew higher, forming a low gray ceiling that neither rained nor cleared, but trapped the mountaintop in a soupy heat. Christy was having one of those days that was more suitable to the Terrible Twos than to a comparatively sedate five-year-old. If it wouldn't break she took it apart, if it was high she climbed on it, if it was low she tripped over it. She refused to take a nap, dropped a bowl of popcorn all over the living room carpet, and left a trail of Leggo pieces from the kitchen to her bedroom. Corky climbed the stairs with muddy paws, and then jumped on the white duvet that covered Laura's bed.

When the doorbell rang at five-thirty, Laura was hardly in the mood for company. She tried to blame her edginess on the weather and the normal hazards of day-to-day life with a puppy and a child. But the source of her malaise could be traced directly back to Sam's visit that morning, and she could not find a way to rid herself either of the unwanted memories his visit had provoked or the unanswered questions.

She had just begun to prepare an early supper in hopes of getting Christy off to bed, and she answered the door with the intention of getting rid of whoever it was in short order. She was so surprised to see Ted Jacobs standing there that she immediately forgot her resolve.

He said, without preamble, "Isabel Bullard said you were having trouble with your computer system. She thought I could help."

He was dressed in running shorts and had a towel looped around his neck, looking like a man who had just one more item of business to check off before he could get down to more pressing concerns — recreation. She said, a little taken aback, "You know about computers?"

"Self-defense." He gave her one of those charming, world-famous smiles. "Back in New York, my computer consultant was also my agent, and every time he came over he would check my log to see whether or not I'd been working. It was easier to learn computers than keep making up excuses."

Laura laughed and opened the door wider. "Well, come on in. I'll take whatever help I can get, and I don't care what you find on my log."

"Actually," she explained as she led the way down the stairs to the office, "it's my fax machine I need the most. If you'll just show me how to get it back on-line . . . Christy!" she exclaimed as she reached the curve in the stairs that allowed her to look down over the office.

Christy was sitting at her drafting board, pencils and paper in a sloppy disarray all around her, intent upon the masterpiece she was creating on Laura's blueprint paper.

Laura hurried down the rest of the stairs. "How many times have I told you not to play in Mommy's office? Look at the mess you've made."

"I'm *drawing*," Christy protested indignantly as Laura swept her off the high stool and set her on the floor. But her aggravation evaporated into interest as she observed the newcomer. "Hi," she greeted Ted, and held out a sheet of paper to him. "Want to see my picture?"

He took it from her politely. "What is it?"

"It's a snowman," Christy informed him. She rounded her eyes and lowered the timber of her voice to make certain he appreciated the significance of what she said next. "A *monster* snowman."

Laura tensed at the words and looked at the drawing Christy had given Ted. Christy had outgrown stick figures a year ago, but no one would be tempted to say she yet showed signs of becoming another Picasso. Still, she had obviously taken a great deal of time with this rendering, and the attention to detail was worth noting. But for all her trouble, the drawing looked like nothing more to Laura than an outsized and particularly savage Pillsbury Dough Boy.

The head was perfectly round and fully half the size of the body, with narrow slits for eyes and two huge canine teeth protruding from a gaping mouth. The shoulders sloped downward and ended in four sharp protrusions that looked like curled claws. The feet too, turned inward the way feet on most children's drawings are, were tipped with straight lines that indicated claws. Laura swallowed hard and glanced at her daughter. This, then, was what had been tormenting her dreams at night?

Ted said, "Well, it certainly is a monster, all right. But I think it's a little early in the season to be wor-

131

rying about snowmen." He offered the drawing back to Christy.

"You can have it for your own," she told him. "I have lots more."

"Thank you," Ted said gravely. "I shall treasure it."

Christy looked pleased. "Now if one comes to your house, you'll already know what it looks like."

Laura said distractedly, "Run up to your room and play now, Christy. We have work to do here."

"Can I have a cookie?"

"No, it's almost dinnertime. Besides, you gave the cookies to—"

She broke off, and Christy's face fell. "The snowmen. I forgot."

And without another word, Christy turned and trudged dejectedly up the stairs. Another time, Laura would have followed her for one of those nice, comforting mother-daughter talks. She was almost relieved that Ted's presence prevented her from engaging in another futile discussion about monsters. And who knows? Perhaps the drawing had been therapeutic for Christy. Maybe tonight there would be no bad dreams.

"Sorry about all this," she said, gathering up spilled papers and pencils. "One of the disadvantages of working at home."

Ted folded the drawing Christy had given him into the pocket of his running shorts and looked around. "Nice view," he commented.

Laura followed the direction of his gaze toward the woods. "I thought so too, at first. But I don't know. I'm not sure I like looking out at those woods all day. They're kind of—well, spooky."

He nodded thoughtfully, still gazing toward the

132

woods. "Some places are like that, especially very old ones. They seem alien, evil, even a little terrifying. Some kind of primal memory, I imagine. Humans don't belong in the forest."

She glanced at him. "Supposedly, we all lived in the forest at one time."

He smiled. "And we've been trying to escape it ever since. The eternal war between civilization and nature."

Then his eyes fell on the computer equipment arranged randomly on her desk and he moved toward it, the subject dismissed. "This doesn't look too complicated. It shouldn't take long at all. Do you have a screwdriver?"

She found a set of screwdrivers and he set to work. Laura sat on the edge of a chair out of his way, feeling awkward and out of place. It would be rude to go back to the kitchen and leave him to labor like a common workman, but she did have other things to do, and as grateful as she was for his help, she wished Isabel had simply given her the name of a qualified technician she could call at her leisure.

She offered him something to drink, and he refused rather absently. He did not seem at all inclined to take the conversational initiative, and Laura searched her mind for some subject of mutual interest. Finally she found it.

"Do you remember what you told us the other night about this mountain being holy ground?" she said. "I mentioned it to a woman I met the other day who claims to be part Cherokee and she said something odd—or implied it, really. That the mountain wasn't so much holy ground as it was taboo, because of the spirit the Indians thought lived

133

here. They called it something that meant 'killer.' "

Ted uncoiled a cable and connected it to the back of the computer. "Minnie Sykes. She's quite a character."

"You've met her?"

He nodded. "Of course, most of what she says has to be taken with a grain of salt. It seems to me she adapts the truth to fit the occasion — a hazard of living in the modern world."

"Do you mean all that stuff about the evil spirit — "

"Oh, that's true enough, at least in legend. But I think she's put her own little twist to it. The thing you have to remember is that the word 'killer' to the Indian would have been a term of respect, not fear. They admired efficiency in the matter of life and death, and Dihi was a name they would give to a mighty hunter or warrior. I don't think they considered it particularly evil; that was the white man's invention."

"Like the Nighteaters," Laura murmured, almost to herself.

He did not seem surprised. Obviously, he had done a great deal of research since he'd been here — which was only natural, Laura supposed, for a writer.

"That's just another name for the same thing," he said. "Do you have anything smaller than this screwdriver? A fingernail file, something with a sharp edge?"

Laura searched through a box marked "accessories" until she came up with a small screwdriver that had been included with an adapter kit she had bought for the VCR. But she was uneasy as she handed him the tool. "You make it sound as though this . . .

134

Dihi was more than a legend. Something physical."

He disappeared behind the desk with the small screwdriver and an even smaller telephone modem. "All I know is that when the government first offered to buy this land from the Indians, their forward scout advised against it. He said something like, 'There are things amongst the woods that are neither man nor beast, so dark and horrible that no man could long survive against them.' Then he went on to tell about boiling springs and sulfur lakes and caves that gave off an eerie glow in the dark and 'a multitude of ghostly specters that float through the night crying out demonic curses.' Things that we would recognize today as swamp gas, geysers, and radiation from uranium deposits."

"My goodness," Laura said softly. "No wonder nobody ever settled here."

He sat up, reaching for another screwdriver. "They tried. The government bought the land anyway — probably one of the few good deals the Indians ever made — and tried to parcel it off. That's how the valley was settled, and the lower mountain. But those who tried to build higher up didn't last long, and eventually the area got a reputation for being cursed. Settlers had enough to worry about without taking on the supernatural, and when you think about how much of their lives were dependent upon the whims of nature, you can understand how they got to be more than a little superstitious. You couldn't give this mountaintop away. Of course, some people were stuck with land they couldn't use, which is how Bullard came by the property for development. But most of it was reabsorbed by the Parks System in 1884, and by the time we discovered the usefulness of ura-

135

nium, it was too late. You can't strip-mine a national forest."

"No," Laura murmured. "I guess not." Then: "You certainly do know a lot about it. You must be planning another book."

She thought she saw just the slightest tightening of his jaw muscles, but that could have been merely a sign of concentration. He said briefly, "No."

She waited for him to elucidate, but he didn't.

He switched on the computer and tapped a few keys, and the printer rattled off several noisy lines. He turned it off. "I like your house," he commented casually. "It surprises me, though. So much open space."

"Most of my designs have an open feel to them," she pointed out. "I think that's what most people want in a house."

"But you?"

She felt herself growing defensive for no good reason. "I've lived in small apartments all my life. Naturally I want something with the illusion of space."

"But not the exposure."

"What makes you say that?"

He gestured. "You haven't even unpacked this room. For most people a home office is a kind of sanctuary, the place they go to feel ordered and secure. It's clear you intend to spend as little time here as possible."

"Maybe I'm avoiding work."

"Another thing." He pulled up another cable and connected it to the back of the fax machine. "All the draperies upstairs are half closed. But you can't close the draperies here without cutting off your source of light. So you avoid the room. Why build a house for the view and then close the draperies?"

She said impatiently, "Did you ever hear of solar heating? It's fine for the winter, but draperies were invented for the summer."

"It doesn't get that hot in the mountains."

"Maybe I don't want my carpets and upholstery bleached by the sun."

"And maybe you don't like the feeling of living in a glass house."

She looked at him coolly for a long minute. "Do you always do that? Dissect people to use as characters in your next book?"

He smiled, a completely natural, unself-conscious expression. "No. Sometimes I do it just for the hell of it. I was a surgeon before I was a writer, remember?"

She replied stiffly, "It's not a very endearing trait."

"So I've been told. But look at it from my point of view. It's a lot more fun than an autopsy."

He slid behind the desk again, leaving Laura with absolutely no reply. Ted Jacobs, she decided, was a strange man, but she wasn't quite sure yet whether that was good or bad.

And then he said unexpectedly, "Do you ever hear things at night?"

She thought her heart actually skipped a beat. She asked cautiously, "What kinds of things?"

He was on his knees, tracing the telephone line from the desk to its junction at the wall. He did not look up. "From the woods."

"Do you mean—a howling sound?"

He looked up at her. His eyes were flat and calm. "Or a scream."

Laura absently massaged the back of her neck, which had grown tight. There was a hollow, shivery feeling in the pit of her stomach. "Mary Beth said—it was wild turkeys."

"There are turkeys in the woods," he agreed slowly. "Also foxes, bears, cougars, snakes, rodents, and over a hundred varieties of birds. None of them make a sound like the one I've heard."

They looked at each other for a long time, each waiting for the other to say more. But neither would.

Then Ted stood and handed the screwdriver to her. "Well," he said. "That should do it. You might want to fax a practice document before you send anything important."

Laura smiled weakly. "Maybe I'll send by partners a picture of a snowman."

When he was gone Laura went back to the kitchen, the unfinished conversation disturbing the corners of her mind like a shadow that moved whenever the eyes were averted. Christy was dragging out a step stool, preparing to search through the cabinets for something to eat, and Laura patiently removed her to the kitchen table. It was already so late that Christy would be cranky by the time she finished the stewed chicken Laura had intended to prepare; she decided to broil it instead.

The Calumit supermarket had apparently never heard of boneless chicken breasts, and Laura grimaced as she unwrapped the whole chicken and prepared to cut it up herself. She wasn't even entirely sure how to do the job. Maybe it would be easier to stew the bird, after all.

Setting her teeth, Laura lifted the meat cleaver and brought it down at the junction of thigh and back with a sickening tear of flesh and crunch of bones. Christy screamed. Laura dropped the cleaver. The chair in which Christy had been sitting clattered to the floor and Christy backed away, tripping over it, pointing at her mother and making choked, terrified sounds that sounded like struggles for breath.

Laura ran to Christy. Her face was ash-white and her eyes a dark blur, and when Laura grabbed her shoulders Christy screamed again—a shrill, high-pitched sound that went through Laura's nerves like a live wire, but at least she was breathing. Thank God she was breathing.

Laura shook her. "What?" she cried. "Christy, what is it?"

More of those choking, inarticulate sounds. Her body was rigid and she kept pointing, staring over Laura's shoulder. She was terrified. "Ch-chicken!" she managed at last. "You killed it!"

Laura went weak. *No more,* she thought. *Please God, no more . . .*

She tried to keep her voice calm as she said, "No, honey, I didn't. It came from the store. I—"

"You did, you did, tearing it apart, ripping it open, pulling off its legs, just like—"

"No, not like—"

"The monsters! Just like the monsters with their teeth and claws—"

"Christy, no!" Laura tried to hold her, and Christy struggled; she shook her again, and Christy burst into tears. Laura gathered her close, rocking her, holding her. She thought helplessly, *Why? Dear God, why is this happening?*

What could she say to a five-year-old whose dreams were more than dreams? She couldn't explain it; Sam couldn't. How could she convince her child the monsters weren't real when her dreams insisted they were and all the reason and rationality of the adult world had no hard evidence to the contrary?

What *had* Christy seen last night? And how had she seen it? Laura wanted to ask her; to try, with patient questioning and calm deduction, to get to the bottom of whatever was haunting Christy's imagination. But she dared not make matters worse with her clumsy attempts at child psychology, and she knew, with a mother's instinct, that she would get no more from Christy than she had already learned. Christy had told what she had seen. The monsters had gotten the chickens, and torn them apart. But was she to go on seeing monsters for the rest of her life?

Laura found there were tears in her own eyes as she pushed Christy away, and she swallowed to clear the thickness from her throat. "Christy, honey, listen. Can you listen to me for a minute, sweetheart?"

She lifted her daughter's chin and forced a smile. Tears still streaked Christy's face, but her eyes were not so wild; her sobs had tapered off to an occasional hiccup. She listened.

Laura said, "Sometimes—animals are our food. We raise them to be food, then we ship them to the grocery store, and then we bring them home and we cut them up to cook them. We have to do that, do you see? Now, Mommy can't put a whole cow on the kitchen table for dinner, can she?" Christy did not smile. "Or a whole pig instead of bacon for breakfast?" Gently, Laura added, "And we have to cut up chickens to cook for supper. Even Corky has to have his food in little pieces," she extemporized on inspiration, "so he can eat it. Do you understand?"

Christy regarded her solemnly.

Laura sighed. "You're right. It sounds pretty bad

140

to me too. I never realized before what barbarians we are. No chicken for dinner tonight, okay?" Maybe not ever again, she thought as she got to her feet. She felt, at that moment, a strong leaning toward vegetarianism.

Christy said hesitantly, "For food? They do it for food?"

Laura did not know what else to say except, "That's right."

"They can't help being hungry," Christy said in a small voice.

"No," Laura agreed softly. "I guess not." Because the world is a big bad place where killing is just a matter of survival and the only thing that separates the men from the beasts is their position on the food chain . . . sometimes not even that.

Christy rubbed the back of her arm across her face. She still looked a little confused, but not quite so frightened. "Maybe it's not so bad then."

Laura got down on her knees again and hugged her daughter. "Okay," she said, smiling as she pushed Christy's damp hair away from her face. "How about a nice bowl of oatmeal for dinner?"

"And cheese toast?"

"And cheese toast."

Christy smiled at her, and Laura felt that familiar melting in her heart, that foolproof mechanism that allows all mothers to endure all pain and count it well worth it for the sake of a smile. Then Christy wriggled out of her arms and looked around.

"Mommy," she said, "where's Corky?"

Laura stood up, whistled for the dog, and peeked around the divider that separated the kitchen from the living room. There she stopped. The heavy front door had not quite closed when she let Ted out. It was still open.

She looked back at Christy in dismay.

Laura stayed up and watched Johnny Carson, going to the door every fifteen minutes to check for Corky. She kept telling Christy that Corky was a smart dog, he knew where he lived, and he would come home. She half-believed it herself. Probably, she suggested, he had just gone down the street to visit his mother and brother at Mary Beth's house, and would come home when he was ready. Christy, of course, insisted that they call the Jenningses right away, but Laura persuaded her to wait until morning. She didn't want Christy to be around when she called, and Mary Beth told her they hadn't seen the dog.

So Christy ritually filled the dog dishes with kibble and fresh water, and went upstairs to say an extra prayer for the safe return of her puppy. And Laura picked up the abandoned doggie toys—a rubber bone, a ball with a bell inside, and an old sock that Christy had knotted into a pull-toy—and placed them in a little pile by the back door. It looked like a shrine.

She dozed on the sofa, one ear still tuned for the smallest whine or scratching at the door, and eventually she was overtaken by fitful, incoherent dreams. The moon shining on the water. Skeletal limbs sketched across the night. A flash of movement. Heart beating. Breath rasping. Stalking. Then running. And what she grasped was small and furry and its frantic cries were cut off with a snap of the neck, and then blood gushed. . . .

She awoke with a smothered gasp, cold with sweat, to find Christy standing above her. Tears traced twin paths down her cheeks and her voice was tiny and trembling as she said simply, "Corky."

Laura took her in her arms, and Christy said again, "Corky." It was a long time before either of them went back to sleep.

At six o'clock in the morning Laura left Christy asleep in her bed and dressed in jeans and ankle-high boots. Her throat was dry, her eyes ached from too little sleep, and her nerves were like knotted bundles of wire, firing off random spurts of adrenaline for no good reason. She couldn't sleep. She couldn't stay in the house. She couldn't go through another night like the last one, and she couldn't face Christy this morning and tell her her puppy was still missing.

She went out the front door, logically assuring herself that since Corky had taken that route, he would have wandered down the street, possibly into a neighbor's yard. That was what she told herself. But she knew that was not what had happened.

A low mist was rising from the creek that ran through her wooded front yard, and little shafts of pale morning sun penetrated the shadows on the street. This was the kind of morning she had come to Calumit for: the smell of pine trees instead of exhaust fumes, the sleepy sound of waking birds instead of garbage trucks. Still, somnambulant, and peaceful. But she could not enjoy the beauty of the breaking day. She barely even noticed it.

She went down the driveway, whistling and calling

softly for Corky. When she reached the street she heard the sound of running feet, and when she turned, Ted Jacobs lifted his hand to her. He looked much as she had last seen him, dressed in running clothes with a towel looped around his neck, and in a moment's disorientation she could almost imagine he had been running all night.

She waited until he drew abreast of her. "We've lost our puppy," she explained. "You haven't seen him, have you?"

He shook his head, his face drawn a little with the effort to catch his breath. His hair was plastered to his head beneath a red sweatband, and his neck and shoulders gleamed with perspiration. "Not a sign. You want some help looking?"

Laura hesitated, then smiled reluctantly. "No, thanks. I think I'd better search the woods, and you're not dressed for it."

Ted looked over her head toward where the woods began, and she knew what he was thinking. If the dog had gone back there, there was very little chance of her finding him.

"He's just a little dog," Laura said defensively. "He can't have gone far."

After a moment Ted glanced at her, and smiled briefly. "Maybe. Well, I'll keep an eye out for him. Good luck."

"Thanks."

The woods at the front of the house were shielded by deadfall, a dumping ground for debris the construction crew had cleared that was now overgrown with vines and brambles four feet high in places. A puppy might have scrambled through that mess, but clearly Laura couldn't. She began to work her way

144

up the driveway, and in a few moments Ted Jacobs was beside her.

"To tell the truth," he said, "I've always wondered what those woods were like. I'll tag along, if you don't mind."

Laura smiled. "To tell the truth, I'd be glad of the company."

They found an entrance that wasn't too overgrown a few yards up, and pushed aside wet branches and clinging grass until the ground leveled out and the woodland absorbed the light. "I'll be damned," Ted murmured. "Would you look at that?"

He indicated a huge, double-trunked oak tree, gnarled and twisted by the ravages of time, with a root system so vast it looked more like a banyan tree than an oak. "That's something you don't expect to see in this part of the country," he said.

"I guess not," Laura agreed. She found herself speaking lowly, as though afraid of being overheard, and quickly shook off the foolishness. She gave a sharp whistle and called loudly, "Corky! Here, boy!"

The deep, heavy silence of the woods absorbed her words and sent back only the faint rustling of irritated forest creatures.

She went forward a few yards and Ted followed, cursing softly when a bramble snared his bare ankle. She called again, listened, and heard nothing. She stopped and looked around, feeling foolish with defeat. The forest was so big. Hundreds upon hundreds of acres of thick gnarled trees and interlocked webs of mountain laurel and not one inch of it distinguishable from the other . . . how could she expect to find one small puppy in this vast primeval wilderness?

But she had found him before. She remembered

145

the panic that assailed her when she had gone into these very woods looking for Christy, the overwhelming hopelessness of the task . . . yet she had found her. Her short legs had not carried her far from the house, and with luck, Corky might be as territorial, or as disadvantaged, as his mistress. Maybe he had not gone far.

And Laura would never forgive herself if she didn't at least try to find him, hopeless as it might seem.

Ted must have read the expression on her face, but he was kind enough not to voice his own thoughts. Instead he gestured toward a break in the bushes. "Looks like some kind of deer trail. We could follow it for a while."

It was a random suggestion, but better than none at all. Laura picked up the flattened path and began to follow it.

"Louis L'Amour said there's a good reason for always sticking to animal trails when you're crossing the wilderness," Ted commented after a time. "Generally, if there were an easier way to get from one place to another, the animals would have found it."

The sound of a human voice was comforting in this alien place, and Laura was glad he had come along. "You don't strike me as the type who'd read Louis L'Amour."

"When you don't know anything about anything," he replied, "you read almost everything."

Another time Laura would have picked up on that, a tantalizing insight into the ego of a successful writer. But the climb was difficult as the trail swept upwards, and the further they went the more palpable the silence of the forest became. Words seemed insignificant. Conversation was inimical. After a

146

while Laura even stopped calling for Corky. It was almost as though she were afraid of what the sound of her voice might disturb.

That was ridiculous, of course. Trees were just trees, shadows only shadows. The moldy, mossy faces of boulders thousands upon thousands of years old were only rocks, sheltering small burrowing creatures who were more afraid of her than she was of them. And yet it felt wrong. Unfamiliar, treacherous, home to things that crawled in the night and peeked out from among the branches with darting tongues and small dark eyes. The air was thick with the cycle of decay and the light was thin, an enemy to this place. They had invaded an alien sanctuary for age-old secrets, the spawning place of human nightmares: the girl who went into the forest and was devoured by wolves, the children who wandered down the wrong path and were baked by a witch—those were but symbols, half-memories of things too savage, too wild and terrifying, to be recalled whole.

Ted was right. Humans did not belong in the forest. And those pioneers who had first tamed the wilderness—had they chopped down the trees and burned out the woodlands merely to build their homes and plant their crops? Perhaps, in part. Or perhaps they had leveled the forest to protect themselves, acting on some instinct they did not even understand that compelled them to be free of the lurking evil within. To escape the forest.

The mist of perspiration was cool and clammy on Laura's skin, and the sound of her labored breathing was eerie, like an echo of some distant beast. Ted, who was obviously in much better shape than she was, fared better, but their feet made too much noise on the forest floor, crashing against twigs and sending small stones scurrying. Laura kept jerking her eyes around, wondering what animals the sound of their approach might alert. Her logical mind knew that any animal would run from them long before they got near, but still she looked. And worried.

She paused where the path dipped into a shallow running stream and braced her hands on her knees, taking a few deep breaths. It was time to turn back. She wanted to turn back. It had been a futile undertaking in the first place. She had tried, hadn't she? But how could she go back and face Christy empty-handed?

She had no choice. She couldn't wander around in these woods all day. It was dangerous up here.

She said to Ted, "How's your sense of direction?"

"Lousy. But I know where we are."

He lifted a hand and pointed through a break in the trees. She felt foolish when she recognized the shape of her own roof, as small at this distance as a doll's house, glinting in the valley below. It only showed what imagination could do, when a grown woman could lose herself in dark thoughts of ancient terrors within sight of her own house.

She noticed that the path formed a fork which drifted downward, and should take them by a more or less direct route straight to her backyard. She said, "We'd better start down. Christy will be up soon and I don't want her to find me gone."

"Laura," Ted said slowly. "Look."

He bent down to retrieve something from the mud at the edge of the stream. The ground all around them was marshy and churned up, as though it might be a favorite gathering spot for deer — or other

148

animals—and the object he had spotted was half buried by mud and debris. He held it out to her.

It was a small leather collar, red studded with blue rhinestones. Christy had picked it out herself because it was shiny and it was red. The catch hadn't come unfastened, nor had it been pulled off intact. The leather was neatly slashed in two.

Laura took the collar with hesitant fingers, a cold tightness gathering in her chest. Ted stepped over the stream and looked around. He didn't bother to call or whistle. They both knew it was pointless.

And then the sounds of Ted's movement stopped. He said in a strange, choked voice, "Jesus."

Laura turned around. Ted was standing stock still about ten feet away, his head tilted back slightly as though looking upward, his arms sagging at his sides. Laura crossed the stream to stand beside him.

"What?" she said.

Ted clutched at her arm as though to turn her away, but too late. Her eyes had caught the direction of his gaze and were riveted there.

A small animal was hanging upside down from a tree branch about eight feet off the ground. Flies buzzed noisily around it, and its fur was matted with mud and blood. Rigor mortis had pulled the gums back from the muzzle, revealing a set of bloodstained canine teeth. The body had been slashed open from throat to groin, and bits of white rib and glistening pink flesh protruded from the opening.

It was Corky.

It was Ted's idea to call the sheriff. At first Laura didn't understand why. She remembered thinking to herself over and over, *It's just a dog, for heaven's sake, the police don't care about a dog*. . . . But the voice in her head that repeated those words was high and thin with hysteria, and when she got home she locked herself in the bathroom and vomited until she choked on dry heaves. Then she called Mary Beth and asked her, as calmly as she could, to please come and take Christy for the day. She did not want Christy to be there when Sam arrived and started asking official questions.

But all her careful planning came to nothing when she turned around and saw Christy coming down the stairs, the hem of her pink nightgown trailing behind her. Laura thought absently, *That nightgown's too long for her. I'll have to hem it up before she trips over it*. Then Christy said, "Corky's dead, isn't he, Mommy? The monsters killed Corky."

Laura looked at her helplessly.

Christy screamed, "They killed Corky! They killed him! I hate them, I hate them, they killed my puppy!"

She turned and stumbled up the stairs.

After that events were a blur. Mary Beth arrived and tried to pry Christy from Laura's arms, but by that time Laura had changed her mind and wanted Christy to stay with her. In the end Mary Beth agreed to stay with Christy upstairs while Laura talked to the police. At that point Laura still wasn't sure why Ted had reported the atrocity, but when she saw Sam's face she was glad he had.

He didn't say anything meaningless like, "I'm sorry," or "Are you okay?" He merely looked at her with quiet solemnity, and his silent presence comforted her more than platitudes could have done.

Then he went with Ted to examine the scene.

Both men were silent on the trudge through the woods. Ted got turned around twice, but as they were never completely out of sight of the house, they weren't really lost. Then Ted said, "There. This looks like it. We were following a trail." Sam didn't need much guidance there. He picked up the sound of the stream and followed it to the tree on the other side and its gruesome ornament.

Ted hung back, and Sam couldn't much blame him. Sam had seen worse in his time, but there was something about kids and animals that could twist the stomach of the most hardened man, and Sam was far from hardened. Perhaps it had something to do with injustice. Most humans, by the time they reached adulthood, had done enough evil or thought enough evil to deserve almost any kind of punishment. But you'd be hard-pressed to find evil in a three-month-old puppy, and a child's pet did not deserve to die like this.

The area around the stream was a churned-up swamp of black mud. Whatever footprints there might have been had been destroyed by Ted and Laura; furthermore, it looked as though this area might have been a watering hole for some of the local animal population. Little else could explain the trampled ground around the stream. Sam searched the area for a few dozen feet, but the thick carpet of pine straw revealed nothing; the broken branches and overturned stones indicated only what he already knew—that something had been here.

The corpse had been impaled upon a stripped branch through the soft flesh above the flank, and hung about eight feet off the ground. Flies buzzed in

151

and out of the abdominal cavity, and the smell of death was like an aftertaste, so well blended with the scent of rotting foliage and decaying earth that was the natural cycle of the forest, it was almost indistinguishable. Sam moved back a few feet and spent a long moment just looking up at the scene.

Ted cleared his throat and said a little uncertainly, "What do you think?"

Sam glanced at him. "I'm open to suggestions."

"Hell, I don't know. There's all kind of weirdness in this world. But if I were writing it, it would probably be some kind of cult. Animal sacrifice, that sort of thing."

Sam looked back again at the grotesque image hanging from the tree. "Maybe." He bent down and picked up a few blood-spattered pine needles, then let them drop. "I don't guess you've ever been hunting."

"No. That's one boyhood pleasure I missed." And then he looked at Sam. "Why?"

"You've never seen a deer dressed out? Or cleaned a rabbit or squirrel?"

Ted replied impatiently, "No, but I've done my share of autopsies. What are you getting at?"

Sam looked at him for a moment thoughtfully. "Nothing," he said. He turned back to the tree. "That poor little kid," he said softly. "She sure was fond of this animal." The quiet words hid the anger he felt, and the swelling sense of frustration which always accompanied the discovery of an act of random violence. This used to be a quiet community. What the hell was going wrong?

He said abruptly, "I'd better get it down before the buzzards start flocking." He caught the lower branches of the tree and braced his foot against the trunk, preparing to hoist himself up. Then he glanced back at Ted, feeling a small twinge of sympathy. A city boy wasn't cut out for things like this. "You can go on back to the house," he said. "I'll handle it from here."

For a moment Sam thought the other man would take him up on the offer. Then Ted said, "That's okay. I'll stay." He took an unsteady breath, and stepped forward to help.

Laura was sitting at the kitchen table when they returned. Sam's mouth was set in a grim line and Ted looked harried and vaguely ill—the look of a man who confronted reality very seldom, and had been dealt too strong a dose of it all at once.

Ted said gently, "The sheriff says it's all right to—dispose of the body. I'll bury it in the woods, if you'll tell me where your shovel is."

"No," Laura said sharply. "Not in the woods. They'll dig it up."

Ted looked startled, and Laura did not know why she had said that. She pressed her fingers to her temples briefly, trying to clear her head. "Ted, I'm sorry. You've been great. I can't tell you how much I—but you don't have to . . ."

He smiled weakly. "I don't get the chance to be a hero very often. Is the backyard all right? Maybe behind the garage, where your little girl can't see me from upstairs."

Laura nodded. It felt wrong, accepting all these favors from strangers; it made her feel helpless and weak . . . like she had been that other time. A victim. But she had learned from that other time that when something horrible happens, something unspeakable and incomprehensible that threatens the fragile supports upon which routine worlds are built, the only defense people have is to do something . . . it doesn't matter what, just something that makes them feel useful, that gives them the illusion, however briefly, of being involved, of fighting back. It was easier to give in to these well-meant kindnesses than to argue, and far less painful for everyone in the end. So she said, "Thank you. The shovel's in the garage."

He closed the back door quietly behind him, and Laura said, "Funny how people are thrown together. I didn't like him much the first time I met him. But I'm sure glad he happened to be around today."

Sam pulled out a chair and sat across from her at the table. "He was the one who found it?"

She took a sip of cold coffee to keep from having to answer out loud, and nodded.

"He said he was running this morning when you told him about the dog. And he just decided to go along?"

"That sounds like an official police question."

"I have to ask, Laura."

"You don't seriously think—"

He released a breath and pushed his fingers through his hair. "No, I don't seriously think."

Laura pushed herself away from the table with an abrupt, angry gesture. "What kind of twisted, sick mind would do something like that?" she burst out. "He was just a little puppy, he never hurt anybody, he didn't even *bark*—" She caught herself as she felt the flood of tears rising, and clamped her lips together tightly. If she started crying now she wouldn't

154

stop, first for an innocent puppy who couldn't defend himself, then for a child whose heart was broken and whose world had been invaded by senseless evil, then for herself, and then she would by crying simply because she didn't know what else to do and she could not allow that to happen. She couldn't.

She stared out the window and blinked slowly, breathing deeply, until her vision cleared. The woods gazed back at her, serene in the knowledge of a thousand hidden eyes.

She said, "Christy thinks there's something out there. Monsters."

"I think there's something out there too," Sam agreed quietly.

She looked at him sharply.

He said, "But I guarantee you it's not monsters."

"What then?" she demanded. She clenched her fists to keep her voice from shaking—with rage, with revulsion, with fear. "What is it that could do something like this? *Who* would do this?"

The lines around his eyes seemed to deepen, but his expression remained unchanged. "I can't answer that now, Laura. But I will. And soon."

Calm words, confident words, spoken like a dedicated officer of the law. But only words.

Laura turned toward the window again, hugging her elbows. "I moved six times after the attack," she said hollowly. "Did I tell you that? Every few months, another address, another set of locks . . . I know it was obsessive, but I couldn't seem to help it. Finally I came here.

"It's not fair," she said tightly. Her fingers dug into her arms. "You do all the right things, you take all the proper precautions, you do everything it takes to

155

be *safe* . . . and it follows you. The perverts with their sick idea of kicks, the crazies with the knives, the drug pushers and the ax killers and child molesters—they're everywhere, aren't they? No matter where you go they're there, waiting for you, and it's just not fair!"

Sam got up and came over to her, and placed a hand upon her shoulder. "No," he agreed quietly, "it's not fair. But all that means is we have to work a little harder to even up the odds."

Sam felt her muscles tighten beneath his fingers, and she lifted her chin a little. "The other night you asked me a question," she said quietly. She turned to look up at him, her expression composed and her eyes hard. "The answer is yes. I have a gun. And I know how to use it."

His fingers exerted a slight pressure on her shoulder, and his tone was low and intense as he said, "I promise you, Laura, it stops here. This is as bad as it gets."

Laura said nothing. She wanted to believe him; desperately, profoundly she wanted to believe. But deep inside, down to the core of her being, she knew the worst had only begun.

And she thought Sam knew it too.

Chapter Eight

Laura took a breath and said, as calmly as she could, "I don't understand."

Carl Bedlow lifted his cap and scratched his head, squinting into the sun beyond Laura's left shoulder. "It's not all that unusual. Sometimes we get in and start blasting and we find these things—natural sink-holes, gas pockets, underground caves . . . you'd be surprised."

Laura could feel her jaw muscles tightening; she deliberately tried to relax them. "No," she said very patiently. "What I don't understand is why I wasn't informed before this. You were aware, weren't you, Mr. Bedlow, that the purpose of clearing this lot was to put a house on it? Do you have any suggestions as to how I'm supposed to design a house with a six-foot-deep hole in the living room?"

His expression was unmoved. "No, ma'am, I don't. You're the architect."

Laura bit back a sarcastic and basically unworthy reply, and moved her eyes over to the construction trailer. A folding table and chairs had been set up outside, and Christy was settled there, occupied with crayons and paper. Occasionally one of the construction workers, when they weren't busy looking for something to do, would stop by and chat with her. The sound of saws and hammers had ceased.

Laura's frustration over the news was far out of proportion, she knew. Her job was to design the houses; let Carl Bedlow worry about how to build them, and Hugh Bullard could worry about how much the delay was going to cost. But over the past few days she had thrown herself into her work with a frenzy; she counted on it to keep her busy, to get her out of the house, to make her so tired at night that she didn't have to worry about going to sleep. It was good for Christy too, who accompanied her on her on-site surveys, and spent a great deal of time at the Jennings house while her mother was working.

Laura was, of course, far ahead of schedule, and as long as the construction crew had been on schedule, all had been as it should be. But this discovery had brought them all to a virtual halt until Hugh Bullard instructed them whether to try to build around the fault—a disastrous possibility which Laura would have to fight—or abandon the site and hope for better luck with the next lot. If, on the other hand, Bullard ordered a geological survey of the entire area, construction could be delayed for weeks. Months.

She knew Bullard's avaricious nature, and that last possibility seemed unlikely, but until he returned from Chicago they were all at a stalemate. Laura had neither the authority nor the inclination to take it upon herself to tell Carl Bedlow to keep his men working.

She said, "You've called Mr. Bullard?"

"Yes'm. Left a message at his hotel."

"I don't suppose you have any idea how big this cave is, or how far back it goes?"

He rubbed his chin. "Well, the blast closed it off,

of course. But it wouldn't surprise me if this whole mountainside was riddled with pockets like this. That's usually the way it goes."

"Great," Laura muttered.

"Now that doesn't mean we're likely to find any more," he added. "The fact is, if you want my opinion—and I'm no expert, mind you—but if I had to guess I'd say the possibility is that we've already built over most of them. There's more limestone at the top of the mountain, you understand, and that's how caves are made—water dripping through limestone."

"I know how caves are formed, Mr. Bedlow."

He nodded. "Then you know what we have here is just a little sinkhole. Might be part of an underground network, might not. But if it's part of a cavern system, like I was saying, the rest of it's a lot deeper, and we're not likely to disturb it with our blasting."

Laura tucked her fingers into the front pockets of her jeans. "Well, that's reassuring. I hope you're right." But even if he was, she was not at all sure she liked the idea of erecting a structure on top of a cavern. No matter what common sense said, she couldn't entirely put out of her mind the picture of a house floating in midair, ready to collapse into a hole in the earth at the slightest provocation.

And when she considered the fact that her own house might be built over just such a fault, she felt a sinking despair. Was nothing on this earth to be trusted—not even the earth itself?

She said, "There's nothing I can do here. Let me know what you hear from Mr. Bullard."

"Right. Just thought you'd want to know the situation."

She turned and walked back toward the construction trailer, trying to put on a cheerful face as she approached Christy.

"Whatcha doing, pumpkin?" she greeted her daughter. But even before she knelt beside Christy, Laura could see perfectly well what she was doing. She had drawn another picture of the grotesque creature she called a snowman, and was stabbing at it viciously with the point of a pencil, shredding the paper. The violence of the act was such that Laura could hardly restrain herself from grabbing Christy's wrist to stop her.

Christy replied grimly, "Killing the monster."

Everything within Laura tightened with a visceral desperation, but she said nothing. A month ago, even a week ago, Laura would have been appalled at such a wanton display of violence from her daughter. But she realized now that if destroying a piece of paper would somehow obliterate the monsters from Christy's mind, Laura would have gladly taken up a pair of scissors and done the job herself.

She also realized something else. If they had still been in the city, Christy would have been in the hands of a top child psychologist long before now. Since Corky's death Christy had become obsessed with the monsters—not talking about them; she was eerily, distressingly reticent to vocalize—but drawing them. More often than not the drawings would end up shredded, mangled, or disfigured in some way. Laura did not know how to deal with that; she didn't have the faintest idea how to begin to ease her child's pain. All she could give was love, and as much understanding as she could. In another reality it would have been all too easy to let a professional take over—and yet a part of Laura was determinedly, selfishly glad such help was not available now. Too much control was surrendered to the so-called professionals of the modern world as it was. Out here she and Christy were on their own, and perhaps that was as it should be.

Laura knelt beside Christy as the paper tore in half, and slipped an arm around her shoulders. "Is he dead now?" she asked gently.

A chill formed around Laura's heart at the force of the hatred in Christy's eyes as she stared at the mutilated paper, but Laura forced herself to conceal her distress. Maybe Sam was right. Children *were* savages at heart, and perhaps the best thing a parent could do was allow them to express that part of their nature without judgments or shame.

Or at least she hoped that was the best thing.

The grimness of Christy's expression began to fade, and after a moment she looked more like the little girl Laura loved—pouting instead of angry, superior in her own grasp of reality. "Don't be silly, Mommy," she said. "I can't kill them with a pencil."

Laura smiled uncertainly. "No, I guess not." And then she asked a stupid, but irresistibly motherlike question. "Why do you want to kill them at all, honey?"

Christy scowled. "Because they're bad. They have to be punished."

"You know, Christy," Laura said carefully, "monsters didn't kill Corky. We talked about that. Corky wandered into the woods and he got hurt. But nobody saw any monsters."

Christy looked up at her. "If nobody saw them," she inquired, "then how do you know it wasn't the monsters?"

Christy's expression was curious and reasonable, but strangely tinged with hope. She *wanted* her

161

mother to prove to her the monsters were innocent. But there was no arguing with a five-year-old's logic.

Still, this was the first time since Corky's death that Christy had talked openly about her monster fears, and it was a sign Laura wanted to encourage. She said, "Why do you call them snowmen, honey?"

There was a touch of impatience in Christy's shrug. "Because they're big and white and fat. And they have great big round heads, like snowmen."

"Like Frosty the Snowman?"

"Not like Frosty. They're mean. Frosty's not mean. And they don't melt."

"How do you know all that?"

Christy hesitated, a small frown plucking at her brow.

"How do you know what they look like?" Laura persisted. "Did someone tell you?"

"No," answered Christy slowly. "I just know it. In my head."

"Do you mean like a dream?"

"Noooo . . . Kind of." Then, her attention span apparently exhausted, Christy gathered up her papers and crayons. "Can we go now, Mommy? I'm hot. I want to go swimming."

After a moment, Laura smiled. "Sounds like a good plan to me. As it happens, I have the afternoon off."

She caught Christy's hand as they walked toward the van.

And then Christy said, "They watch me at night."

Laura stopped walking. "What?"

"They sit in the woods and they watch my house. While I'm sleeping."

Laura's throat closed up in helplessness as she stared at her daughter. Christy's brow was puckered

162

with worry, and she looked up at her mother. "You won't let them get me, will you, Mommy? You won't let them come in my house?"

Laura knelt down and hugged her daughter hard, squeezing her eyes closed. "No, baby," she said huskily, after a moment. "I won't let them get you. I promise."

Then she straightened up, and forced a bright smile. "Now, how about that swim?"

"Subhumans." Deputy Lars Greesom kicked aside a wad of newspaper and scowled at the soiled carpet that was uncovered. "That's what they are. Goddamn subhumans. Ought to be taken out and shot, if you ask me. Or drowned at birth, just like you do with deformed animals. Goddamn subhumans."

Sam edged between an overturned chair and a motorcycle with the front wheel missing, moving toward the kitchen. It looked as though the rats had gotten to the chair, and oil from the motorcycle had soaked through the matted nylon carpet. Broken venetian blinds hung by a corner from one window; the other had been boarded up with plywood. The holes in the wall might have been made by a fist or the careless moving of furniture; Sam suspected the former. Beer bottles and oily rags were everywhere. A pile of dirty clothes decorated the top of a projection television set, and unwashed dishes were piled on top of the mammoth stereo speakers.

"Smells like a shithouse in here," Greesom said, curling his upper lip in distaste as he nudged a paper sack half filled with rotting take-out food out of his path. "Goddamn animals. How can people live like this?"

Sam opened the refrigerator. Except for an open can of beer that gave off a sour fruit odor, and something unidentifiable wrapped in tinfoil, it was empty. The sink was filled with crusty dishes, and when he turned on the faucet a few roaches scuttled away, but only a thin stream of brownish water came out.

He pushed open the torn screen door and went out onto the back stoop, where the two children were huddled together under the watchful eye of his other deputy, Jeff. Jeff was twenty-two and had been on the force for less than a year; he was good on traffic patrol and highly efficient at filling out forms, but the finer points of police work still sometimes eluded him. He hovered over the two children as though he were guarding an armored truck.

The girl might have been six, with matted mouse-colored hair and beads of black dirt around her neck. The sty that had caused her left eye to redden and swell half shut was the least of her problems. Her brother was about three and, from the multiple scabs that covered his thin body, appeared to be recovering from chicken pox. One arm was wrapped tightly around his sister's waist, a thumb was stuck in his mouth, and his eyes were big and fearful. Both children smelled of rotting teeth and dried sweat and unwashed clothes.

Sam sat down on the step, at eye level with the girl, and smiled. "How long've you been locked up in here, sweetheart?" he inquired gently.

The girl shrank back and refused to answer.

"The mailman said it'd been at least a week since he'd seen either one of their folks," Jeff volunteered, and Sam shot him an impatient look. He knew what the mailman had said; that was why they were out here.

He tried again. "Did your mama fix you supper last night?"

The child hesitated, then slowly shook her head.

"What about the night before?"

She said nothing.

"Well, I'll bet you're pretty hungry," he said easily. "How'd you like for Deputy Goetz here to take you out for something to eat?"

She shook her head, this time more adamantly. Her brother clung to her. "I ain't—supposed to leave. M-mama'll be mad. I d-don't wanna get a whupping."

Sam smiled. "We'll fix it up with your mama." His eyes traveled, as casually as possible, over the child's stained shirt and shorts to her bare legs, which were far too thin and crisscrossed with elongated bruises. "Is that what happened to your legs? Did your mama give you a whipping?"

She said nothing.

"Daddy?" Sam prompted. "Did he hit you with his belt?"

The little boy started to cry.

Sam stood up. "Take them to the hospital," he said to Jeff. "Get them checked out. Have the county send somebody from social services to meet you there."

Jeff nodded, and bent down to pick up the little boy. He cried harder and clung to his sister, and the girl pleaded, "Don't make me go, mister, I ain't suppose to leave. I don't want to go!"

Sam reached out a hand, but the child flinched away and started sobbing. He knelt beside her. "Nobody's going to hurt you, honey." It was hard to keep his voice gentle with fury and disgust churning in his stomach; hard to smile at the terror in the girl's eyes. "We're just going to have a doctor look at you and then get you something to eat. Don't you worry about your mama, we'll tell her where you are. She's not going to whip you, I promise."

Jeff pried the boy away from his sister and took the little girl's hand. "I don't want to go," she sobbed. "Please don't make me go!"

Sam had to turn back into the house as Jeff carried them away. Lars Greesom was standing in the kitchen, looking as grim as Sam felt.

"I don't know, Lars," Sam said quietly. "Sometimes I think there's got to be a Hell. Seems like that's the only fit punishment for what we do to our children."

Greesom looked for a moment as though he didn't know what to say. Then: "You want me to put out an APB on Kellerman's truck?"

"Yeah."

Sam's eyebrows were drawn together; his shoulders were slumped, and the word had sounded more like an afterthought than a dismissal. So Greesom hesitated.

Then Sam straightened, his mouth set in a thin line, his jaw muscles tight. "But first," he said, "I want to know how a man who's never held a steady job in his life can afford a big-screen television, two VCRs, and a thousand dollars worth of stereo equipment. We're going to tear this goddamn place apart."

"Do you mean to tell me," Laura said slowly, deliberately into the phone, "that you've known about this all along?"

Hugh Bullard's voice, traveling down the line from Chicago, sounded brusque and impatient. "Of course I knew. What kind of fool would start a project this expensive without checking out what he's getting into? It's that fool Bedlow's fault. If he'd been blasting where I told him to instead of worrying about some goddamn chunk of granite, none of this would have happened. Leave the rocks there, I told him. That's what rock gardens are for. But he had to go get creative on me. He—"

"That chunk of granite, as you call it," Laura said tersely, interrupting, "was an eight-foot boulder that was positioned right in the middle of the living room, as you would have known if you'd bothered to look at my plans before you approved them. I told you that was a hard lot to work with—"

"Well, now you don't have any lot to work with," Bullard replied, effortlessly making it sound as though it were all her fault. "What you've got to do now is figure out what we're going to do with a quarter acre of ground with a goddamn blast hole in the middle of it."

"Correction." Laura's hand tightened on the receiver. "You've got to figure out what to do with it. I'm not drawing another line until I find out exactly what I'm building on. I don't want any more surprises."

"Now you hold on just a minute. Are you implying some kind of negligence here?"

"Not at all. I'm simply pointing out that when a building collapses, it's usually the architect people start pointing fingers at, not the developer."

"Come on, Miss Kane, I expected better than that from you. Nothing's going to collapse and you know it."

"And even if it does, it won't be your fault."

The words sounded petulant, even to Laura, and the minute she spoke she regretted them. She was overreacting, and she knew it as well as Hugh did. There was no evidence at all to indicate that the ground on which the development was being built was unstable enough to cause a collapse; the worst that could happen was a leaky basement or a cracked ceiling, and those were risks builders took every day. She wasn't angry at Hugh about the sinkhole; she was angry because he had built a luxury community on the edge of a dark, unfriendly forest where things howled in the night and people slaughtered household pets and children couldn't sleep for fear of being watched by malevolent eyes. And she was angry at herself because there was nothing she could do to change any of that.

Still, in the face of Hugh's remonstrative silence, she persisted stubbornly. "I need to see the geological survey maps before I go any further."

Hugh made an exasperated sound. "What good do you think that will do you? *I* looked at the map and all it told me was that there was an underground stream running through the mountain. The surveyor didn't bore a hole down there and trace its course, you know; he could only lay out a general direction. Nobody can predict every twist and turn or every cave it's formed. According to the map there are no major depressions or openings this far down, so now you know everything I know. Sure, you're going to run into a sinkhole now and then, but what builder doesn't?"

Laura's silence was stony.

"Oh, hell, look at the maps if it will make you feel any better. My wife will give them to you. Top file drawer on the left."

"Thanks, but there's no hurry," Laura replied smoothly. "I can wait till you get home."

His voice held a subtle warning. "Don't hold me up over this, Laura."

Laura smiled mirthlessly, enjoying the small power play. "I'm three houses ahead of you, Hugh. Now all you've got to do is figure out where to build them."

But as soon as she hung up the satisfaction of one-upmanship vanished. The work in which she had taken such comfort was temporarily suspended. Now she was feuding with the man who was not only her boss, but her neighbor as well. Christy was napping and the house was too solemn, too quiet. It reminded her of a museum, or a great sunlit tomb, and she was nothing but a microbe of dust in the middle of it.

Laura had thought an afternoon spent playing with Christy in the pool would relax her and put things in perspective. It had the opposite effect. The sound of splashing water and childish laughter echoed hollowly against the vast backdrop of wooded mountains and empty sky, as though they were the last living beings on a deserted planet, mocking their fear by pretending to have fun. And the woods, dark and silent, watched with the grim patience of absolute certainty. This mountain had been here long before they arrived, and would endure long after they were gone.

She longed to hear the sound of a truck lumbering past, a horn blasting, a distant siren wailing. Whenever a plane passed overhead, which was all too seldom, she bent her head back to follow its progress as though it were the last hope for a doomed civilization. Whatever had made her think she could be happy living in a place like this, cut off from the rhythms and rigors of a living, thriving society? What had been so appealing about this isolated, wooded lot where even the sounds of her next-door neighbors were too far away to hear?

It was amazing, the difference one small pesky puppy had made. Amazing how much she could miss him after having had him for such a short time. Without him, the house seemed bigger, emptier, and somehow more vulnerable. Footsteps echoed, shadows seemed deeper, and small noises — the crack of a branch, the clatter of the icemaker — made her jump. Mary Beth had offered to give them the last of the litter, but Laura would not even consider it. For Christy's sake and her own, it was best to have no reminders. She was beginning to realize, slowly and reluctantly, that she hated this place, and it would take more than the replacement of a lost puppy to change that.

She went over to the picture window and stood for a moment looking out. The pool was a sheet of silver-blue in the middle of a terraced garden, and oaks and elms cast ragged shadows over the park-lush grass. Today might be a good day to start those flower beds she had planned. But the thought of going out there, all by herself, and turning her back on the woods, made her uneasy.

A low vibration, like distant thunder, caused the windowpanes to shudder and startled Laura. The blasting had started again. Apparently Hugh had placed a call to Bedlow as soon as he had hung up with her, and no time was being lost after all. Either Hugh had decided what to do about the ruined lot, or had given orders to blast away the side of the mountain out of spite. The thought should have brought an ironic smile to her face, but it did not.

After a moment, she pushed the button that closed the vertical blinds and turned away from the window, sealing off the harsh afternoon sun, and the view of the woods beyond.

Sam did not consider himself a very good detective, which was why he was so perfectly suited to small-town police work. Big-city crooks might have the time and energy to try to outwit the cops, but most folks, when moved by the urge to commit a crime, did not. In a small and relatively isolated community, where people adhered to predictable — though by outside standards, sometimes bizarre — patterns of behavior, there were few unsolvable mysteries.

In Sam's term of office there had been two murders. The first was committed by a wife who had been beaten one too many times by her alcoholic husband; Sam had picked her up at her sister's house an hour after a neighbor had discovered the husband's body. She was drinking Sanka and watching soap operas. The second had been a hit-and-run with half-a-dozen witnesses. Sam had caught up with the teenage driver, who was too drunk and too scared to put up much of a protest, half a mile outside of town.

The fact of the matter was that people who committed crimes didn't plan on getting caught, and in their arrogance — or confusion — they were more likely than not to simply ignore the obvious. It was therefore generally the simplest solution that was the correct one. Ted Jacobs might think in terms of satanic cults, and Laura of psychopaths, even the deputies were beginning to form theories about mad hermits in the woods. Sam's theory was much simpler. More obvious.

After twenty-five minutes of searching they found it: two packs of neatly baled homegrown stuffed in a duffel bag in back of a closet. Sam sat back on his heels and smiled faintly. "Gotcha," he said softly.

Greesom's eyes gleamed. "You think he's growing that stuff around here, Sheriff?"

"I wouldn't be a bit surprised."

"Hey," Greesom said excitedly, "I read in the papers awhile back how the cops discovered a whole drug lab right under the ground. Fellow had a trapdoor in his backyard, like a storm cellar, and he had electric lights and cable TV and everything right down there. You think maybe Kellerman's got something like that going on?"

Sam hid a smile as he replaced the evidence and zipped up the bag. "I kind of doubt it. More than likely, he's got a field cleared out back in the woods someplace, and that's exactly where he is right now — tending his crop."

Greesom looked disappointed. "It wouldn't hurt to check, though, would it?"

Now Sam grinned. He felt so good he couldn't help it. "No, it wouldn't hurt to check. And if you don't find any trapdoors in the backyard, maybe you could take a ride up Hog-Back Road, see if anybody up that way's spotted Kellerman's truck coming and going. When you get back to the office, I'll have a search map drawn up."

Greesom looked doubtful. "I don't mean to say nothing against you, Sam, but if we start searching this mountain piece by piece, we can plan on passing the case on to our grandkids still not solved."

"That's what you call job security, Lars." He swung the strap of the duffel over his shoulder. "But don't worry. We're not going to cover the whole mountain—just the part that backs up against the Heights."

Lars frowned. "How come?" And slowly his face cleared. "Oh, you think one of them—"

"I think," Sam said, "that if I had me a nice little patch of illegal crop growing up there, I'd do my damnedest to cause some mischief to anybody who got too close. And that's where Kellerman all but drew us a map himself."

Lars nodded thoughtfully. "Yeah, makes sense. But it's still an awful lot of ground to cover."

"Then I wouldn't waste any time."

But Sam didn't really expect they'd have to spend too much time searching the woods on foot. The way he had it figured, the answer would come much more easily than that.

The afternoon mail brought Laura a collection of bills, two magazines, and a package from Ben and Hilly. it was a small hardcover book entitled *Ghosts and Legends of the Great Smoky Mountains*, and the flyleaf inscription read, "Just a little something to read before bedtime. Happy Housewarming!"

"Thanks a lot, guys," Laura muttered.

But the house had been cleaned within an inch of its life, Christy was watching *Sesame Street*, and Laura could not find anything else to do. She sat down on the sofa and began to flip through the book.

The collection of tales proved to be as bland as oatmeal and just as comfortable in their trite, reassuring way: lovers leaping into a gorge, an Indian Princess lost in a cavern, a long-dead Confederate soldier appearing to warn his daughter of danger. Then she turned a page and saw a chapter heading

173

that made her heart stop. *The Nighteaters of Calumit Mountain.*

She had to blink, and focus her eyes before she could read the text.

"Yeti, the Loch Ness Monster, werewolves, and vampires . . . of all the tales of mythical beasts around the world, none is as elusive, nor as persistent, as the legendary Nighteaters of Calumit Mountain in northeastern Tennessee. The creatures, described as huge, white-skinned, with hideously enlarged skulls and phosphorescent eyes, have apparently made their home in this mountaintop wilderness for several centuries, although reports of similar creatures have been made from as far west as the Rocky Mountains and north into Canada. Although Indian lore is sprinkled with references to the beasts, the earliest written account comes from the journal of Lever Foulks, a trapper and explorer who crossed the Calumit Mountain area in 1640."

"Mommy, the monster! The snowman monster!"

Christy's shrill cry caused Laura to jump and drop the book, her heart leaping to her throat. She half leapt off the sofa, only to find Christy standing right behind her, looking over her shoulder.

"Christy! Honey!" She sank back onto the couch with a dramatic sigh of relief. "Don't sneak up on Mommy like that. You scared me half to death."

"Mommy, look!" Christy scrambled around to pick up the book, which had landed face down on the floor. "It's them, it is! Look!"

Christy jumped on the couch and held the book in front of Laura's face, pointing. Laura took the book from her and looked at it.

The caption read: "Artist's rendering of the Calumit Nighteaters." The sketch was of a darkly

174

wooded area, in the center right of which an upright creature loped, as though moving furtively from tree to tree. Except for the grotesquely exaggerated head and the obvious luminosity of the skin, the drawing was similar to those famous impressions of Sasquatch, but that was not what made Laura's blood run cold. The large, sloping body shape, the almost perfectly round head, the clublike feet and hands complete with claws—it was, detail for detail, exactly as Christy had described her snowmen monsters. It was, in fact, only a more sophisticated version of the drawings Christy herself had done over and over again.

Laura stared at her daughter. Christy's pigtails swung forward as she examined the drawing—not with shock or repugnance, but with critical interest, the way a child might study a picture of Santa Claus or the Easter Bunny and compare it with her own conceptions of the creature. She wasn't afraid. But Laura was.

And perhaps what shocked Laura most was how *little* shock she felt. She had known all along, hadn't she? Somewhere, in some dark secret part of her, hadn't she always known that Christy wasn't suffering from an overactive imagination or a child's equivalent of stress syndrome? Hadn't she known with a mother's instinct struggling to rise above an adult's denial that Christy was reporting only what she saw, telling only what she knew to be the truth? And Laura knew it because *she* had seen it too, in snatches of dreams borrowed from Christy: running, hunting, a scar of blood across the face of the night. . . .

No. And there an adult's mind jerked her away from the precipice of possibilities. No, if she believed that, she would have to believe that her little girl was

175

in communication, somehow, with these alien creatures, these monsters of evil that killed at random and cut through the night with their bloodthirsty howls. . . .

The chickens. How do you explain the chickens?

And she couldn't believe that. She couldn't believe that her daughter was connected, in whatever incidental way, to these inhuman beasts, that she was being singled out for torment by some malformed murderous animal. . . .

But she knew. Before you even told her, she knew Corky was dead.

Christy was just a little girl. A sweet, innocent, basically *good* little girl. What knowledge did she have of evil, of monstrous killers? Why should she, and no one else, be troubled by the dreams, the visions, the certain knowledge of something as outrageous as this? A little girl's mind should be filled with dreams and fairy tales; she should not *know* about the bad things.

But she did before, didn't she? She knew about the worst thing that could ever happen to a little girl, when she almost lost her mother. . . .

There were other explanations, Laura knew there were. Sensible, comfortable explanations. Her head was spinning and she couldn't think of them just now, but she knew there were explanations. . . .

No explanations. It's true. It's really true. There's something out there. . . .

Christy looked up at her, a puzzled expression on her face. "Course it's true, Mommy. Didn't you believe me?"

Laura drew an unsteady breath and put her arms around her daughter, hugging her hard. "I believed you, honey," she said, closing her eyes.

"Of course I believed you."

The doorbell rang, and Christy cried, "Doorbell!" as she scrambled out of her mother's arms. Laura sat on the sofa and took a moment to compose herself. She didn't even remind Christy to check to see who it was before she opened the door. She sat staring at the open book and trying to dispel the queasy, shaky feeling inside.

"Hi, Sheriff Sam!" Christy exclaimed. "Do you want to see the monster book?"

Laura got up quickly. "Not right now, Christy." She went to the door and placed her hands on Christy's shoulders. Her smile was frozen and automatic, but she made an effort to turn it into something more genuine as she looked at the man in the doorway. "Well, well. What is this? I don't believe I've ever seen you out of uniform before; I almost didn't recognize you."

He grinned, gesturing to the pale blue sports shirt and dark slacks he wore. "Sorry. My plain brown suit was at the cleaners."

She was glad he was there. His presence brushed across her like a cool breeze on a sultry day, and she felt the tension leave her shoulders as she stepped away from the door. "Come on in. It's kind of a relief to know you're not here on official business."

"Actually," he said, pushing the door closed behind him as he stepped inside, "there's this great Disney movie playing at the Twin I've been wanting to see. I thought if we left now, we'd have time to get a bite to eat and catch the first show; be back before Christy's bedtime."

What a strange thing it was. The awful, gut-wrenching dread she had felt only a few minutes ago faded away beneath the sound of his voice, and the

177

presence of monsters, which had seemed so real and possible before the doorbell rang, now seemed . . . not ridiculous, but irrelevant. She glanced, very briefly, at the sofa where the open copy of the book still lay, and again felt that prickle of alarm, for she knew what she had read and she knew what it meant, and nothing had changed because Sam was here . . . and everything had. In the simple, straightforward, quietly confident world of men like Sam, there was simply no room for things that went bump in the night. And she would feel foolish even talking about them. For that, and nothing more, she was desperately grateful.

She did not even consider refusing his precipitous invitation. Her lips tightened in a rueful smile and she said, "Lucky you. I was planning to have dinner with the Uruguaian Ambassador, but he canceled at the last minute. Christy, run upstairs and wash your face and hands, and bring a sweater. It might be cold in the theater."

At Christy's suggestion, they had grilled cheese sandwiches at the drugstore counter, and not once during the course of the meal did the talk turn to monsters, or sheriff's business, or things that lurked in the woods. It was as though, upon leaving the mountain, they stepped into another world; a world in which Christy laughed a lot and grilled cheese sandwiches tasted like something prepared by a cordon bleu chef and normalcy—indeed, mundanity—was something to be treasured above all else.

The theater was filled with children and the constant murmur of parents "ssh"-ing them; Christy sat on her knees between Sam and Laura, and asked no more than the usual number of questions. When the scary part came Christy edged toward Sam, and he put his arm around her shoulders and bent his head to whisper something reassuring to her, and Laura thought, *This is a good man. A really good man.* Looking at him, she smiled, and for the first time since coming to Calumit, she felt completely content.

It was a little after nine when they got home. Dusk was gathering in the pockets and corners of the mountain and Christy was fighting sleep with a step-by-step replay of the movie.

"Come in," Laura invited as she unlocked the door and quickly punched out the code that disengaged the alarm system. "Make yourself at home while I get Little Miss Muffet here ready for bed. Then I'll make some coffee."

Christy giggled. "I'm not a Muppet! I'm a little kid!"

"Thank Sheriff Sam for the nice time, and say good night."

"Thank you for the nice time," Christy repeated dutifully, then looked up at her mother. "Do I have to go to bed now?"

"You do. Say good night."

"Good night." She hung her head and trudged toward the stairs.

"Sweet dreams, high-pocket."

"I'll be be back in a minute," Laura said. She caught up with Christy and tickled her, and Christy laughed, running from her mother, all the way up the stairs.

"She was asleep before her head hit the pillow," Laura announced cheerfully as she came back down the stairs. "Too much fun for one evening, I guess."

Sam stood as she came into the room, a book in

his hand. It took Laura only a moment to notice the book was the one she had been reading before he arrived, and a pall fell over her as she recognized it.

He said, "I guess this was the monster book Christy was talking about."

It was a casual comment, and Laura could have let it go at that. The book had been left open to the section on Calumit Mountain, but he had heard all the old legends before. He could have no idea of the significance that particular passage had for her.

She came over to him and took the book from his hand. She tried to keep her voice light as she said, "Christy's been obsessed with monsters since we moved here. I don't know what to do about it."

"I think that's a phase most kids go through at one time or another."

She opened the book to the page with the drawing, and held it out to him. "Not just any monster," she said. "This one."

He looked at the page, then back at her, puzzled. "I don't understand."

"Most legends have their basis in fact," she said, making an effort to keep her voice steady. "What if—"

"Laura, you don't really think—"

"Then explain it," she insisted urgently, her hands tightening on the book. "Explain what happened to Corky, and Christy's nightmares, and the chickens! Can you explain that?"

"A fox or a bobcat could have gotten to the chickens," he said, though a shadow came over his eyes, as though he were still uncomfortable remembering that incident.

"What about the Jennings dog run? Did a fox tear that chain-link apart?"

180

"Laura . . ."

She took a breath and gave a short shake of her head, infusing her voice with calm. "Look, I know it sounds crazy. I'm not saying I believe in monsters. But you said yourself this area has never been fully explored—not in all these hundreds of years. What if there's some kind of animal up there, something we don't know about, something that *looks* like this. . . ." She indicated the picture again.

He looked at her soberly. If she had never admired anything else about him, she would have been forever indebted to him then for the effort he made to at least appear to take her seriously. "Then why," he replied reasonably, "after all these years, would this animal suddenly be making itself known? If there really were something out there, don't you think we'd have found some evidence of it before now?"

Laura couldn't immediately think of a reply to that, perhaps because she wanted so very badly to believe he was right.

"Laura," he said gently, and took a step toward her. "Animals didn't tear up the Jennings dog pen, and animals didn't kill Corky and hang him from that tree. Only a man could do something like that. And I think I know who it is."

She seized on that hope immediately, and allowed it to wipe out everything else. "You do?"

He nodded. "It seems one of the locals has got a marijuana field planted up here somewhere, and he's not above a few dirty tricks to keep people away from it. He's not the most upstanding member of the community as it is, and I wouldn't be surprised at anything he does. But we're on his trail now, and expect to have him behind bars before the end of the week."

Laura's relief was so overwhelming that she was

momentarily mute. But then she glanced down at the book in her hand and she couldn't help it; a shiver went through her. "What if you don't?" she said lowly.

His puzzled silence was the only reply, and she looked up at him. "What if you don't catch him?" she repeated. "What if you're wrong? What if it's not the same person or—"

"Then that's my problem, isn't it?" he said quietly.

"But—"

"They never caught the guy who attacked you, did they?"

It was more of a gentle statement of fact than a question, and Laura made no reply.

"Sometimes the bad guys get away," Sam said. "But sometimes—*most* of the time they don't. So let this be my problem, okay, Laura? Can you do that?"

There was such tender insistence in his voice, such strength in his eyes, that Laura felt a lump rising in her throat. She tried to smile. "I don't know. I'm not used to . . ." She had to clear her throat. "Depending on other people. It never seems to work out."

He lifted his hand, and touched her hair. "Maybe this time it will."

And she heard herself replying, "Maybe it will." And in that moment she knew the relief of letting go, of letting someone else be responsible, of trusting another person with the essence of her fears. And although all she had really done was to give Sam permission, in her mind, to do his job, it felt like something much more important than that. It felt wonderful.

And he must have sensed it, or seen it in her eyes, because he smiled. "I'm a pretty good cop, Laura. Don't worry."

She smiled back. "I'm not."

For a moment they just looked at each other, a comfortable moment that measured the tentative yet inevitable changes in their relationship. Then Sam glanced at his watch. "Well," he said, "if I'm going to get a head start on crime in this little metropolis, I'd better get going. Early day tomorrow."

It was on the tip of Laura's tongue to ask him to stay. For a little while, maybe longer . . . maybe longer than that. What was it about Sam that made things seem so manageable, so in control, so sane? She felt safe when he was around, and she wanted that feeling to last.

It was almost as though he read her thoughts, for he smiled at her, and said, "Don't worry, Laura." He placed a finger under her chin and kissed her gently on the lips. "Good night."

"Thank you," she said softly. "For everything."

She locked the door behind him and set the alarm. In the middle of the night she was awakened by the piercing howl, a cacophony of howls, that somehow seemed worse than ever before, as though the woods themselves were mocking her newfound complacency. She squeezed her eyes tightly shut and tried not to be afraid. She tried to remember what Sam had said, and it helped a little. He wasn't worried. He would take care of things. He knew what he was doing. Everything was going to be all right. She was determined to believe that.

Christy awoke and came padding into her room, rubbing her eyes, and Laura pulled back the covers and took Christy into bed with her. It was a bad habit to start, she knew, but she didn't care. Sometimes mommies needed company too.

Chapter Nine

Sam was at his desk every morning by six o'clock. Even on busy days, which were rare in the Calumit County Sheriff's Department, nothing ever happened before eight o'clock, and Sam enjoyed those early morning hours in which to sip his coffee, visit with his deputies, and ease into his day.

It was barely seven o'clock when Deeanne Kellerman came striding in, slamming the door behind her. She was a twenty-four-year-old woman who looked closer to thirty, with bad skin and hair that had been too much abused by peroxide; she was thin-faced and small-eyed. Her slim figure was encased in a denim halter top and a pair of yellow stretch pants which might have looked sexy except for the way the elastic cut into the soft roll of flesh around her waist and cast a greenish tint on her too-white skin. She dangled a cigarette between her fingers, and dripped ashes on to the floor as she marched up to Sam's desk.

"Where's my kids?" she demanded. "They said you got my kids here, and I'm here to tell you I want 'em back and right now!"

Sam leaned back in his chair and cast a sidelong warning look at Deputy Greesom, who started to rise. Greesom settled back and Sam said, "Welcome back, Deeanne. Understand you've been out of town for a couple of days."

"That ain't none of your business. Where's my kids?"

"Where's Jim? You seen your husband since you been back?"

She took a quick angry drag off the cigarette, spilling another half inch of ash on to the floor. "I don't care if I never see that bastard again. He knew damn well he was supposed to stay home with the kids, and what did he do but run off and leave them. I'll tell you something else, Mr. High-and-Mighty Sheriff." She leaned forward on the desk until Sam could smell the odor of her cigarette breath and the sweat of the last man she had been with. "This ain't god-damn Russia, you know! You can't just bust into a person's house and take her kids away and get away with it. So you better get them kids out here right now where I can see them or I'm getting myself a lawyer, you hear that?"

"That might not be a bad idea," Sam agreed, "getting yourself a lawyer. But you're wrong about the way it is in this country. How it is in this country is that we have laws to protect children who can't stick up for themselves. And what that means is that we *can* just walk into a person's house and take their kids away, and we can take them so far away you'll never see them again. We can also lock their folks up for criminal neglect, abuse, and abandonment, and it's going to take a mighty good lawyer to get you out of that."

The faintest trace of uneasiness came over her face, and she straightened up. "What the hell're you talking about? I didn't abandon my kids. I

185

didn't leave 'em on nobody's doorstep, did I?"

"No. You locked two children up in a house with no food and nothing to drink but muddy water for a week that we know of. Both of them had scars and bruises that you're going to have to think real fast to explain to the county prosecutor. If we hadn't found them when we did, they might have died, did you ever think of that?"

Her eyes went sharply to his, and there seemed to be a trace of fear in them.

Sam rested his forearms on the desk and said gravely, "I'll tell you the truth, Deeanne. I've got enough on you right now to put you under the jail, and don't think I'm not of a mind to do it. It's going to take everything I've got to talk those folks down at social services into even letting you see your kids, much less ever take them home with you again. But then again, I've been thinking." He picked up his coffee cup and glanced at the contents thoughtfully before sipping. "If what you say is right, and if it was Jim that was supposed to be minding the children while you were gone, maybe it's really him we should be looking for."

"That's what I said, ain't it?" She ground out the cigarette under her heel and nervously dug in her purse for another one. "I'm the one that came looking for them, ain't I? You got no cause to be talking jail to me. It's him!"

"Where is he?"

"How the hell should I know?"

Sam sat his coffee cup down with a thump. "Listen to me, Deeanne. We found almost four pounds of pot wrapped up in the back of your bedroom closet, so you can add possession to that list of charges I just mentioned, and believe you me, that's no laughing

186

matter. We know Jim's got himself a field planted hereabouts, and *you* know where it is. So here's the deal. You cooperate with me and maybe you'll walk out of here. You stand there and play dumb, and the next time you see daylight will be on the way to the women's prison. What'll it be?"

Deeanne lit the cigarette with a snap of her Bic and blew out a stream of smoke. "I don't know what the hell you're talking about," she muttered.

Sam glanced at Lars. "Deputy, would you mind escorting this young lady to our holding cell?"

Lars was on his feet before Sam even finished speaking, and Deeanne jerked away violently as he started to take her arm. "All right, all right!" She glared at Sam, but there was more fear than anger in her eyes. "All right, so I know where he's planted the stuff. That's all you want to know, right? But all that shit you said before—you'll let it drop, right? And you'll get my kids back?"

Sam pushed a sheet of paper and a pencil toward her. "Why don't you draw us a map?"

She hesitated, then bent over the paper. "It's up near Jefferson Holler. You take the switchback till it forks, then he's cut out a little footpath. It ain't hard to find, I been up there once or twice. He never took much pain to hide it because nobody ever messes around back there in them woods. Here." Sullenly, she pushed the paper toward him. "Now, when am I gonna get my kids back?"

Sam examined the drawing for a moment, then tucked the paper in his pocket. He looked at her coldly. "When Hell freezes over, if I have anything to do with it." He stood up and started for the door. "Lock her up, Lars. I'll meet you in the patrol car."

187

"Hey, you can't do this! What the hell do you think you're doing? You bastard—"

Sam stepped outside and shut the door firmly on the noise.

Laura awoke that morning, looked in the mirror, and discovered her hair was in desperate need of a stylist, she had three new wrinkles, and she was five pounds overweight. She had definitely let herself go since coming here. She made a face in the mirror and turned to adjust the shower, muttering, "And I thought dating a nice man was supposed to make you feel better about yourself."

Dating. Was that what she was doing? It sounded so corny and old-fashioned, yet . . . that was okay. Families were corny and old-fashioned too, but last night she, Christy, and Sam had felt like a family, and she liked that. She had never imagined she would, but she did.

Maybe, she reflected as she arched her shoulders and let the soapy water sluice down her back, it was time to slow down, to take a good long look backwards at her life and put things in perspective. Maybe that was what she had really been looking for when she came to Calumit. Security, stability, all those good old-fashioned values she had never had a chance to grasp before. A peaceful resting place. A chance to settle back and realign her priorities.

And maybe putting her trust in a man like Sam was not such a bad place to start.

Morning cartoons were gibbering on the television set in the kitchen alcove when Laura came down, and Christy was pulling out a step stool, preparing to search for her own breakfast. "Morning, pumpkin.

188

No climbing on the cabinets." Laura swept her daughter off the stool, kissed her on the head, and opened a cabinet.

"Morning, Mommy," Christy replied cheerfully. "Can we go swimming this morning?"

"Better wait until this afternoon."

"But the water's warm!"

"I know, but the air isn't. How about Cheerios and bananas?"

"Peanut butter toast." Christy opened the back door. "It is too warm out here. It's—"

She broke off with a sound that sounded first like disgust, then escalated to a cry of horror. "Mommy! Mommy, come quick!"

Laura rushed to the door.

Lying against the threshold was what she, at first glance, took to be an exceptionally large cat, or a battered toy animal with most of the stuffing gone. She almost bent to touch it before she saw the distinctive ring tail and mask and knew it to be a raccoon. She recoiled in surprise, and then she saw what had caused Christy to scream.

A long slash divided the animal's midsection from throat to loin, and it had been completely gutted.

Part of Calumit County's vehicular allotment was a sturdy jeep, and that was what Lars and Sam used to climb the unpaved mountain roads indicated on Deeanne Kellerman's rough map. Without it, they would have been forced to take the last three or four miles on foot. Kellerman had chosen his hideout well. In some places the only sign that there was a trail at all was the faint impression of tire tracks between the rocks. As the jeep bounced and climbed in the direction Deeanne had indicated, Sam couldn't help drawing a little map of his own in his head. They were moving west now, behind and above Minnie Sykes's place, skirting the Heights at a diagonal. He had to admit it would be rough for a man to navigate the woods between here and the Heights, where most of the mischief had occurred, but not impossible. And to a man like Kellerman, a fortune in weed would be worth any amount of trouble to protect.

"It don't seem like anybody's been up here in a while," Lars commented, turning the wheel sharply in a futile effort to avoid a big rock. "Not since the last rain anyhow."

Sam had to agree with him, which was disappointing. Finding the field was one thing, but it was Kellerman he was really after. And even though he had known it was too much to hope for to find the man with the evidence in his hand, he liked to wrap things up neatly.

"Looks like we're about to run out of road," Lars said.

Sam pointed. "Look."

"Well I'll be damned." Lars down-shifted and slowed. "Kellerman's truck."

He pulled the jeep behind the muddy blue pickup, which was parked where the rutted trail came to an end with no effort having been made to conceal its presence. Early morning shadows waved gently back and forth across the cab, but otherwise everything was still. As a precaution, Sam radioed their position back to the office, and they left the jeep cautiously.

Lars kept his hand on the butt of his pistol as they approached the truck, but Sam didn't expect any trouble at that point. A man like Kellerman lacked the subtlety for an ambush; he would have opened fire the minute they approached if he had seen them. Sure enough, the truck was empty.

Lars relaxed. "Maybe he's got a camp set up around here somewhere."

"Maybe," Sam agreed. But he was uneasy. The man had been missing for a week, his truck was abandoned in the middle of nowhere, and the morning silence was eerie. Not wanting to, he moved forward into the woods.

The crude footpath Kellerman had cut was not hard to follow, nor was it difficult to see why he had chosen this spot. Nature had been more than cooperative with Kellerman's ambitions. Less than a hundred yards into the woods there was a natural clearing bordered by two streams; no heavy equipment had been required to clear the plot, and irrigation was achieved by means of a gasoline-powered pump and four green garden hoses. The field covered less than an acre, just right for a lazy man and even an acre represented vast riches to a man like Kellerman.

"Well, there she is," commented Lars with satisfaction as he surveyed the rows of ankle-high plants. "Not bad detective work, Boss."

Sam grunted. His eyes were fixed across the field, near the stream, where four or five large buzzards were circling and diving. There was a queasy feeling in the pit of his stomach, and he told himself it could be anything: a dead fox, a bobcat, anything except what he knew it was.

"Do you want to burn it now?" Lars asked.

Without answering, Sam started across the field.

The buzzards scattered at his approach, but by the time he reached the stream he didn't need them for guidance. He could smell it. Death and rot lay over the air like a foggy curtain.

He waded through the stream, which was calf-high in places, then grasped a root to pull himself up the slippery bank on the other side. When he straightened up something bumped against his face; something cool and rigid, yet covered by an oddly smooth surface. He looked up.

Jim Kellerman was hanging upside down from an oak branch overhead. His clothes were in tatters and his eye sockets were nothing but empty holes decorated with strings of flesh where the buzzards had plucked at them. But that was not the worst. By far, that was not the worst.

Through a buzzing in his head, Sam heard Lars splashing across the creek behind him, the puffing of his breath, and his grunt as he pulled himself up on the bank. And he heard Lars stop breathing.

The body had been torn open from throat to groin. Broken shards of ribs stabbed through the flesh in places where the rib cage had been peeled backward to expose an empty chest cavity. As Sam watched, a beetle crawled out of that dark hole, balanced itself for a moment on a sagging tendon, then plopped to the ground.

"Oh, man," Lars said weakly behind him. "We are in deep shit." Then he stumbled away, and vomited into the bushes.

But it was a long time before Sam could even avert his eyes.

Laura called the sheriff's office, but Sam was out on a case. She hung up without leaving a message, and then wondered why she had called at all. *He can't help you,* an irrational, half-panicked voice chided. *This has nothing to do with him. Nobody can help you. . . .*

She sat on the edge of a chair at the kitchen table, looking at the closed back door and trying to blot out the disgusting thing that lay beyond. They had come to her *house.* The bastards had marched right up to her door and no one had known, no one had stopped them. They were taunting her. This time the back door, next time . . .

Christy snuggled up to her, laying her hand on her mother's knee. Her voice was soft with awe and worry as she said, "The monsters did it."

Laura put her arm around Christy's shoulders, and looked down at her. "Why, baby?" she inquired, trying to keep her voice steady. "Why would they do something like this? Do you know?"

Christy's brow puckered as she thought over the difficult question. "Because," she answered slowly, "they're sorry. They're sorry they ate Corky. That's why."

After a moment, Laura nodded, and kissed the top of Christy's head. "You stay inside until I get back," she said.

Then she went to the garage to get the shovel, and she buried the creature in a soft patch of earth she had intended to turn into a flower bed. There was no one around to do it for her this time, and she had learned a long time ago she had to take care of herself.

It took two hours for the D.A. and the coroner to arrive from Winston, forty miles away. By that time Sam and Lars had taped off the scene and gathered what evidence they could, which wasn't much. Kellerman's wallet, with over three hundred dollars in it, was still in the back pocket of his jeans. His gun, an old-fashioned hog-leg of the type favored by most men around the mountain, was found some distance from the body, but showed no evidence of having been fired.

"He might have been taken by surprise," Sam told Doug Evans, the district attorney. "Or he might not have been as ready to use it as he thought and dropped it trying to run away. Whoever it was caught up with him right over there." Sam jerked his head toward the east, where the contour of the land sloped toward a tangle of blackberry bushes. "There are signs of a struggle and blood all over the ground."

"Struggle, hell," Lars put in. He was still shaken and sallow-faced, and he spoke in rapid, clipped syllables punctuated by darts of his tongue over the surface of his lips. "It was a goddamn massacre. Ground's all churned up, bushes pulled out of the ground—what about the scars on the trees, Sam? What do you make of that?"

Doug Evans glanced at Lars, then said, "We'll get pictures."

The coroner was zipping up the body bag and instructing his men on its safe transportation back to the van, which hadn't been able to make the climb all the way up the trail. Sam waited until he was finished to inquire, "What do you think?"

Will Jakes wiped his small, wire-framed glasses and replied, "I think it's a damn shame that when a man goes to meet his Maker, he can't do it all in one piece." Then he shook his head, his eyes following the progress of the sagging body bag. "Been dead three days or so, I can't be more exact than that. His neck was snapped, I'd say that was the cause of death, then he was disemboweled—heart, lungs, liver, intestines, every soft tissue in body." He paused a moment, as though pondering the depths of the desecration. Then he shook his head again and said, "I can't tell you much more than that until I get him back to the lab—if then. The bastards didn't leave me much to work with."

"What about the incision?" Sam persisted. "Can you give me a guess on what kind of knife was used?"

Jakes frowned. "Come on, Sam."

"Just a guess. Was it neat, like a surgeon's scalpel, or—"

"Hell, no. It was a mess. You could see that for yourself. Matter of fact, I'm not even sure it *was* a knife."

"What do you mean?"

"I mean," replied Jakes, fixing Sam with small blue eyes magnified out of proportion by the double-thick lenses of his spectacles, "that man's body wasn't cut open so much as it was torn open, like . . ."

"Like what?" Sam's voice was sharp.

But Jakes shook his head. "I'll let you know when *I* know." And that was all he was going to say.

When Jakes was gone, Doug Evans stood beside Sam and looked out over the field. "At the risk of jumping to conclusions," he said, "it looks to me like you've got yourself the beginnings of a nice little drug war going on here."

Sam said heavily, "Yeah. Looks like it."

"And you haven't had any signs of anything like this before now?"

All Sam could think about was a cocker spaniel puppy, hanging upside down from a tree. "No."

Doug said gravely, "This is bad business, Sam. You want some help from the state boys?"

With difficulty, Sam brought his attention away from the memory of a slaughtered pet and focused it on Doug. "No," he said. "Not for a few days. Not until we hear from the coroner anyway. I've got Kellerman's wife in custody, maybe she can give us a lead. I'd like to keep this thing contained as long as I can."

Doug nodded. "Good idea. The less publicity the better. Sometimes these crazies get their kicks out of reading about themselves in the paper. You can count on my office, Sam. But," he repeated sternly, "this is bad business. Don't be a hero."

Sam smiled faintly. "Nobody ever accused me of that."

Doug looked around for another moment, then shook his head. "Peaceful up here, isn't it?" he murmured. "Who would've ever thought?"

Laura's words echoed in his head. *They're everywhere, aren't they? No matter where you go they're there, waiting for you.* . . . Sam's fists tightened in his pockets, and he felt his back molars crunch together as he thought, *But not here. Not here, damn it, not in my town, not while I'm on watch* . . .

Doug went to direct his photographer, and while they were busy at the tree where the body had been found, Sam walked down the hill to the actual murder site. Lars had not been exaggerating in his description of the place. A well-contained war might have been fought here. Blood was splattered in an eight-foot perimeter. The ground was gouged and trampled into such a state that even footprints were impossible to discern. Undergrowth had been uprooted and fallen branches crushed. The bark from a nearby pine tree had been chipped away in several irregular places as though something heavy had

196

bumped against it repeatedly. He stood some distance from the site, so as not to disturb the photographer's prints anymore than he had already done, and he was overwhelmed by the sheer magnitude of it all. The scene before him did not represent a common murder, but a frenzy of violence. No one man could have done this much damage. Not even a man struggling for his life . . .

He lowered himself to his haunches, looking over the ground for nothing in particular, and an absurd memory kept fluttering around in the back of his head. Rabbit hunting with his dad, cleaning the catch on the back porch. Cold fingers, a bloodstained hunting pouch, steam rising from the incision their knives made down the midsection of the limp animals. "First clean out the guts," his dad would say, "then reach up in there and pop out the heart—"

Lars spoke up anxiously behind him. "What do you think, Boss? Any leads?"

Sam picked up a small blood-spattered twig, examined it for a moment, then snapped it between his fingers. He got to his feet. "I think," he replied, "that it's not simple anymore."

He felt very tired.

Chapter Ten

Ted Jacobs was a compulsive runner. He ran in the early morning, when the fog was so heavy it swallowed up his steps and the air he was breathing was fifty percent water; he ran in the hazy midday with humidity weighing down his legs and clogging up his lungs; he ran through the deep still shadows of early evening. In New York he had done seven miles a day without pausing, but in the hilly, oxygen-thin mountains he was barely able to break three before his muscles turned to rubber and his breath gave out. Still, he ran, pushing himself, not because he wanted to, but because he needed to. He hadn't been much of a surgeon; God only knows he wasn't a writer. But he was a damn good runner.

At five o'clock in the morning daybreak was barely a promise. In the valleys a thin band of gray was beginning to paint the horizon, but here in the higher elevations the sky was a murky black and the shadows were as deep as pits. Ted had noticed that the nights seemed to last longer in the mountains, and the days were all too short. He told himself that was one explanation for his early morning insomnia. The other, more obvious, explanation was that he was in the first stages of a clinical depression.

So he ran, hoping to exhaust himself, trying to blot out the memories and the guilt. But even he knew he couldn't run from what was inside his head, and everywhere he went the face followed him, sometimes angry, sometimes cynical, sometimes merely sad. Always accusing.

When he had first moved here his course had followed a circular path downward from his house toward the new construction, often taking the footpaths and unpaved roads around unfinished houses. Lately, though, he had started running uphill, toward the woods. It was a shorter course, and far more difficult, but that was not why he had chosen it. Those woods, dark and menacing, had always fascinated him. Since he had entered them with Laura and discovered for himself just what kind of evil could find its home there, they had also terrified him. He never wanted to go there again. So he went there every day.

By the time he reached the end of the paved street in front of Laura Kane's house, his lungs were on fire and his vision was blurred with sweat and strain. He paused, as he always did, stretching his hamstrings as he bent forward with his hands on his knees, struggling to draw in deep breaths. And as he always did, he turned his eyes toward the still darkness of the woods.

And he saw a movement.

From his vantage point he could see around Laura's house, into a portion of the backyard. Because he was focusing on the woods behind the house, he caught only a glimpse of the movement out of the corner of his eye, and at first he thought he had imagined it. There was more light now, but the shadows that stretched across the clearing of the yard were inky. When he turned his gaze toward those shadows he saw nothing, but a chill came over him nonetheless. A renewed pump of adrenaline made his chest hurt. He straightened up and started to turn away. And then he saw it.

It burst out of the shadows less than a hundred yards away, huge, white-skinned, naked. At first he thought it was a man, but then he knew it couldn't be. Its head was oversized and almost completely round, swallowing up its neck and its arms swung below its knees. It ran—no, loped—away from the house and toward the woods, and it was all so fast, such a blur of shock and half-clear impressions, that in another instant Ted would have convinced himself he had seen nothing at all, but at that moment the creature stopped, and looked at him.

There was no sound but the quick hot pounding of his heart and the hiss of his breath through his teeth. In the darkness phosphorescent red eyes gleamed and lips curled back from narrow canine teeth. It looked at him, it pinned him with its gaze, and a terror deeper than any Ted had ever known shuddered through him and left him frozen. Then it turned, and in another moment was swallowed up by the shadows of the woods.

Ted did not know how long he stood there, wet with perspiration, choking on his own breath, wanting to run and unable to move. *Not human.* The words kept spinning about in his brain, tinged with horror and repulsion and the undeniable certainty that he had seen it, with his own eyes he had seen it and it was *not human. . . .*

There was a part of his mind that knew he could not have seen what he thought he had, a part that desperately wanted to shroud the memory in logical explanations and reassuring science, but that part was eclipsed by the power of primal fear. Even now it could be circling around, stalking him from behind, preparing to leap out from the black sanctuary that had spawned it and rip him apart, and everything inside him screamed for him to run. Then his eyes fell on the house, sleeping in the shadows of dawn, and his heart gave a powerful lurch that exploded icy prickles of adrenaline over his skin. *It had come from the house.*

He wanted to run the other way. He didn't want to know, he didn't want to remember, he didn't want to tell anybody what he had seen. He didn't want to ring the doorbell and have no one answer, he didn't want to walk to the back of that house and find . . . who knows what. He wanted to leave this place and forget what he'd seen, to pretend it had never happened, to turn his back on the bad things just as he had been doing all his life.

Then a face surfaced in his mind, mocking, cynical, accusing. He made himself turn toward the driveway. Then he was running. The ninety seconds that he leaned on the doorbell, waiting for a movement inside the house, were the longest of his life.

The sun was fully up by the time Sam arrived at Laura's house, spreading a grayish pink haze across the backyard, leaving the woods in black shadow. On foot, he traced the course Ted Jacobs had described from the edge of the woods to the barbecue patio that surrounded Laura's kitchen, on the off chance that he might spot something—anything—that would give him a clue as to who he was dealing with. As expected he found nothing—nothing except for a few dew-wet footprints smeared on the flagstones of the patio, and the grisly offering at the back door.

Offering. That was a strange word for it, but it was the one that had sprung to his mind the minute he looked down at the gutted squirrel lying against Laura Kane's threshold. Now, examining it again, he was reminded of an old barn cat his family had had when he was a boy. It was a good mouser, and kept itself fat on the rodents on the corn crib, but had the peculiar—and, as far as his mother was concerned, disgusting—habit of bringing a dead mouse or snake to the back door at least once a day and leaving it there for Sam's mother to find when she swept the stoop. Of course she would pitch a fit and go after the cat, if it could be found, with a broom, but his father used to chuckle and explain that the cat was just doing his job. It felt sorry for its adopted family, who were such poor hunters they couldn't catch mice for themselves, so it'd bring them their dinner every day as if they were a bunch of helpless kittens who needed looking after. Sam remembered that his father, if he was the one who happened to spot the mouse first, would always praise the cat lavishly, and wait until it had stalked off with its tail held proudly in the air before burying the offering. He said an animal couldn't be blamed for doing what was natural to it.

And that, for some reason, was what this scrawny squirrel with its guts ripped out reminded Sam of.

He checked the yard and the patio for bloodstains, but there were none. The animal had apparently been dead for several hours, and thoroughly drained. He looked again at the footprints, but couldn't tell much about them. The sun had already dried the edges, leaving few clear impressions. From what he could extrapolate, the prints were at least as large as his size tens, and maybe wider. On one there was a clear impression of a big toe. The perpetrator had been bare-foot.

He went back inside the kitchen, where Laura was waiting with Ted Jacobs. Laura was pouring coffee, wearing a football-jersey-type nightshirt that barely covered her thighs, and Jacobs was sitting at the table, shirtless, staring into his own cup. Looking at them, Sam felt a stab of jealousy that was so unexpected and so inappropriate it embarrassed him, and he cleared his throat abruptly before he spoke. Even then his voice sounded sharper than he had intended.

"You should have called me sooner."

Laura looked started as she turned, a mug of coffee in her hand. "I called as soon as—"

"I mean before." Impatiently he took the mug she held out. "You said this has been going on for the past three days. You should have called me out the first time it happened."

Laura glanced at Ted, and Sam knew that she would not have called him at all had not Jacobs insisted. The realization gave him a hollow feeling.

She said, "I did. But you weren't in, and then . . ." She turned to refill her own cup. "I knew you were busy."

The words left volumes unspoken. Though no details had been released, it was impossible to hide a murder in a town the size of Calumit. Sam thought the papers might have used words like "brutal" and "mutilated body."

Three days of combing every inch of that field, of interrogating Kellerman's less-than-grief-stricken wife until he was hoarse, of examining the activities of each one of Kellerman's associates, and he was no closer to a suspect than he had been the moment he found the body. Three nights of poring over photographs and

203

autopsy reports and lying awake at night, turning over possibilities in his mind and knowing there was something he had missed, some piece he was not considering, something he could *do* . . .

He had promised Laura. The worst of it was that he had promised her she would be safe. Now he could see her drawing into that shell of self-defense she had built around herself, and no, that wasn't the worst. The worst was he couldn't blame her.

He sat down across the table from Jacobs. "You say it was about five-fifteen when you saw this man running into the woods?"

Ted met his eyes evenly. "It wasn't a man."

"A woman then?"

Ted was silent for a moment, and then he said, without ever wavering in his gaze, "I told you what I saw."

It wasn't like Sam to create hostility in a witness, and he could not excuse himself for doing so now. Another time he might have sympathized with the courage it took for Jacobs to tell a story like that and then stick to it; now the man's unaccountable persistence only annoyed and frustrated him.

Sam took out his notebook. He rarely took notes, and did so only when he wanted to intimidate or impress someone. He despised himself for the gesture now, but once again couldn't seem to help himself. He said, "It's still pretty dark even at five-thirty."

"There was enough light to see."

"But you couldn't tell whether it was a male or female."

Ted Jacobs stared at him. "No."

Sam glanced at his notebook. The page was blank except for a series of concentric circles he had absently drawn while pretending to listen. That was exactly how this case was shaping up too: a series of never-ending circles. "What made you come to the house?" he asked.

"For heaven's sake, Sam." Laura's voice held the slightest tinge of impatience as she sat down between them, cupping her coffee mug with both hands. "He told you that. He saw someone. . . ." She stumbled a little over the word. "Something running away from the house, and thought there might have been a break-in, and what would you have done? Of course he came here, and when he told me . . ." She glanced down at her coffee, nervously pushing her hair over her shoulder. Her voice was low as she finished. "I knew. I looked on the back patio and—it was there, just like it's been for the past three mornings. And then Ted made me call you, and here you are, and that's all we know."

She sounded tired, defeated, and the deep violet hollows under her eyes gave her face a haunted, pinched look. *Three days,* Sam thought. *She's been dealing with this for three days, and never a words . . .*

He made himself turn back to Ted. "What size shoe do you wear, Mr. Jacobs?" he asked casually.

It was a moot question, because Sam had already observed that Ted Jacobs's feet, now encased in running shoes, were smaller than his. But the other man answered without hesitation, "Eight. And if you want a straight answer you might do better to ask a straight question. No, I haven't been bringing dead animals to Miss Kane's back door on my morning jogs, and no, I'm not making up stories just to get my name in the paper. I didn't kill her dog either, if that's what you're thinking."

Laura turned accusing, disappointed eyes on him. "Sam, why are you doing this? I told you, it was Ted

205

who insisted we call the police. He *saw* the—the thing that's been doing this! This is the first real proof we have—aren't you in the least bit interested in that?"

Sam pushed up from the table abruptly. "What am I supposed to think?" he demanded. "You give me some story about a giant two-footed animal with a round head and red eyes—"

"I didn't say it was an animal," Ted said quietly.

"You said it wasn't a man! Damn it, you write fiction for a living, but I've got a crime to solve. A man's been murdered—"

He broke off, knowing he had said too much, and knowing it was too late. Laura looked up sharply. "Do you think this has something to do with—with the murder?"

Sam said nothing.

After a moment, Ted spoke up dryly. "At the risk of putting myself back on the top of the list of suspects, I'd be willing to bet the murdered man was found eviscerated, just like these animals have been. Just like the dog."

Sam could feel Laura's eyes on him, and he could feel her fear. He refused to look at her. He took his coffee cup and made a pretense of refilling it. He said to Ted, "You're not a suspect."

"Why not?"

Sam turned to him, and there was a note of resignation in his voice as he replied. "Because, unless you're stronger than you look, you couldn't possible have killed Jim Kellerman."

And because of what the coroner's report had said. It had been buzzing around in the back of his mind like a pesky insect, and he couldn't seem to get rid of it no matter how hard he tried. *The wounds do not appear to have been inflicted by any known instrument or tool. On gross examination the possibility of an animal attack cannot be ruled out.*

Sam thought about Brett Howard, whose remains had been crushed into splinters. He thought about Corky, and about the slaughterhouse that once had been Minnie Sykes's chicken yard. And he thought about Nighteaters. How could he not?

Ted said, "So he was eviscerated."

Sam heard Laura's small intake of breath. "Yes," he replied.

Laura said softly, "You said . . . it was Kellerman who was doing these things. But it wasn't. I knew it wasn't, not after the first day, because he was dead. And now . . ." She pressed her lips tightly together and gripped the coffee cup as though it were an anchor.

Sam felt a sharp twisting in his chest as he looked at her. He sat down at the table again, leaning forward urgently. "Look," he said to Jacobs. "It was dark. Early morning light is the worst kind, it distorts things. You were what? A hundred yards away? And you'd been running, maybe a little light-headed. So what you thought you saw may not be exactly what you saw. But if you'll just think, just try to give me a better description . . ."

For all of the other man's assumed savoir faire, Sam could see a slight tremor to Jacob's hand as he lifted his coffee cup, and there was fear far in the back of those steady eyes . . . not fear of the law, or of what Sam might think, but fear of what he had seen, of what he could not yet fully make himself believe he had seen. Fear of what could have happened, had almost happened, could yet happen. Sam knew that feeling, and he tried not to let it influence his judgment. But a blind man could see that Ted Jacobs was

207

telling what he believed to be the absolute truth.

He replied, "What I saw was a primate, but not like any we know. It was larger than a gorilla, and completely hairless. White. Its head was—" He dropped his eyes a little and shook his head. "I can't describe it. Engorged, round, about one and a half times a normal human head, and if it had a neck I didn't see it. Its arms were heavy, but it was crouched down so I couldn't see how long they were. Its whole body was covered with a thick layer of adipose tissue—fat—but it was strong. You could tell by the way it moved. It looked like . . ." He turned to Laura. "It looked a lot like that picture your little girl drew me of the snow monster."

A moment of tacit understanding passed between Ted Jacobs and Laura that excluded and infuriated Sam. Laura's eyes were shocked and frozen; Ted's eyes were dark and troubled. But before Sam could react Ted turned back to him.

"I'll tell you something else," he said quietly. "I'd be happy to agree with you. I *could* agree with you—if it hadn't looked at me. I saw its face, its eyes, and it was like . . ." The repulsion, the shrinking from remembered horror was clear in his face. "It was like looking into a mirror and seeing that all your features have melted off. It was like opening your front door and stepping off the edge of a cliff. It was grotesque, it was unnatural, it was . . . horrifying. I can't explain it better than that. I expected to see a man, but I didn't. What I saw wasn't human," he finished lowly, then lifted his coffee cup and drank without meeting Sam's eyes.

Sam looked at him for a long time. Nobody had to remind him that he was talking to a scientist, a born observer, a man who chronicled details for a living.

208

The average detective could not ask for a better eye-witness account than Ted Jacobs had just given, nor was there any denying that the events he had recounted had shaken Jacobs profoundly. Every instinct Sam possessed insisted Ted Jacobs was telling the truth. But he was *wrong.*

Laura got up and left the room. She returned in a moment with several books. She opened one of them and handed it to Ted. "Is this what you saw?" she asked.

Sam did not have to look at the picture. He saw it in Ted's eyes, and in Laura's when she looked at him. The silence was as heavy as a shroud.

Nighteaters.

Then Sam exploded tightly, "Damn it, will you stop this? I've got a real murder on my hands, a real psycho out there carving up animals and people and using them to decorate the countryside. . . . I need *evidence,* and you're giving me fairy-tale monsters and Abominable Snowmen! Don't either of you realize this is serious?"

Laura said slowly, "Not the Abominable Snowman. But maybe something like it."

She looked at Sam, and the expression in her eyes was hard, and calm, and quietly, fiercely determined. Yet there was a trace of a smile on her lips as she gestured toward the books and said, "I like to know what I'm up against. So I've been doing some reading. This mountaintop isn't the only place creatures like these have been seen. And I'm not just talking about your Yeti and Sasquatch and Bigfoot either, but all over the world—China, Mongolia, Malaysia, Africa, even Maine, for heaven's sake. Wherever there are mountains. They're all basically the same—big, two-footed, apelike creatures that live in the woods and feed at night. The only difference between this and—and others is that the Calumit creature is white and hairless, and it—" Her voice caught slightly. "Eats meat. The others don't. But what I'm saying is that if hundreds of people from dozens of different countries have described the same kind of beast for centuries, there's got to be some basis of truth there. Maybe . . . I don't know, maybe a whole species we just haven't discovered yet. But *something.* Something real."

Her voice was frantic, but not hysterical. Her eyes were blazing, but with cold, hard insistence rather than mania. Sam looked at her and he thought, *I've lost her. I made a promise I never should have made and I broke it and now I've lost her.* He felt as close to despair as he was ever likely to get.

Ted was looking at Laura with knotted brows and a troubled interest in his eyes, and Sam did not expect any help from that quarter. He said, as calmly as he could, "So you're talking about some kind of animal."

She nodded.

"Laura, these tales have been circulating for centuries, you said so yourself. Are you telling me that this thing has been around for two hundred years or more? Be reasonable. Nothing lives that long."

"You don't know that. A housefly only lives a day or two. A parrot can live over a hundred years. Every species has a different life span."

Sam looked at her helplessly, and then Ted spoke up. His voice was hesitant, but his words were not at all what Sam wanted to hear. "It doesn't have to be a single animal. It could be a whole tribe. For generations."

"Christy always refers to them in the plural," Laura agreed.

Sam turned to Jacobs. "You're telling me that a

whole tribe of monsters has been living on Calumit Mountain for hundreds of years and no one has ever seen them? Do you want to explain how something that big could have stayed hidden all this time?"

Laura answered. "But they *have* been seen, by everyone who goes into the mountains. That's how the stories got started."

"But they're just that, stories. Something like that wouldn't be hard to prove. After all these years, they'd be bound to leave some sign—even if it was nothing more than a carcass or a skeleton of their dead. Some hunter would have spotted one and shot it or—"

"No one hunts in those woods," Laura said, interrupting. "You said so. No one *ever has,* don't you see? It's easy to stay hidden when no one is looking."

Ted added, "You said you used to hunt. Did you ever come upon a bear carcass, or a deer? Even a skeleton? Did you ever know anyone who has?"

Sam could see that this was getting out of hand. "No," he admitted, "I can't say that I have."

"Large mammals usually seek privacy before dying," Ted said thoughtfully. "Even then, the carrion-eaters make short work of them. Just because you don't find any remains doesn't mean there was never anything there."

"The last I heard," Sam said coolly, "doctors were supposed to be trained in science. So give me a scientific explanation for this undiscovered species of yours."

"I can't," Ted said bluntly. "Not entirely. But we thought all the primates had been cataloged until the African mountain gorilla was discovered in 1901. The mega-mouthed shark wasn't even a legend until a fisherman pulled up his net in 1976. I don't guess it's entirely out of the question to imagine there are a few

211

species on this planet we aren't familiar with yet."

Ted hesitated, and lifted his cup. Discovering it was empty, he set it down again. "Maybe it's not a new species. Maybe it's a mutation of an old one. I don't know. I only know what I saw. And what I saw was fast, and powerful, and savage. In short, a very strong, very efficient killing machine."

Sam looked at him, and an involuntary chill gripped him. He remembered Kellerman, swinging upside down from that tree like a slab of meat. He thought of Laura, living here all by herself.

Laura said softly, "Christy says they're hungry. We started tearing up the mountain and drove the game away, and now they're coming out of the woods . . . hungry."

Sam rose abruptly. "This isn't getting us anywhere. There aren't any monsters out in the woods. What you saw was a man," he told Ted, "and it was a man who killed Kellerman and has been playing these dirty tricks on Laura. Why, I don't know. But I'm going to find out."

He nodded curtly to Ted, and Laura followed him out of the room. She caught his arm before he reached the front door. "Why?" she demanded. Her hair swung around her shoulders and her face was set in angry, defensive lines, her eyes dark smudges of emotion. "Ted Jacobs is no liar. You were here with Christy, and the chickens—you heard what she said and you saw what happened and you couldn't explain it! You couldn't explain what happened to the Jenningses either, or to—to Corky, and now. . . . Why won't you listen? Why won't you even consider that I might be right—or even a little bit right?"

Sam wanted more than anything in the world to draw her slim form into his arms and comfort her, to

212

tell her once again that everything was going to be all right, that he would *make* it all right. But this time he owed her the truth.

"Because," he said quietly, "if I believe that there are monsters in the woods, things that can come in and kill at will, strong enough to tear a man apart and smart enough to knot a vine and hang him from a tree . . . if I believe that these things have been living out there for hundreds of years and nothing has ever stopped them, then I'm helpless. There's nothing I can do. I've got to believe that what I'm up against is something I know. Something I can do something about. Something I can *see*. It's just got to be, that's all."

Laura took a breath, hugging her arms to herself. "It came to my *house*, Sam," she said tightly. "I'm scared."

He cupped his hand around her neck and held it there briefly. "I know," he answered. And that was all the comfort he had to offer.

After three cups of coffee Ted felt some of the effects of physical shock begin to dissipate. He wasn't quite so cold, and his hands had almost stopped shaking. But still, whenever he brought the picture of that thing to mind, his heart would start pounding and his mouth would grow so dry he could hardly swallow.

How had it come to this? An old woman's ramblings, a little girl's nightmares, myths and superstitions . . . and now he was seeing things that could not possibly be there.

Could they?

Laura came back in, and for a moment neither one of them spoke. The weight of an unwilling alliance hung between them like an anchor chain. Neither one of them wanted to believe the possibilities that had been thrust before them, and neither of them could think of a way to avoid believing.

After a long time Ted asked soberly, "What are you afraid of, Laura?"

She hesitated, then forced a shrug and a brief smile. "Aside from things that hide in the woods and tear people apart, you mean?"

His expression remained grave, and she looked away. Picking up a sponge, she began to wipe spilled coffee from the counter. "Being helpless," she said after a moment, lowly. "Being defenseless. Maybe . . . of just being afraid."

Ted fingered the cover of the book before him. "For me," he said softly, "it's ineffectiveness. And for your friend the sheriff . . . I think it's just not knowing. Funny. I thought that here, of all places, I wouldn't have to be afraid of anything."

She turned around, leaning her palms on the counter. "Do you ever miss New York?"

He smiled dryly. "Right now, muggers and street shootings and an apartment with six locks on the door sound pretty good to me."

She swallowed visibly. "I'm not sure how much longer I can stay here."

He nodded, feeling an overwhelming wave of fatigue as the effects of the adrenaline surge began to drain away. "Better the devil you know, I guess."

Then he got to his feet. "I think your boyfriend is jealous of me."

She looked surprised, and vaguely indignant, as though the mere mundanity of the statement had caught her off guard. "What?"

"He has no reason to be." And then he explained. "I lost a lover last year."

Again she looked confused, disoriented by the change of subject. But she managed, "I—I'm sorry."

Ted's voice was vague and reminiscent. "His name was Craig, and he was the smartest man I ever knew. He was the writer, does that surprise you? Oh, I wrote down the words, but the stories were his. I haven't written a single coherent sentence since he left."

He paused, helpless for a moment against the swift backward spinning of time. And then he said, "Once he called me a coward. And he was right."

He turned toward the back door, and made a small gesture toward what lay beyond. "I'll take care of—that."

Laura cleared her throat, once again focusing with difficulty on the change of subject and tone. "You don't have to."

He looked at her, and smiled faintly. "Yes," he assured her softly, "I do."

Chapter Eleven

"Jesus, Cathy, you sure have a weird idea of fun."
Scott played his flashlight beam over the slimy-looking
walls of the cave, and grimaced when a cockroach half
the size of his fist scuttled across the circle of light.

"Oh, come on, Scott, where's your sense of adventure?" She was a few feet ahead of him, with her own
flashlight, but even so her voice echoed. "I used to
play in this cave when I was a kid. When you told me
abut the one your dad's people uncovered the other
day, that's what reminded me."

"That wasn't a cave, it was a sinkhole. Anyway, we
should get out of here. This is private property."

Her laugh had an eerie, disembodied quality in the
close confines of the cave. "Your father owns it,
dummy. So what's he going to do, put you in jail?"

Scott brushed a spiderweb out of his hair and
looked back over his shoulder. The chamber in which
they were standing was about six by eight by five feet
high, and the exit was a four-foot circle of diffuse
greenery and sunshine just a few paces away. He could
still hear the sounds of hammering and somebody's radio tuned to a country-western station. The cave, as it
turned out, was across the road and back in the woods
a ways from what his dad referred to as "Phase Two" of

the project, and it was a wonder nobody had stopped them from coming in here. Not that Scott was worried, and what he had told Cathy about private property was just a ploy to get her out. The plain fact was he didn't see what was so fascinating about a hole in the ground filled with bugs and bat shit, and he had planned to work on his tan this afternoon.

"It sure seemed a lot bigger when I was a kid," Cathy commented, still playing her flashlight over the wet walls. "Granny says this whole mountain is tunneled out with caves, but this is the only one I ever found. She said—"

"To keep your ass out of here, I'll bet." Scott came to stand beside her, but the usually sweet scent of her was spoiled by the smell of mildew and rot.

"That too." She giggled, leaning into him as he put his arm around her waist. "But mostly she talked about Indian legends and stuff. I forget now." She jerked her flashlight as the ground seemed to shudder in response to an explosion from outside. "God, was that dynamite? What are they doing anyway?"

"Clearing out a new road," Scott replied absently. "Can we go now? It's cold in here and there's dirt and shit all down the back of my shirt."

"No, there's something I want to show you first." She caught his hand and moved forward a few inches, casting the flashlight beam before her. "It used to be around here somewhere. . . . There."

The light stopped on what appeared to be a crack in the rock, but on closer examination Scott saw that it was actually two cracks, divided by a thin slab of rock, like a swinging door that had gotten stuck in the middle.

"There's another chamber through there," Cathy explained. "Come on."

217

"Good Christ! You expect us to crawl through that?"

She hesitated. "Well, it did look bigger when I was a kid," she admitted. "But we can get through okay. Just suck in your breath."

The opening on the right side of the flat rock did look big enough to squeeze through, but just barely. The last thing Scott wanted to do was try, but ever since that incident in the woods he felt he had been walking on shaky ground with Cathy, as though he had to prove himself at every turn. And it was funny. Since the episode in the woods he wasn't nearly as reckless as he once had been. He still had nightmares about it sometimes.

But when she flashed him a smile and teased, "Chicken?" he had no choice. He scowled.

"Hell, if you don't mind getting bat shit in your hair, I don't. Lead the way."

The opening was only about four feet high, and they had to scrunch down and squeeze through sideways, one leg at a time. Cathy got her tennis shoe stuck at one point, and had to pull her foot free of it. Scott was careful not to make the same mistake.

Cathy held on to his arm as she put her shoe back on. "Isn't this neat? I used to have little tea parties here, with acorns for cookies and leaves for plates. I thought it was the greatest place in the world."

Scott looked around. The room wasn't much different from the one they had left, except that here he could stand up straight . . . and except that it was darker. He could no longer hear the sounds of hammering and voices from outside.

He muttered, "Yeah, it's great. Now come on. Let's go."

"That's the trouble with you rich kids, you've got no imagination. A *normal* person could just look around and—oh!" Another explosion shook the ground, hard enough to send a shower of dirt and loose pebbles down on their heads.

Scott grabbed her hand. "Okay, that's it. We're getting out of here before this whole place falls in."

"Scott, look!" She was shining her flashlight overhead, presumably to check the solidity of the roof. What she had discovered was a large hole in the rock overhead, and by the way the light picked up glints here and there another room seemed to be located overhead.

"Christ," Scott muttered.

"I never knew that was there before. I guess when you're a little kid you're too close to the ground to look up much." Her beam moved to the wall, and the irregular outcroppings of rock there. "I bet I could climb up."

"Girl, you're crazy. You don't know what the hell's up there. You might get stuck. This whole place is getting ready to cave in—"

"I'll just peek. Just to see what's up there."

And before he knew what was happening, she handed her flashlight to him and got a foothold on the wall, balancing precariously as she pulled herself up by the rim of the hole. "Hand me my flashlight," she said.

Muttering to himself, he did.

"Wow." Her voice sounded hollow and far away. "It's *huge*. It just goes on forever. Hey, maybe we've really found something. Like those Lorelei Caverns in Virginia?"

"Lurray," Scott corrected impatiently.

Her foot fumbled for another hold, and she boosted

herself up until she was sitting on the edge of the hole, her feet dangling from the ceiling.

"Now how are you going to get down, smart-ass?" Scott taunted.

"It stinks up here," Cathy commented. "Like something died."

Scott felt a chill. "Come on down," he said urgently.

He grabbed for her foot, but she swung both her feet up over the rim and called back, "You come up and get me!"

"Cathy, I'm not kidding!" His voice was hoarse. "Come down *now!*"

"You're such a wimp. All city boys are."

He could see the faint round circle of her light bouncing off the walls overhead. A pressure was building in Scott's chest that was more than anger and tasted like fear, and he shouted, "God damn it, Cathy!"

Her light stopped moving. Her voice was half a whisper, echoing down to him. "Good God. What is *that?*"

A lot of things happened at once, and Scott wasn't sure which was first. There was a sound, a roar, a scuffling, lurching movement; Cathy screamed. The distant thunderclap of another explosion and the sharp report of cracking rock, a black shower of falling earth, and something hit him hard on the shoulder, knocking him down. Things were falling. The place was breaking up.

He could hear Cathy screaming and he screamed back, pushing himself to his feet and shielding his face with his arm against a pelting of small rocks. *"Cathy!"*

It lasted only seconds, less than that, but he could hear her screaming, and he could hear the thing she was screaming at, hissing, slashing, growling. And then, abruptly, she fell through the opening, she literally flew through the opening, head first, landing against Scott and knocking them both off their feet.

"It's there, it's there, something's up there!" She was babbling hysterically, half sobbing and half screaming. Another shudder shook the cave, and a huge boulder split away from the wall and crashed not three feet away from them. Scott grabbed her hand and started to run.

They were six feet away from the narrow opening that led to the outer chamber. The earth was cracking and splitting around them; there was blood in Scott's eyes and somewhere he had lost his flashlight. He hit the wall of the cave with both hands; Cathy was screaming in his ear and clawing at his arms, and he pounded the wall until he found it, the opening, the door. He grabbed hold and hoisted himself into the opening. Cathy was clinging to him, trying to pull him back. But only one of them could go through at a time so he flung her off. The opening seemed to be smaller than it had been before; he scraped his knees and his knuckles and there was a moment, an awful moment, when his hip became wedged and Cathy was screaming and clawing at his ankle on the other side. With a mighty heave, he pushed himself through, then turned back for her.

That was when he saw what had happened. The rock that bisected the opening had cracked, and even now was shifting, starting to slide downward. Eventually it would seal off the opening.

"Cathy, hurry!" he screamed, and reached through the opening.

She got her arm through, and her shoulder and part of her head. Sharp pieces of gravel were raining overhead, and the distant circle of light that defined the entrance to the cave was foggy with dirt and debris. "Damn it, hurry!"

She edged one knee through.

And then he heard it. A wet, rumbling animal sound, like the low growl a bulldog gives before it attacks. Cathy screamed, and he could see part of her face as she turned to look backwards, the terror in her eyes, the wild disbelief. And then she went rigid; her body jerked.

He grabbed her T-shirt with one hand and her bare arm with the other. Her hand wrapped around his wrist and her nails dug in and she was writhing, screaming, slipping away from him.

"Cathy!"

The material of her T-shirt ripped as her head and torso were jerked backwards through the opening. Her fingernails slid down his arm, leaving slippery rivulets of blood, and she screamed, "Scott—help me! God, no . . . oh, God, *no* . . ."

He grabbed her arm with both hands, and he was screaming too. Her arm twisted and jerked, and he held on against the force on the other side, but it was as though her whole body were being tossed back and forth; the tendons of her arms strained and stretched and her fingernails clung, but it was no use, she was being torn *apart*. . . .

The screams stopped. Her arm went limp. There were only inches left in the opening now, just enough room for her arm and his. And helpless, horrified, Scott watched as her arm was wrenched from his grip, flopped brokenly against the rock ledge for an instant, and then disappeared on the other side.

Early in the afternoon, Hugh Bullard, by now returned from Chicago, came by with the survey maps Laura had requested. "Is this going to make you feel better?" he demanded. "Can we get back to work now?"

Another blast echoed and Laura said, "Sounds to me like we're already back to work. What are you going to do with the vacant lot?"

He shrugged. "Right now, we're using it as a dump. Eventually we'll cover it over with topsoil and sell it as a double lot."

"And hope the people who buy it don't decide to put in a pool."

"That'll be their problem, won't it?"

"Don't you have any ethics at all?"

"Very little," he confessed cheerfully. "Now, what I want you to do is see what you can put on the lot next to the sinkhole. Try to keep it down, because whoever buys it is going to be paying for a double lot and we don't want to price ourselves out of the market. Think you can have something for me by tomorrow morning?"

For a moment Laura just stared at him, but she didn't have the energy for a fight. She said, "I'll see what I can do."

She should have been glad for something to occupy her mind, but she couldn't concentrate. She spent the afternoon sitting at the drawing board, making desultory sketches and tearing them up before they were finished. Sunlight splattered over her papers and made yellow patches on the oak flooring, and the day outside was a bright emerald. Christy was playing on the swing set and, with the window open to the breeze, Laura could hear the rhythmic creak of the chain as Christy swung back and forth. It was a still summer afternoon, peaceful and pretty, and it was hard to imagine that evil of any kind could afflict this place.

Evil. Was that what it was? Maybe it was human nature to fear what one didn't understand, but how could anyone understand something like this? It hunted at night and killed indiscriminately and taunted them with evidence of its slaughter. It was sly enough not to get caught, and strong enough to tear chain-link as though it were chicken wire, and it *came to her house*. How was she supposed to fight something like that?

She was angry. Her child was being threatened, her home, her peace of mind. And it didn't matter whether the threat came from a madman or a monstrous deviant from the bowels of the forest, *this was her place*. She had worked for it, built it, planned it to be a sanctuary of peace and refuge in which she could contentedly live out the rest of her life. Now it was being invaded, and that wasn't fair.

Yet more than once that afternoon she picked up the telephone to call Philadelphia. And something — pride, most likely — always prevented her from making the call.

About four o'clock in the afternoon she was ready to give up on the plans. She got up from the drawing board with the idea of making a pot of coffee, and suddenly she was invaded by a wave of nausea so strong that she had to grip the back of a chair to steady herself. It swept over her in wave after terrifying wave, more than just sickness; it was a black feeling of loss, of horror, of soul-penetrating sorrow, and all she could think was *Christy*. It was coming from Christy.

Panic surged through her bloodstream and strengthened her limbs, and she stumbled toward the glass door and jerked it open. Christy fell into her arms, her face wet with tears.

"They're dead, Mommy," she cried. "The babies—they're all dead. I didn't want them to die, but the babies—"

Laura held her daughter tightly, her heart beating hard. "What babies, honey?" she inquired hoarsely. "What babies . . ."

"Monster babies," Christy said brokenly. "They didn't do anything bad, it's not their fault. . . ."

A chill went down Laura's spine, and she hugged Christy harder. "It's all right," she whispered. "I know. It's all right, sweetie, we're going home. We're going far away from here. . . ."

About twenty minutes later she heard the sirens, a great many of them but she did not want to know what they signified. First she called Hilly in Philadelphia. Then she called the airline and made reservations for a morning flight out of Washington.

At five o'clock, her telephone rang. It was Joe McCallough from the security office, and in a panicky voice he told her about the cave-in and insisted she bring the geological survey maps to the site right away.

It was almost dark when the man in charge came out of the cave and went over to speak to the sheriff. They kept glancing over at her, but Minnie Sykes did not have to look at them to know what they were saying. Her girl was dead. They had gotten to her, those things. And she was dead.

Two other men came out of the hole, carrying pick-axes and shovels. Their faces were white beneath the streaks of dirt, their eyes shell-shocked. One of them stumbled off behind the bushes, and in a moment

Minnie heard retching sounds. Her lips tightened.

This place, she thought. *This black, wicked place.* She could smell the evil rising up from it like sulfur seeping out of the ground. Death. Squalor. Decay. The very earth on which she stood was crawling with it, and from such malignance were those creatures spawned. For centuries they ravaged, they disappeared. And no one stopped them. But now they had taken one of her own. Now it was too much.

A whole crowd of people had gathered around. Two police cars and an ambulance. Those Heights people, in their well-fitting clothes, running around trying to look helpful, their eyes straining for a glimpse of the gore. Some town folks too, bringing their ropes and shovels and strong backs. For a while they'd tried to talk to her, bringing cups of coffee, saying stupid, patronizing things. Now they left her alone. They were all fools. They didn't have the first idea what they were dealing with. If they had they would have covered their faces and run from this place screaming.

That pretty woman, the one who had come to her house, she was there. She looked scared, different from the others. Maybe she knew. Minnie had tried to tell her. And Scott. He knew. He sat on a camp chair with his mother hovering over him and his father marching around giving orders like a captain who had lost his ship. Yes, the boy knew. His face was streaked with blood and dirt and his arm was bandaged and he just sat there, staring into space. The mane of golden hair in which he'd always taken such pride hung in limp strings over his face and his shoulders, and he hadn't said a word; he just sat there and stared blankly into space. Minnie didn't feel sorry for him. He was alive.

When she was nine years old Minnie had seen one

of them. It was dusk, her brothers had finished before her, and she was left out in the corn field alone, hurrying to pick the last of her row so she could get to the house for supper. Her mother was making fried apple pies that night, and there wouldn't be any left if she was late. She looked up, and there it was, squatting across the creek from her, lapping up water like a dog.

She must have squealed, or made some noise, because it looked up; it lifted its huge, balloon-shaped head and fixed her with its fire-red eyes and made a low, rumbling sound. It got to its feet, bigger than a man, with skin the color of curdled milk and as slimy as a white worm, and she saw its huge, misshapen male member dangling between its legs and the glint of fangs as it spread its lips. She was so scared she lost control of her bladder, and a puddle formed in the dusty soil between her feet and splashed onto her ankles. Then it raised its arms and let out a sound, a peal, a roar, a screeching growl that jarred the marrow of her bones. She ran the half mile to the house without once stopping for breath.

Her brothers whooped at her story. Her father scowled and said nothing. But her grandfather nodded sagely and said, "To see a Nighteater at dusk, it's a rare thing. It's a sign of blessing, and means you're destined for great things."

Minnie Sykes had not been blessed. But she knew what her destiny was.

The sheriff started walking toward her. His uniform was rumpled and stained with perspiration and his shoulders sagged; he looked old. But as he drew nearer, he straightened his shoulders, and looked her in the eye. Minnie had to admire him for that.

"I'm sorry, Miz Minnie," he said. "They were able to break through, just enough to get a flashlight in. I'm

227

afraid your granddaughter didn't survive the cave-in."

He paused there, as though waiting for her to say something. Waiting for her to scream, or cry. She didn't, of course.

"We'll keep working to recover the body," he said awkwardly, after a moment.

"No need. Dead is dead." She looked back toward the dark hole that had swallowed her grandchild, and her chin jerked. "Damn fool girl," she said thickly. "Damn fool."

If he was shocked at her words, he had the good sense not to show it. His tone was gentle. "Why don't you let one of my deputies drive you home now?"

She turned her eyes back to him, but it took longer than she would have liked to focus. Then she straightened her neck, and set her shoulders, and brought her mind away from the past and to the task at hand. "Thank you kindly," she said stiffly. "But you got your job to do, and I got mine."

Sam watched as she walked away. A murmur began to ripple through the crowd as the news spread, and someone cried out softly. She thought it was Scott Bullard's mother.

He felt stunned, drained, battered down by too much too soon. This was a freak accident, he knew, it wouldn't happen again in a dozen years, yet in combination with the other freak accidents and inexplicable acts of violence that had taken place over the past few weeks, it seemed to be part of a dark, ugly picture whose borders he could not see. *I should have retired three years ago*, he thought. *I should have never stood for reelection. I'm not as sharp as I used to be, and this is a game for the young.* He had his eyes on a little plot of land at the foot of the mountain, a sweet piece of bottom land that would be perfect for fruit trees. Maybe he'd put up a few greenhouses and try his hand at organic gardening. Strawberries, maybe. He would be good at that. He would be happy doing that.

He felt a light touch upon his arm. Laura said softly, "Sam?"

Spotlights had been set up to supplement the fading daylight, and their fluorescent hue gave her face a parchment-white quality. Her hair was beginning to come loose from its braid, and her eyes were dark smudges of fear and anxiety. In answer to her unspoken question, Sam shook his head.

Her voice was strained and tight, like her face. She spoke as though begging for a denial. "You—found the body?"

Sam hesitated. There was an uncertainty between them, almost an awkwardness, that could be traced directly back to their last encounter. He didn't want to tell her the truth. But he couldn't avoid it.

"The opening was too narrow to get a man through. But they were able to find—an arm. Apparently it was severed in the initial cave-in. They figure. . . ." He had to stop there, and clear his throat. "The rest of the body must be buried beneath the rubble. We'll start digging again in the morning. I didn't figure there was any need to tell Miss Minnie the details," he added tiredly. "There's no way the girl could have survived."

He saw the rest of the blood drain slowly from Laura's lips. She made a small, smothered sound, and closed her eyes briefly. When she opened them again her eyes had a dull, flat look, and the small lines around her mouth were clearly visible

"Tore her apart," she said hoarsely. "That's what Scott kept screaming, remember? 'They tore her apart.' He kept screaming it over and over, and then he stopped talking at all."

229

Sam felt every muscle in his body tense. "Laura, the boy was in shock—"

A small shudder went through her, and then she looked at him. The haunted look in her eyes was slowly replaced by fatigue, the deep, soul-numbing kind that Sam himself felt. "I know," she said heavily. "It's just that—I knew her, and it's so much. This— and everything else . . . it's too much."

Her voice cracked, and she brought her hand to her throat, as though to rub away a pain or hold back a cry. Sam wanted to reach out to her. He said instead, lowly, "This was an accident, Laura."

She looked toward the cave, and did not reply.

After a long moment she seemed to gather her energy, and pulled her eyes away from the cave entrance. "I'd better go. Christy is with Mary Beth and . . . I'd better go."

"Laura," Sam said firmly. "This had nothing to do with Kellerman, or the dog, or any of the things that have been happening to you. It was an accident."

She turned back to him. For a moment she looked as if she believed him, or wanted to believe him, but it was only for a moment. The dark, heavy look was back in her eyes. "We're leaving tomorrow," she said. "We're going home. For a few weeks, maybe . . . maybe longer. It seems like the best thing to do."

Sam looked at her for a long moment. Then he said quietly, "So that's it. You're running away again."

Her eyes moved slowly away from his, over the surrounding landscape, across the frightened, uncertain faces of the people who were huddled around the scene of the tragedy. "It wasn't supposed to be like this," she said softly. And then her eyes, and her voice hardened. "Damn it, *it wasn't supposed to be like this.*"

She looked as though she wanted to say more, but

230

the words were choked off. Her hands tightened into fists, her shoulders squared, and she walked away.

For a long moment Sam stood there alone, watching her disappear into the shadows. Then, abruptly, he turned back to his job.

Chapter Twelve

Laura said nothing to Christy about Cathy. In answer to Mary Beth's question, Laura glanced at the children and shook her head slightly; Mary Beth's eyes flashed with shock and tears and she turned away.

But in the car Christy asked in a small, solemn voice, "Did the monsters eat Cathy too, Mommy? Just like Corky?"

Laura looked at her daughter. The small white face, the big troubled eyes, too scared, too knowing. A stab of fury and helplessness went through her, and she had to grip the steering wheel to keep her hands from trembling. *She's only a child, goddamnit,* she thought. *It isn't fair. . . .*

Laura said, as steadily as she could, "Cathy was in an accident, sweetheart. She went into a cave and was hurt very badly by falling rocks."

"She's dead," Christy said.

Dead. That word should not be in the vocabulary of any five-year-old. But within the space of a few short weeks, Christy had had the opportunity to use it twice.

"Yes."

Three times, Laura remembered abruptly. This afternoon, when she had come in crying. *The babies are dead*. Laura remembered the awful blackness, the empty sick feeling that must have been only a reflection of what Christy had felt, and it drew a shudder from her. Christy had known about Cathy. Somehow she must have known, there was no other explanation. All Laura knew was that she did not want to go through anything like that ever again; she could not let her child go through that again. And she wouldn't.

She reached over and took Christy's hand. Despite the warm night, her hand was cold. So was Laura's. "When we get home," Laura said, forcing energy into her voice, "we're going to pack our suitcases. Tomorrow we're going on an airplane to see Uncle Hilly. That'll be great won't it? To see Uncle Hilly and Ben again?"

Christy was silent for a moment. "Uncle Hilly doesn't have a pool. Or a swing set."

It occurred to Laura for the first time that Christy might be as tired of moving as she was. "No," Laura agreed carefully, "but it's time for a visit, don't you think? Don't you miss Ben and Hilly?"

After a moment, Christy turned her head and looked out the window. Her voice was sad. "I liked our new house, Mommy."

Laura swallowed hard. *So did I,* she thought. *So did I.*

It was about that time that she heard, even over the sound of the engine and the tires against the roadway, the howling. It was louder, much louder than ever before, and earlier in the night. It had a piercing, cacophonous quality to it, dozens of voices raised to the moonless sky, baying, screaming, high and low, fading out and gathering strength and beginning all over again. Christy turned frightened eyes to her, and strained against the confines of her seat belt to get near her mother. Laura held her hand hard as she pulled into the driveway. Then she locked the doors and rolled up the window, and they did not get out of the car until the sound had died away.

Ted Jacobs took a glass of mineral water out onto the back deck. He had been cutting back on his drinking lately in hopes that might help his insomnia, but tonight he knew it was a futile gesture. His mind was full of dark heavy things, and sleep was an idea beyond the realm of possibility.

His house was diagonally across the lake from the Bullards. Tonight that house was dark, a shadow upon shadows, and he knew why. *Tragedy strikes again,* he thought, and wished there were something more potent than mineral water in his glass.

From the first day he had come here, he had known this place was cursed. Until now, he had thought he carried the curse with him. Now he knew it was real.

He had been among the first to buy into the development, and had seen it before the bulldozers came in; dark, stoic, foreboding. Eternal. Even now they sat perched in their little glass houses, the new superimposed upon the old in an unnatural defiance of what should have been, and it was as though history itself mocked them. The forest waited. They were only temporary.

Today he had driven to Bridgeton, a small university town a hundred miles away, in search of books of cryptozoology. What he had found were answers he did not want, answers, wrapped deep inside the dark mystery of logic, that all of them had been afraid to face. He kept thinking, *I should have known. I, of all people, should have known.* And why hadn't he? For with the answers came other questions, ironic in nature, equally as terrifying as the truth. How far would the

234

human mind go to avoid reality? Just how fragile was their grip, after all, on that tenuous thing men of science like to call reason? How could it have gone this far?

Over the car radio on the way home he heard about the cave-in. He didn't want to stop. He shouldn't have stopped. He had no reason to even go past the site. But he saw the slow intermittent flash of the ambulance dome, and he turned down the narrow street.

The police were sealing off the area. The crowds were beginning to disperse. It didn't take him long to find out what had happened. Everyone he passed wanted to tell him. Hugh Bullard was looking right at him, and Ted had to go over to him.

"They want to take Scott to the hospital," Bullard said without preamble. "You're a doctor, what do you think?"

"I don't practice medicine anymore," Ted reminded him. "I think you'd better do what the paramedics say."

"Just look at him," Bullard insisted, growing more agitated by the minute. "Just go on over and have a look."

So, much against his will, Ted did.

"He won't talk to us," Isabel said, stroking her son's hair. "I keep thinking he'll snap out of it but . . ."

Ted knelt beside Scott. The boy had apparently been treated for shock, but beyond that Ted did not know, and didn't want to guess. He said softly, "How's it going, Scott?"

Scott looked up at him. He licked his cracked lips. He said hoarsely, "Man, it was bad. I kept trying to tell them . . . wouldn't listen . . ."

Isabel gave a small gasp, and Ted glanced at her briefly. He said to Scott, "I'm listening."

Scott began to shake his head, slowly, back and

forth, making harsh sobbing noises that swallowed all words. Ted looked at Isabel sympathetically. "It'd probably be best if he spent a night at the hospital. For observation."

He started to get to his feet. And then Scott spoke. The words went through Ted with a chill that he couldn't shake, even now.

"That thing . . . it kept tearing at her, ripping at her, screaming . . . I tried to hold on but it kept pulling her . . . I tried to tell them, man, don't go in there, but they—it was eating her. It was eating her *alive*."

Ted took a swallow of the mineral water, and it scraped against the back of his throat like sawdust. A picture was beginning to form in his mind, terrible and clear. He wished he could have left some of his questions unanswered.

Because now he knew what was hiding in the woods. And it frightened him more than any monster could have done.

There should have been relief in the act of packing suitcases, but there wasn't. The decision was made, the worst part was over. In a few hours they would be safe. Everything was going to be all right. But was that reproach she saw in Christy's eyes, or merely fatigue? Laura remembered when Christy's face had been awash with sunshine, her every movement bright and bouncy, her conversation nonstop energy. Now her face was hollow and her movements subdued, her eyes tired and worried.

Damn it, I have no choice, she thought. *I have to get her away from here. I have to get us away from here. Somewhere we'll be safe.*

"Sometimes bad things happen in the city too,"

Christy said, folding her Strawberry Shortcake night-gown on top of her suitcase.

Laura just looked at her helplessly.

She got Christy into the bathtub, and laid out her clothes for the plane trip, and made a game of picking the three toys that would accompany them to Philadelphia. When Christy was tucked in and drifting off to sleep, she made one last tour of the silent house, turning off the downstairs lights, setting the alarm, making mental notes to herself to empty the trash in the morning and run the dishwasher. The house, so carefully planned and lovingly decorated, seemed to accuse her with every step. *Running away again?*

She poured herself a large glass of wine and went back upstairs, deliberately ignoring the inner voice that taunted her. She tried to take some kind of reassurance from the suitcase packed and ready at the door, the flight schedule she had copied down waiting atop the bureau. But all she felt was cowardly, and ashamed.

This was supposed to be her home, her final stop. Here she was to make her stand, to live out her life the way it was meant to be lived. But once again she was on the move, and no, it wasn't fair, but what was she supposed to do?

So I'm not perfect, she thought angrily, and took a big gulp of wine. *I'm not James Bond and I'm not Luke Skywalker and I can't scale tall buildings in a single bound. I'm just an ordinary person trying to get along the best I can, and when I'm scared I do the only thing I know to protect myself.*

And she was not going to continue beating herself up over this. The decision was made. It was for the best.

She filled the sunken tub with water and turned on the jacuzzi controls, and took the glass of wine into the bathtub with her. The jacuzzi was definitely something she would miss, she thought as she sank back into the water. She would miss a lot of things.

She did not know how long she stayed there, but it was long enough for the water to ease away most of her tension, and for the wine to start to make her drowsy. She rested her head against the bath cushion on the ledge of the tub and closed her eyes, concentrating on nothing except the soft whoosh of the water jets.

And then, in a simultaneous explosion, it happened. The sharp report of bursting glass, the klaxon of the intruder alarm, screeching with a deafening blare in her ears. The lights, automatically wired into the alarm, flared on all over the house. And Christy's voice, almost drowned out by the raucous peal of the siren, screamed, "Mommy! Mommy!"

The wine glass shattered on the tile as Laura lurched out of the tub. Precious moments lost scrambling for her bathrobe, pulling it on. She cried, "Christy, stay where you are! I'm coming!"

She pulled open the bathroom door and raced through the bedroom. More glass breaking. An *explosion* of glass. She whirled, ran across the room, jerked out the drawer of her nightstand. It tumbled onto the floor and she knelt, fumbling through the scattered contents, until she found the gun. Bullets. Where were the bullets?

"Christy, don't move! Stay in your room!"

She found the ammunition box, jerked it open. Half the contents scattered onto the floor. *Christy . . . oh, God, please . . .*

She found three bullets, forced them into the chamber, and snapped it shut. She went first to Christy's room. Christy was sitting up in bed, her hands clamped to her ears, crying. Laura flew across the room and embraced her with one arm swiftly. "Hush.

238

Hush, baby, it's all right. Stay here. Just promise Mommy you'll stay here. Don't do anything. Just *stay here*."

She tore herself away from Christy's entwining arms and pulled the door closed behind her. She ran to the head of the stairs, and stopped. The living area below was brilliantly illuminated. Nothing moved. The siren was beating in her ears, deafening her. The gun was sweaty in her hand and jerked with every heartbeat. She steadied it with both hands and flipped off the safety. She started to move down the stairs.

Then she heard it. A howl. *A howl.*

It was in her house.

Sam was at the security gate when the call came in.

"I don't know," Joe McCallough was saying, his voice tight with agitation. "I don't *know* what she wanted with it. It was just pure luck that I happened to see her. Most of my men were out at the site, you know, and I was coming back to relieve the guy on duty at the gate, and I happened to see a flashlight beam from the storage shed. When I went to check it out, there was Miz Sykes, stuffing those big pockets of hers with bundles of dynamite and fuses. I tried to stop her, but she had a shotgun, and I'll tell you the truth, she looked just crazy enough to use it too. She kept saying 'They got my girl. Do you think I'm going to let them get away with that?' And then she started talking about getting them where they slept, and blowing them to kingdom come, and short of pulling my pistol and shooting her where she stood, there wasn't nothing I could do. She took off back through the woods, and I came back here and sent a couple of my men after her, but it's God's good guess where she went and if they'll ever find her in the dark."

Sam rubbed the tight muscles at the back of his neck. "Christ," he said. Would this night never end?

"I thought you might want to leave a man back at the cave," Joe suggested, "in case she had in mind to go back there and blow it up. She was in a pretty bad way, no telling what she might do."

"Right," Sam muttered absently. "Good thinking."

Joe peered at him, his brow wrinkled with worry. "Who do you suppose she meant by 'they'?"

And then the buzzer on his security board sounded.

Joe turned quickly back into the gate house, scanning the panel. "It's Laura Kane's house," he said. "Intruder alarm."

Sam was already in his car.

Ted Jacobs was about to go back into the house when he heard the alarm. For the past hour, maybe more, he had been sitting on the deck, holding an empty glass and indulging in the only form of self-defense he knew; intellectualization.

It never failed to work. Standing over the operating table with the patient hemorrhaging: follow the book, step-by-step, remember the procedure, then if the patient died at least it wouldn't be his fault. Ask the questions. Answer them. No problem was insurmountable as long as it could be faced with cool, calm reason.

Or almost none.

A horrible mistake. A cruel insanity only man could devise when the face of evil could not be distinguished from that of the unknown. Superstition, legends, fear . . . it should not be so surprising. After all, they had all lived in the forest once. Perhaps they had not left it quite so far behind them as they thought.

He had been wrong. He liked to think of himself as a scientist, but he had been wrong.

For the first time, intellect failed him. Cold, calm reason did not make the monster go away. It only grew, larger and more possible than ever. And he knew he would not sleep tonight.

Neither could he stay outside when he knew, with his heart and his soul and his mind he knew, what lurked just behind the sheltering shadows of the woods. So he turned to go inside, and then the screeching wail of a burglar alarm split through the night.

The sound carried clearly down the sloping side of the mountain, an anachronism of modern technology in a primeval world. Ted's first thought was, *Someone forgot to punch out their code.* But the shrieking didn't stop after a few seconds, as it would have if the alarm had been accidentally tripped, and his second thought, as he felt his muscles tense up in a flight-or-fight response, was, *Ignore it. None of your business. That's what we've got security guards for.* He didn't get involved. He had made a career out of not getting involved.

But as the desperate, wailing sound went on and on, it became impossible to ignore the direction from which it came, and the implications it shrieked out with every breath. It was Laura Kane's house. And whether he liked it or not, he was already involved.

Her progress down the stairs seemed interminable, gripping the banister with one hand and the gun with the other. Her heartbeat, choking off her breath. A voice, pounding inside her head. *Run. Take Christy and get out of here.* . . . But where could she run? They were out there, waiting. They were in here, searching. Furniture crashing. Glass shattering. The angry, pained, bone-tearing howl competing with the scream of the siren. Her office. *It was in her office.*

A rivulet of bathwater trickled down her spine like

an icy chill. She made her feet cross the living room, toward the spiral stairs that led to the office. *God help me. Don't let this be happening. Don't let me see it. . . .*

And the other voice: *Run.*

I can't, I can't, there's no place to go. . . .

She reached the top of her stairs. She forced herself to put her foot on one tread. And then another. And another. She looked down into the office.

It was a demolition area. One glass wall had shattered inward. The floor was strewn with glittering glass and mangled wooden blinds. A bookcase was overturned, and several heavy wooden file cabinets. Their contents added to the rubble of destruction on the floor. Her drafting board was crushed into splinters, papers shredded, pencils scattered. She took another step downward, gripping the pistol. And then she saw it.

It was crouched in the center of the room, its hands clasped to the side of its bulbous head, its mouth opened in a howl of rage. Its pendulous breasts swung forward as it moved, still in a half crouch, occasionally swinging an arm out as though to strike at the source of the deafening noise.

For a moment Laura just stood there, transfixed in horror and awe. The smell of it filled the room and reached her even on the stairs—a smell of refuse and gaseous decay, nauseating, repulsive. The ripple of its flesh in the bright overhead lights, the glint of sharp, brownish teeth, the harsh grunting noises that came from it between howls. It was alien, malformed, hideous, and every instinct she possessed revolted and recoiled in shock . . . and yet it was something more. And it was that indefinable twinge of recognition, of something horribly familiar, that held her paralyzed, frozen in the amber of her own denial, until it was almost too late.

She must have made a sound, or perhaps it merely smelled her fear. Suddenly the creature spun around, its nostrils flaring, its narrowed eyes pinning her. With incredible speed and agility for its bulk, it lunged toward her. Precious seconds were lost as she stood there helpless and staring, and then it hit the staircase with a force that shook the treads beneath Laura's feet and caused her to reel backward. With a cry, she lifted the pistol in her hand and fired blindly.

The bullet went wild and the beast attacked the staircase again, grabbing the rail with both hands and shaking. Bolts rattled; the entire structure trembled. Laura cried out, and had to lower the pistol as she flung out a hand against the wall to balance herself. She was going to fall. *She was going to fall right into the arms of that thing.*

It backed away, emitting a deep, rasping howl of frustration. And then, before Laura could turn and run, it lunged again. She didn't think. She lifted the pistol and fired.

The recoil stabbed through her shoulder and a bright patch of torn flesh appeared on the upper arm of the beast. It didn't appear to notice. It kept coming. She fired again and missed. It was halfway to the stairs and still coming. She squeezed the trigger again and again in rapid succession, and nothing happened. With a cry of rage and terror, she threw the gun at the creature with all her might. It bounced off the white torso harmlessly.

"No! Don't hurt my mommy!"

It was Christy, her shrill voice piercing over the sound of the alarm, her small body thrusting against Laura's legs, squeezing past her on the stairs. "Go away from here!" she screamed. *"Don't you hurt my mommy!"*

"Christy, no!" Laura grabbed for her, but only a

243

handful of nightgown floated through her fingers as Christy pushed herself between Laura and the monster.

The beast actually stopped its advance, turning its gaze on Christy. Christy plunged down the steps, her small fists raised, screaming at it. Laura lunged after her and caught her arm, but the forward momentum was too much; Laura stumbled and went to her knees and Christy plunged forward, tumbling down the last three stairs and hitting her head on the overturned bookcase as she struck the floor. She lay still and silent at the feet of the beast.

No more than a second could have passed, but for Laura it was a vignette frozen forever in time. Her baby, lying facedown amidst the broken glass with a dark patch of red seeping through the veil of her hair. Her own scream echoing over the incessant wail of the alarm. And that creature, poised in movement with its head cocked at a peculiar, almost thoughtful angle, looking down at Christy.

Laura pushed herself to her feet and stumbled down the stairs, but she was too late; she never had a chance. The beast took one step forward and with a single swipe of its arm, snatched Christy up.

"Christy!"

Laura reached the bottom of the stairs, tripping over broken glass and scattered books. She flung out her arms, pushing herself forward, but she caught only air. The thing with her daughter in its arms turned and plunged through the shattered glass door, out into the night.

Chapter Thirteen

Laura's feet slipped on the decking that surrounded the pool and she went down onto one knee, but she didn't feel the pain of the jolt. She was on her feet again, running and screaming, although she knew it was hopeless as the creature disappeared out of the milky circle of light cast by the house flood beams and was swallowed up in the shadows. Still she ran, terror and fury pumping strength through her legs and her lungs; she ran into the darkness of the lawn and toward the woods where she knew it had gone, where it had taken *her child.* . . .

And suddenly something grabbed her arm, spinning her around, almost jerking her off her feet. She lashed out wildly with her fists and her nails, kicking and screaming and prepared to battle to the death, but the grip held firm and a voice shouted, "Laura! Stop! Laura, it's me!"

Vaguely she recognized Sam's voice, but she didn't cease her struggles. "Let me go! Let me go, you fool, it's Christy! It's got Christy!"

He wouldn't release her. She beat at him with her fists, twisting against his grip. "Stop it! It's Christy! *It's got my baby!*"

Sam got both arms around her and held her tightly against his chest so that she couldn't move; she could barely breathe. His own voice was hoarse and ragged as he said, "I know. I saw. God help me, I saw it."

It seemed to Laura great blocks of time were lost after that, though in fact no more than ten minutes had passed. She had changed from her bathrobe into jeans and a sweater, but she could not remember when. The house was filled with people, but she did not know where they had come from. Two sheriff's deputies and a security guard were downstairs, inspecting the damage to the office. Ted Jacobs was applying antiseptic to Laura's feet, which had been lacerated by the broken glass. Mike Jennings had heard the intruder alarm and come to investigate. He had met Carl Bedlow on the way.

Joe McCallough came through the kitchen entrance with one of his assistants. He glanced at Sam and shook his head. "There's blood on the patio and a little way into the yard. It could be hers." He nodded to Laura. "And it's too dark to see much else."

Sam came over to her, her gun in his hand. His face had a grayish tint and his brow was furrowed. "How many shots did you fire?"

"Three." Her voice was steady, though tight and low. "Two missed. The other one—didn't even slow it down."

Sam glanced at the revolver. It was a .38 Smith and Wesson, commonly known as a Lady Smith because its light weight and easy maneuverability made it a preferred self-defense weapon by women. Laura's firearms instructor had recommended the gun, but she knew its limitations.

Sam said, "A bullet this caliber wouldn't necessarily stop the average man."

"It wasn't a man." Laura's voice was calm and deliberate, and she didn't look at him. She didn't have to. "You know that." She reached for her shoes and socks.

Ted said, "Your feet are in pretty bad shape. You shouldn't—"

"I'm going to look for my baby."

"We're forming search parties right now. There's no need for you—"

"You're not doing anything." Laura jerked on a sock and tied a tennis shoe with short, jerky motions. "You're standing here talking and looking while my little girl is out there in the dark and . . ." But no. She wouldn't think about it. She couldn't. If she thought about it she would start screaming, and if she started screaming she would never stop, not ever. So she set her jaw and pulled on the other shoe, directing ferocious concentration on the effort it took to tie the laces.

"You're not going to do any good wandering out there in the dark yourself. You're in no shape—"

Laura pushed to her feet, closing her fists to keep her voice from shaking. "You think she's dead, don't you? You saw what happened and you know what that thing can do and you think it's too late! You're not even going to try! You—"

"Stop it!" Sam grabbed her shoulders as her hysteria rose, and his voice was harsh. "You know I'm not going to let anything happen to Christy, damn it, you know that!" His fingers tightened on her shoulders in a bruising, desperate grip and he repeated, *I'm not going to let anything happen to her,* do you understand that?"

She saw the determination in his eyes, and the fury of a man whose instincts had betrayed him and who

247

would move heaven and hell to make things right again. It was a powerful, terrible thing, and the force of it penetrated Laura's panic and gave her strength — but only for a moment. Because she saw something else in his eyes and it reflected too well what she felt, what she knew, deep down, must be the truth: fear. Fear that it was too late, that nothing could help Christy now, that the creature who had taken her was too brutal and too quick to be stopped. They had seen what it could do. They knew what it left when it was finished. And Christy was only a little girl. . . .

Laura glanced at Ted, but he wouldn't meet her eyes. They were hoping, all of them, but only because they couldn't bear to face what they all knew, deep down, to be the truth. And self-deception was a fragile thing, not meant to withstand the trauma of sharing.

Sam released his grip on her shoulders slowly. "Laura, Please." His voice was strained and low. "I don't want you out there."

Because he didn't want her to see what he knew he would find. And for a moment, just a moment, Laura felt weakness seep through her and she did not want to see either. She wanted to crawl away somewhere and hide and make her mind a blank; she wanted to go upstairs and pull the bedcovers over her head and sleep, long and deep, and when she awoke Christy would be bouncing on her bed, demanding breakfast. It would all go away. If she tried hard enough, she could make it all go away.

Then she straightened her shoulders, and swallowed hard, and started toward the kitchen. "We'll need flashlights," she said.

Mommy.

She stopped in mid-stride.

It went through her like a beam of sunlight seeking

out the dark corners of her soul, slow, thorough, certain. A rush of warmth, a breath of air, a hundred scents and sounds and feelings . . . Christy. She was filled with the essence of Christy.

The tiny voice came inside her head again, so clear that she let out a cry of welcome and whirled around, expecting to see Christy standing right behind her. *Mommy, where are you?*

Laura closed her eyes against the flood of joy that burned them, wanting to laugh out loud, to shout, to fall to the floor and thank God . . . *Christy*. It was Christy!

"I'm here, baby," she whispered, and let the tears roll down her cheeks. "Oh, sweetie, I'm here!"

Sam touched her arm, and the look of despair on his face made her laugh. She clutched his arms, laughing, gasping, weeping for joy. "She's alive!" she cried. "Oh, God, she spoke to me — she touched me — I heard her! She's alive!"

The expression on Sam's face went from dread to confusion to, far back in the far depths of his eyes, the faintest glimpse of hope. He said hoarsely, "Laura for God's sake — "

Ted came close and spoke quietly, as though she couldn't hear him. "She's hysterical. I think we'd better . . ."

Laura merely shook her head and brought her hands to her face, as though to restrain the flood of wonder and joy that held her in its grip. Sam looked at Ted, and then at Laura, and for the second time in less than an hour, he found himself doing battle with the impossible . . . and losing. Maybe he needed to believe as badly as Laura did, maybe he was remembering a little girl who answered questions that weren't spoken and could see things that were happening miles away. Maybe it was simply the look on Laura's face—transported, rapturous, filled with wonder and relief. It was the look of a mother who is holding in her arms a child she had believed was lost.

He looked back at Ted and he said quietly, "No. I don't think so."

Sam touched Laura's shoulder. "Are you sure? Are you absolutely sure?"

At first she only nodded wordlessly. Sam could feel the fine tremors in the muscles of her back. And then she whispered, closing her eyes, "Yes. Oh, yes."

Suddenly she gasped, and her eyes flew open. "I can see it—I could see where she was, just for a minute . . . dark and cold and—and wet. Water dripping on the rocks, I could hear it, and the smell—dank and filthy, like a grave." She looked up at him, desperate and anguished. "Oh, Sam, she's so scared! We can't leave her in that place!"

"We won't," Sam said. He gripped her shoulder briefly before dropping his hand, and the muscles in his cheek tightened. "We won't."

Lars Greesom came in. He carried a canvas pouch and had a coil of rope and two guns slung over his shoulder. "Here's the rest of the emergency equipment. The forest service said they couldn't get a chopper down here for a couple of hours. Do you want me to start rounding up volunteers?"

Laura gripped Sam's arm urgently. "That may be too late! She's out there, hurt and—she's okay now, but we can't wait!"

The deputy cast Laura a hesitant, questioning look, and Sam went over to him. He spoke lowly, so as not to be overheard by the others milling about, and quickly. His plans, such as they were, were only one step ahead of his words.

250

He said, "Get hold of Wilt Jeffries and see if he'll give us the loan of his dogs. But I want you or one of the boys to handle them—not Wilt. I don't want any civilians out there. This is not just a lost child, it's a kidnapping."

And there he hesitated. How much could he tell Lars? What right did he have to send men out there who probably wouldn't be coming back without even telling them what they were facing? But he couldn't take the chance of having this get out, of having the woods littered with the bodies of curiosity-seekers and *National Enquirer* types . . . not now. Not yet. Not until at least *he* knew what he was dealing with.

He said, with difficulty, "This isn't a normal situation. It's dangerous. Make sure the forest service people know that too and keep their people off the ground. Helicopter searches only. The only men I want out there are the ones with weapons and training; make sure they're armed and ready to use it. Divide the woods in back of the house into quadrants and send them out in teams, and this is important: Each team is to go no more than five hundred yards into the woods, then come back to the house and report. That's *all.*"

Lars looked uncertain, and reluctant. "I don't understand. Why?"

Because, Sam thought, *they're called Nighteaters. There's a reason for that. They're waiting out there in the dark where we can't see them and maybe it's only one and maybe it's a dozen but they're out there. . . .*

He said, "We can't do any more than that until morning. Tonight we look for signs, that's all. At daybreak—" *when it's safe* "—the search starts."

As clearly as if he had spoken the words, Sam knew Lars was remembering the search for Brett Howard.

251

"It's gonna take a peck of people to search that whole mountain. If the little girl's hurt, like she said . . ."

Sam glared at him. "What?"

Lars lowered his eyes and said nothing.

"I'm leaving you in charge," Sam said. He knelt on the floor and began going through the contents of the pouch. A first-aid kit, compass, and a buck knife went into the pockets of his field jacket. He clipped a hand-held radio onto his belt.

"Where're you going to be?" Lars asked in a tone that implied he already knew the answer.

Sam held up a canvas canteen. "Fill this for me, will you?"

"You can't be thinking of going out there by yourself?"

Sam checked both guns. One was an AR-15 semi-automatic, good for long range and by logic, his best choice. The other, a riot gun, was a 12-gauge pump that could splatter a man inside out at twenty yards. Neither of them had night sights, but then the Calumit County Sheriff's Department had never had much call for a weapon so equipped before. He would have liked to have taken them both, but the extra weight would only slow him down. The 12-gauge felt good in his hands, powerful and accurate, and he could only hope he had made the right choice as he loaded his pockets with shotgun shells.

"Now, listen here, Sam. You and me've been friends too long for me to just let you go marching out there by yourself. You said we're supposed to work in teams and that's just what we're going to do. You need a backup."

The holster on Sam's belt held a Glock 17 with a full clip. Sam added two more clips to his belt and got to his feet, pulling on the field jacket. He wouldn't

252

look at Lars. "I know what I'm doing. And I'm not coming back without her." It sounded like bravado, like the kind of thing Clint Eastwood would say before storming a hill or gunning down the bad guy. Sam would have laughed in the face of another man who uttered those words, but he didn't even have the emotion to spare on embarrassment now.

He did know what he was doing. This was his county, and he was sworn to protect it. That thing, that creature, whatever it was, had invaded his territory and left a trail of blood behind, and he was going to destroy it.

And he was not coming back without Christy. It was as simple and as terrifyingly complex, as that.

"Sheriff."

It was Ted Jacobs, and Sam tried to conceal his impatience as he turned to him. One look at the other man's taut face and shock-darkened eyes mitigated some of Sam's annoyance as he remembered that there were only three people in this room who knew what they were really up against. Ted Jacobs was one of them.

Jacobs said, "I'm going with you."

Sam hoisted the rope coil and the shotgun onto his shoulder, dismissing the other man without another glance. "I don't need you out there."

"Maybe not," Ted replied evenly, "but I need to be there."

Sam picked up a big torch and put a smaller one in his pocket. Frustration grated on him like the tick of the clock, seconds wasted, minutes slipping by while he stood there powerless. He said, "Do you know how to use a gun?"

Ted replied quietly, "I won't need one."

"You're a goddamn fool." Sam brushed by him.

In the kitchen he stopped to fill his canteen, and Laura was standing by the door. She was wearing a lightweight jacket and had a flashlight in either hand. Sam couldn't stop her. He couldn't tell her that, by trying to save her daughter's life, she might be only endangering it, that her presence would only slow him down, that he needed to concentrate on Christy and nothing else, and even then he could make no promises. If he refused to let her come with him she would only go by herself, and he couldn't argue with her. Christy did not have the time.

So he pushed open the door and Laura hurried out with him. Ted Jacobs took one of the flashlights from her hand and followed, and Sam did not even spare him a glance.

His eyes were focused on the place where the light ended and the forward trees rose like the spires of some dark cathedral, and his mouth was dry with terror. His first prayer was that he would find Christy. His second was that he would not see again the thing that had taken her. The third was that, if he did see it, he would be able to live long enough to kill it.

Chapter Fourteen

Their progress was slow, both because of the dark and the uncertain terrain, and because each of them paused periodically to search the circle of his own flashlight beam, hoping to find something the others had missed. After a time their lights were joined by others sparking in the woods like distant fireflies, small beacons of humanity that were both desperately reassuring and frightening. The more people there were thrashing about in the woods, the greater chance they would stir up something best left alone. More death. More savage shrieks in the night. More of the monstrous unknown.

They had only one chance of finding Christy alive, and Sam thought they all knew that. If she had been abandoned, or somehow escaped, within the fifteen or so minutes between the time she had been taken and the time Laura had first claimed to hear her voice, she might be within reach. The thing had been moving fast, but even it could not have gone more than a mile in a quarter of an hour. It was a fragile theory, almost preposterous in its faultiness, but wasn't the whole incident preposterous? An alien monster ravaging a house and stealing a child, a distraught mother's mystical communication with that child . . . But it was all Sam had. Confronted with hundreds of square miles of midnight-black forest and an enemy whose potential he could not even begin to guess, Sam was ready to grasp at any hope. *Christy, honey, just stay put,* Sam thought. *Whatever you do, just don't move.*

They moved on a straight course from the house into the woods, following the direction in which Sam had seen the creature running, with no more justification than the fact that an animal will usually follow a set path coming and going, deviating by no more than a few inches from the trail created by its own scent. Again, it was a frail hypothesis, but they had to start somewhere.

Once they had spotted a splash of blood on the carpet of dead leaves before them, and Sam's chest had clutched with elation and dread. At least they were moving in the right direction. But for the past twenty-five minutes they had seen nothing.

The radio at his belt crackled, and Sam flipped on the transmitter. He tried to keep the anxiety out of his voice as he spoke sharply. "Yeah."

Lars's voice was faint and shot through with static; already the hills and valleys were beginning to break up the signal. A few more hundred yards and the radio would be useless. "—dogs," Lars was saying. "Acting crazy, won't go more than a few yards in the woods. Worthless damn mutts, can't do anything with them. You want me to call that man in Chattanooga with the search-and-rescue team?"

Without meaning to, Sam met Ted Jacobs's eyes. Jacobs looked surprised. "No," Sam said. "Dogs won't do any good."

"Say again?"

"Forget the dogs," Sam repeated, more loudly. "What about the choppers?"

"Not even off the ground yet. They said. . . ." Sam lost the rest of the transmission in a garble of static.

Sam stared at the radio in a moment of tightening frustration. Then he said, "Do what you have to."

"You're breaking up. Are you coming back?"

"No," Sam said. "Out."

For another moment the three of them stood there, silhouetted by the circle of light their flashlight beams cast on the forest floor. If Lars had followed Sam's instructions, most of the search teams would be turning back soon. They could expect no help from the dogs or from choppers, at least not for a while. Hopelessness lurked in the shadows like the ancient Medusa, waiting to turn them into stone if they ever once looked it in the face. Yet a decision had to be made. If they went much further there would be no turning back.

Sam could not meet Laura's eyes as he spoke. "Look, Jacobs. I think the best thing for you to do is take Laura back to the house. We're not making any progress this way and—"

"So that's it?" Laura's voice had a peculiar atonal quality, and her words were all the more cutting for the lack of emotion. "Get the helpless female out of the way before she swoons. Goddamn it, Sam, you belong in the eighteenth century."

Ted said, "You're right about one thing though. We're not making any progress this way. We need to split up, cover more ground."

"That's the stupidest damn thing I've ever heard. I said before, nobody's to be out here alone—"

"Isn't that what you suggested only a moment

257

ago?" replied Ted mildly. "That we go back and leave you alone?"

Sam was not going to fall into that trap. Too much was at stake to waste energy on intellectual one-up-manship. "Look," he said plainly, "I don't have the time to be polite. You're in the way, both of you. You're costing me time, and it may be time that little girl doesn't have. The plain fact is, I don't need you."

Ted said quietly, "You may need me more than you know."

And before Sam could reply, Laura swung her flashlight around and started walking away.

"Laura! What are you doing?"

Caught in the beam of his flashlight, Laura turned around. Her face had an eerie luminescent glow in the artificial light. Her hair was silver and her eyes dark shapeless smudges. She said coldly, "You're wasting time."

Sam walked the few steps toward her. He wanted to touch her, but he didn't dare. She looked brittle enough to break. He said quietly, "I'm sorry, Laura. I don't mean to push you out. It's just that I'm used to taking care of things."

She replied simply, "So am I."

And the decision was made.

Sam turned back to Ted. "All right. We'll each go twenty-five feet in a different direction. Keep an eye out for the other flashlights. The minute you lose sight of one turn around and come back. We'll meet back here in five minutes."

Laura walked off into the dark.

She had gone about six steps when the beam of the flashlight started shaking so erratically she couldn't see. She had to stop, gripping the flashlight with

258

both hands and gritting her teeth, desperately fighting back the wave of despair. It came to her out of nowhere that she might never see her daughter again. It had been over an hour since that brief contact, that sweet certainty, and maybe it had been nothing after all, maybe she had imagined it, maybe she had felt only what she so desperately needed to feel. Christy was gone, and five years was such a short time. From infancy to toddler to preschool just like that, in the blink of an eye, and Laura had always planned on so many more years, she had taken them for granted. To have a child, to love her, to watch her grow and share her discoveries . . . Five years was not enough. It just wasn't. And she couldn't let Christy go now, she *couldn't*.

"Over here!"

Laura didn't know whose voice it was, but when she turned she saw the wave of a flashlight, and another beam moving toward it. A leap of her pulse choked off her breath and she started running toward them.

Ted was kneeling on the ground in front of a large indentation in a rock outcropping. Sam dropped to one knee beside him and ran his finger over the leaf Ted held up, examining the smear beneath the light.

"It's blood," Sam agreed, "still sticky. Less than an hour old."

"There's more of it smeared on the wall in there." Ted directed his flashlight toward the rocks, and Laura saw that it wasn't just a shadow or an indentation behind him she had seen, but a small cave.

Sam got up to look inside, and Laura followed. The cave wasn't very large; the three of them standing shoulder to shoulder filled it. They all had to stoop, but not by much. It was conceivable that a large animal could have come in there.

Ted played his light over the rough, mossy walls until it illuminated a dark streak that looked like mud. Sam examined it and said nothing for a moment.

"It could have come in here, hiding," Sam speculated, though without much conviction.

"Or Christy could have," Laura added, trying to keep her voice from trembling. "Her head . . ."

But she didn't go on. The thought of a lost little girl with a head injury was not very comforting, but it was their best hope. And even at that, all they had discovered was another dead end. Christy was not here now. They didn't even know whether she had been here. Were they tracking a little girl or the monster that had taken her? They couldn't afford to be wrong, and they could never be sure.

Ted said, "Look."

He shone his flashlight on the opposite wall, where, midway down the wall, another opening appeared. Sam moved close, joining his beam to Ted's as they bent down.

"It goes straight down," Sam commented.

"I can't see the bottom, can you?"

"It's hard to tell."

Laura shivered. The small closed place suddenly seemed oppressive, and at the same time too vulnerable. The air was old and tainted and filled with the refuse of things that crawled and slithered; that creature had been here, she was sure of it. The residue of evil it had left behind was almost palpable.

She said, "Let's get out of here. We're wasting time."

Then Ted said, "Look. There's something on the ledge."

"I don't see anything."

"There."

"It's probably nothing."

Ted straightened up. "I think we should check it out."

"What the hell for?"

Laura protested, "Christy would never go into a place like that, not even if . . ." Not even if she were terrified, hiding, running for her life? Laura looked at the dark, ragged hole again. If she had fallen . . .

Ted looked at her. "I don't think she did go in there, not by herself—not of her own free will. I'm sorry, Laura," he said quietly, "but I think that thing still has her. It wouldn't carry her into the woods just to let her go, and there's no way she could have escaped."

Sam turned on him angrily. "What the hell are you trying to say?"

"Just listen to me for a minute. Just think. What does an animal who's wounded or carrying prey—" he flinched only slightly over the word "—do? Where does it go?"

The question was directed to Sam, and he answered it, though with obvious reluctance. "That depends. It usually looks for some place private, safe. Its den, maybe, or its burrow. Are you saying—"

"I'm saying this thing—or these things—live in the caves," Ted replied calmly. "It's the only thing that makes sense. That would explain the white skin, and the night vision, and the fact that they're rarely ever seen. It would explain," he added, and

261

so quietly it was almost to himself, "a lot of things."

Laura said hoarsely, "Like why Cathy Sykes was killed." And she was remembering that cold dark place, water dripping. . . . *Oh, God, Christy* . . .

"Let me go down there," Ted said. "We have to check it out."

After a moment Sam shifted the rope coil off his shoulder. "I'll go."

Ted held his gaze. "Have you ever done any rappelling, Sheriff?"

"What's that got to do with anything?"

"I have. Which I guess makes me somewhat less than useless, doesn't it?" Ted took the rope from him and began fastening a harness.

Laura turned toward the entrance, looking out into the lighter darkness beyond. The trees stood like gray ghosts marching in formation, their leaves rustling like shrouds. "It's right behind my house," she said softly. "This place, if this is where they live . . . I built my house right in the middle of their nest."

Sam looked up from winding his end of the rope around a small rock projection for better leverage. He said, "We don't know anything. And this isn't the same cave where—well, where the Sykes girl died."

"No," Laura agreed. But somehow she didn't think that mattered.

Ted slipped the rope over his head and tightened it around his chest. He handed his flashlight to Laura. "Try to keep the beam on the left side of the wall," he said. "That's where I thought I saw something."

She nodded, and Ted backed into the dark hole, holding the rope with both hands. She edged to the opening and sat on her heels, shining the beam down and to the left of Ted's face. Sam stood behind her, braced and holding the other end of the rope. She saw the rope jerk and tauten as Ted stepped off into the air. Her flashlight reflected off nothing but grayish-black rock.

"Okay!" Ted called up, just as she was about to shout to him. "Let out the slack."

Sam began to feed the rope.

For a time there was nothing except the sound of Ted's shoes striking the surface of the chimney. Laura angled the flashlight to shine deeper into the hole, but from her position she could only see about four feet down. The rope made a scraping sound over the ledge as Sam released more tension.

Laura spoke abruptly, her voice low. "I never should have had Christy. I thought I was being so modern and competent. I thought of all the women in the world I was the one best qualified to raise a child. What I was being was selfish. I wanted it all, and I never thought about what I had left over to give . . . like a normal family life, a childhood. I used to nurse her at my desk. She was attending board meetings when she was three months old. She never had a chance to be a kid."

She released a shaky breath. "She never asks about her father, you know that? She thinks it's normal for mommies to be alone. I've *raised* her to think like that. And then . . . moving every few months, never getting a chance to make friends. God, I've put her through so much."

Sam was silent for a moment. Then he said, "My parents weren't perfect. Were yours? I guess if we had to be licensed to have children, the population would die out in about a generation. Nobody's a perfect parent, Laura," he said gently. "Nobody does all

263

the right things all the time, though I think you've probably done them better than most. We just have to keep on doing the best we can because we're human, and maybe the best part of being human is to want the impossible for our kids."

Laura's lips tightened against a sudden trembling and she closed her eyes briefly. "I just want her back," she whispered. "I just want her *back*."

The sounds of Ted's movement stopped. He called, "I'm at the bottom. Hold on, I want to look around."

Sam shouted, "Damn it, Jacobs, get back up here!"

There was no reply. Sam swore softly and let out more rope when Ted tugged.

After only a few minutes, Ted pulled on the rope again. Laura balanced the flashlight on the ledge and went to help Sam draw him up.

Ted hoisted himself over the edge and slipped the harness off. His clothes were dirty and damp in places, but otherwise he appeared unharmed.

"Well?" Sam demanded impatiently. "Did you find anything?"

Ted reached into his pocket and withdrew something, handing it to Laura. Sam directed his flashlight beam on her hand as she examined it.

Laura's breath caught in a sound that was half wonder, half despair. The scrap of material was about six inches long. It could have been part of a ruffle or a sleeve. Soft cotton, with its distinctive pale pink stripe . . . "Christy's nightgown," Laura whispered. "The one she wore to bed tonight." She closed her hand around the cloth and couldn't say any more.

Ted looked from Laura to Sam. "There's more," he said quietly. "Footprints on the floor—big ones. There wasn't enough light for me to see where they lead, but there's another tunnel down there. I think what we have here is a cavern system. It probably runs underneath this whole mountain."

Laura's throat tightened convulsively. "She's down there. That thing—took her down there."

Ted said, "The chimney is only about twelve feet deep, and there are ledges on either side. The footholds may be too far apart for Laura, but you and I could probably get down without the rope."

"Christ," Sam said softly. He had never expected this. Not this.

Laura lifted her head. "I'll go first then," she said. "You two can bring the rope."

Sam looked at Ted. His respect for the other man was raised a notch when Ted volunteered, "I'll start down; send Laura a few feet behind me on the rope. I can help guide her to the handholds."

After a moment, Sam nodded.

Without another words, Ted started back down the chimney. Sam helped Laura adjust the harness around her waist. And he tried one more time. "You could wait here. There's no reason for you . . ."

She just looked at him.

Sam reached for the pistol at his belt. "Take this, then. We don't know what we're going to find down there."

Laura shook her head and touched the zippered pocket of her windbreaker. "I've got my own gun. Reloaded and ready to use."

He started to point out that her weapon had not proven very effective against the creature before, but then he stopped. He thought she knew that. And he thought that it might not be such a bad idea for each

265

of them to save a bullet for themselves, or for Christy, if they were too late.

He loved her so much in that moment that this chest ached.

He held the rope tight until he heard one set of footsteps strike the bottom, then another. Laura called up, "Okay!" He retrieved the rope, tied the three flashlights to it, and lowered them down. When they were received safely, he let the rest of the rope fall into the abyss.

"We're going to shine all three lights on the walls," Ted called up. "You should be able to see okay."

"Hold on," Sam replied.

He went to the entrance of the cave and breathed deeply for a moment of the fresh night air. It had begun to rain lightly, and the drops splattered on the overhead leaves like the footsteps of tiny animals, creeping through the branches. The night was as dark as any he had ever known.

He took the buck knife from his pocket and slashed a mark on the nearest tree, with his best representation of an arrow pointing toward the cave. Then he took his radio off his belt and placed it beneath the tree, protecting it as much as he could with the overhanging branches, and flipped the transmitter on. For as long as the batteries lasted, it might provide some kind of signal. But those were routine, by-the-book precautions; he didn't really expect them to do any good. He knew, as he suspected Laura and Ted had known from the beginning, that they were completely on their own.

For a moment he stood there, feeling the rain on his face, listening to the whisper of the breeze. The only thing he had ever asked from life was that he know what he was getting into. Now he was about to walk in tthe biggest unknown any man had ever faced, and he was scared.

He turned and went back into the cave.

Chapter Fifteen

Laura had never wondered what Hell was like; she had never believed in it or cared. But now she knew. Hell was a night so black no eye could penetrate it, cold with a dampness that clung to the bones, and it smelled like death. It was filled with echoes of whispers no voice made and the scuttling of creatures so alien the mind could not even imagine them. Hell was as old as the first primitive man who had sought refuge in the dark ancient crevices of the earth, and its memory was stamped in terror upon the unconscious of every human who had lived since.

Once Laura had been afraid of the woods, but they were only the portal, a shadowy reflection of what lay beneath. This was the real horror. This was the birthing place. Before the woods were even seedlings, this place had been. Before Man had first crawled out of the slime of primal ooze, this place had been. Forests had died and new ones had begun. Great beasts had risen and withered away. But the rocks endured, unscarred, unchanged. And even now the walls seemed to murmur, *We had you once. We can take you again.*

They were in a cavern, not large by the standards of such things, but high enough that their heads were in no danger of scraping the ceiling, and wide enough in most places for them to walk abreast. The footprints in the thin layer of clay at the bottom of the chimney led unmistakably across another threshold, into a black corridor that dipped and climbed, twisted and turned, narrowed and widened again. The footprints faded out on the hard rock floor, but the three of them continued to move forward. There was nothing else they could do.

Their combined flashlights illuminated an oval no more than three feet in front of them, and they moved very slowly, feeling their way along the walls in spots. Laura's socks were damp with blood and every step sent needles of pain through the soles of her feet, but she didn't mind the pain; she concentrated on it. That kept her from thinking about other things.

Sam said to Ted, "You knew about the caves, didn't you? You were looking for them. That's why you wanted to come."

It was a moment before Ted replied. "I suspected. Like I said, it was the only thing that made sense. As for why I wanted to come . . . well, that's a longer story."

They walked on through the dark, with their sliding, halting, shifting gaits, like zombies feeling their way up from the grave. Minutes passed, long and suffocating. Cold dampness seeped through Laura's windbreaker and prickled in her fingertips, crawling along the back of her neck.

Laura said, "No bats." Her voice echoed, even though she spoke softly. "Did you notice that? Bats are supposed to live in caves."

It was Ted who replied, and only after a long ominous silence. "Maybe not in this one."

Bats, handfuls of them, would make a convenient meal for cave-dwelling carnivores. Laura tensed against an icy shiver.

Their three flashlight beams, wavering and separating, looked like disembodied spirits floating along the cave wall. Even the air they breathed was thick with menace, tasting of rich wet soil and ancient rock, different from the outside air, only another reminder that they did not belong here. They were the aliens here, they were the invaders. They were walking into a trap from which there was no turning back.

And the silence. The silence was as heavy as the air, as oppressive as the dark. It rang with secrets, sharp-pointed arrows of truths that had been hidden too long. Guilt. Fear. Mistakes.

Laura's voice was low and shaky. "It's our fault. We shouldn't have come here. Tearing down the trees, bulldozing the mountain . . . we should have left it alone. We should have left *everything* alone."

It was a moment before Sam replied, tersely, "People have got a right to live where they want."

But his words had the bite of an accusation. Laura knew what he was thinking, what everyone had been thinking since Hugh Bullard had moved up here with his heavy equipment and his grandiose schemes for turning the wilderness into a paradise for people with too much money and not enough sense to realize what they were doing. They did not belong here. They had no place here. The mountain had been safe before they came here.

And then Sam spoke again, in a voice that was husky with suppressed bitterness. "Hell, do you think you're the only one that ever went looking for a safe place? Why do you think I ended up back here? We're all looking to be safe from something."

But there was no safe place, because the monsters were everywhere. She should have known.

Laura made a misstep on the sloping cave floor and pitched forward slightly. Sam caught her arm with far more force than necessary, and the inertia of his movement flung her back against the cave wall. "Damn it, be careful!" he shouted. "Don't you think we've got enough trouble without you breaking your leg?"

Ted swung his flashlight around to them, and in the illumination of his beam Laura stared at Sam. His face was taut and his eyes were angry; his hands bunched into fists.

Ted said, "Is everybody okay?"

Slowly, and with a visible effort, some of the tension left Sam's shoulders. He said briefly, "Yeah. Okay."

Ted turned his light away, but Laura did not move. And neither did Sam. He lifted his hand, rubbing at his jaw. "I didn't mean to shout at you."

His face was in shadow now, but the anguish in his voice was clear and sharp as he said lowly, "Damn it, Laura, I *knew*. Somewhere deep inside, all this time, I knew what was happening, I knew what these things were doing, but I was too scared—too stubborn and scared—to face up to it. If I had, if I had just once been able to take a chance on something I couldn't see, Christy might be here today. I promised to keep you safe." Now his voice was so low Laura could barely make out the words. "And I didn't."

Laura reached through the shadows for his hand. Her fingers brushed his sleeve, and drifted downwards until they touched his wrist. She said quietly,

271

"Christy was the one who really knew. I didn't believe her either."

His voice was heavy with an exhaustion deeper than physical. "I never knew about taking things on faith before. Never was able to . . . believe in things. Like Christy. And you. I should have. God damn it all. I should have."

Laura wanted to comfort him, but there was no comfort. For either of them. Slowly, she leaned forward until her forehead rested on his shoulder; after a moment his hand curved around her waist, and she felt his exhalation on her hair. Tired, worn out, overwhelmed, they rested against one another for a brief time. Then they started moving again.

Sam was in the lead when suddenly he stopped. "There's an overhang," he said. "Be careful." He braced his hand against the lowered ceiling to show them its height, and ducked under. He had only gone a few feet before he stopped again. Ted and Laura, coming up close behind him, immediately knew why.

The stench was overwhelming. Laura was reminded of hamburger left out too long to thaw on a hot day. Ted remembered an open-air meat market he had visited once in Mexico. For Sam the image was much simpler and more accurate: a slaughterhouse. Sick-sweet, rancid, not yet to the point of putrefaction but close. Dead things.

Sam took a step back, extending his arm to keep the others behind him. Laura could hear the soft hiss of his breath as he lifted his flashlight briefly to the point where the wall gave way into another chamber. He shifted the flashlight to his other hand and slid his pistol from its holster.

"Sam, no!"

He shrugged off her restraining grip and moved slowly forward.

But Laura was right behind him, joining her flashlight beam to his as they moved into the small chamber. What she saw caused the flashlight to tumble from her fingers and her breath to freeze in her throat. She wanted to scream. But she couldn't.

It was Cathy Sykes. Her eyes were glazed open and her face was sculpted into a mask of eternal agony, lips pulled back over blood-coated teeth, features distorted. There was only a dark stump where her right arm should have been, and her chest and abdominal cavities were sunken, collapsed into an empty vacuum of shredded ribs and clinging strands of muscle. Sam's light lingered for only a moment, as though in that first instant he was too stunned to move it, then he jerked the light away. But that brief glimpse was enough. The image was imprinted for a lifetime.

Laura stumbled back, flinging out a hand to support herself. Her fingers brushed something soft and furry and then she did scream, propelling herself forward. Ted caught her arm before she fell, but she pushed him away, wiping her hands on her jeans in a desperate effort to clean them and looking around wildly. She tried to choke back the tiny sobbing sounds that kept leaping to her throat.

Ted directed his light to the wall behind her, where her hand had gone. And then, slowly, joined by Sam's beam, the light moved around the chamber.

Every wall was stacked with bundles of some sort, four feet high from the floor, crisscrossed like firewood. At first Laura didn't understand. And then she saw that those bundles were the bodies of small animals. Squirrels, possums, raccoons. On the floor larger animals were spread out: a deer, a medium-sized dog, some kind of cat. And Cathy Sykes.

Ted said softly, "It's a bloody food locker."

Laura pushed past him and stumbled out of the chamber.

She slid down onto the floor, drawing up her knees and doubling her fists against her mouth to choke back sobs and bile. She was shaking uncontrollably. *Christy,* she thought. *My God, Christy . . .* Her child was in the hands of the creatures that had built that gruesome mausoleum, and Laura was helpless to reach her. Even now it might be too late, even now. . . .

Sam sat down beside her and slipped his arm around her shoulders, drawing her close.

"How can they live?" The words were uttered from deep within Laura's throat, almost swallowed by rage and horror. "How can those vile things *live?* If there's a God in heaven or any kind of rightness to the world, they shouldn't, they shouldn't even be allowed to live. . . ."

"I know," Sam said softly. "I know."

"Christy. Maybe the next room we come to she'll be there, cut up like that—"

"Laura, don't."

"But how do we know?" she cried. "How can we—"

Mommy, don't be scared.

Laura caught her breath. "Christy!"

She felt Sam's muscles tense and she raised a trembling hand to silence him. All her energy, all her concentration, was focused inward, desperately searching, hoping. "Christy," she whispered. "Oh, baby, where are you? Talk to me, please. . . ."

Don't be scared, Mommy, the little voice repeated. It seemed to Laura Christy was so close she could smell her. *The mother monster is taking care of me. They like me.*

A chill went through Laura that felt like icy fingers, squeezing off the pump of her heart. "Christy, baby, tell Mommy where you are. Think, honey," she whispered desperately. "Tell me where you are so I can come get you."

There was nothing but an answering confusion. And then, almost fretfully, *My head hurts. I want to go home.*

The contact faded away.

Laura released a shuddering breath. Her heart started beating again, with such force that it hurt. "She's okay," she managed after a moment. "She's okay but—it still has her. And she's not even scared." Her breath made a hitching sound in her throat. "Why isn't she scared?"

Sam was silent for a moment. "Maybe . . . it's like anything else. Not so bad, once you look it in the face."

She started trembling again, violently. Sam chafed her arm, holding her close, and his expression was intense. "Laura," he said, "I'm sorry, but you've got to be sure. It's important. And—you've never been able to . . . well, to talk to Christy like this before, have you?"

Laura shook her head, gulping for a deep breath, trying to steady her voice. "Not—like this. Not that I could hear her in my head. But . . ." And she looked up at Sam, finally managing to control the shudders. "She's never been lost and hurt before. Nothing like this has ever happened before."

After a moment, Sam nodded. It was not an easy acceptance, but it was firm, an indication of commitment from which there was no turning back. And with that gesture a bond was formed between them, something to hold on to now and for the rest of their lives.

He said, "Then she's alive. We know that much at least. Could she tell you where she was?"

Laura shook her head, leaning against him. "She's warm." She spoke on an instinct without knowing where the impression had come from, but knowing just as surely that it was right. "She's lying on something soft, and warm. . . . But it's dark, and the sound of dripping water . . . . I think she's still down here, somewhere. She said. . . ." Her throat closed up with an abrupt clicking sound. It was a moment before she could speak again. "She said it was taking care of her."

Sam's arm tightened around her. The silence was long and heavy.

Ted Jacobs had come out to stand beside them. Sam glanced up at him. He seemed to wrestle with a decision for a moment, and then said brusquely, "You seem to know more about these things than any of us, Jacobs. What do you think?"

Ted looked at him for a moment as though the question did not register, and Sam repeated, more forcefully, "What the hell *is* it we're after?"

A frown drew the edges of Ted's brows together. He seemed distant, preoccupied, and greatly shaken. He said softly, almost to himself, "A very strong, very efficient killing machine."

His eyes went to Laura, then to Sam. The expression there, flat, numb with shock, and wholly resigned, made Laura want to recoil, and she wasn't sure why.

His tone was as dull as his eyes as he said, "I think

276

you know what they are, Sheriff. I think we all do."

No one said anything. Somewhere, very far off, Laura thought she could hear water dripping. Seconds spun out.

Then Ted straightened his shoulders, and looked Sam straight in the eye. Laura thought she saw the faintest hint of a smile. "You're going to make me say it, aren't you? I guess I deserve that." He knelt beside them, and his voice, though it still seemed hollow, was very calm.

"In 1926," he began, "a doctor by the name of Evert Clausen wrote a book of essays about unusual diseases. One of them had to do with the years he spent here in Calumit during the last part of the century, and a woman named Alice Cobb who gave birth to a deformed male child. Dr. Clausen diagnosed the condition as cephalonia and giantism, which I think was probably fairly accurate. In his own words, though, 'It was the most monstrous thing I'd ever seen, and I could only pray God would take it quickly and mercifully from this life.' "

Ted paused, gathering a breath. His face was eerily illuminated by the glow of the flashlights, distant and introspective. Laura stared at him, confused and uncertain.

"Clausen wasn't surprised when, a few days later, he learned the child had died. Some years after that, the stories started—howlings in the night, strange things going on out at the edge of the woods, where the Cobb place was. The child hadn't died, you see. it had been kept locked up, for over fifteen years, in a shed at the back of the house."

Ted looked at Sam, then at Laura. His face was sober, his eyes unreadable. "Idiocy is usually an offshoot of cephalonia," he explained. "And giantism—

well, it's a very painful condition. The joints and tissues strain to lengths they were never meant to reach, the body is incredibly large and out of proportion, often there's some deformity of the spine . . . and the victim suffers almost constantly. It's rare that anyone with that condition lives beyond his twenties. But the diagnosis was made a long time ago, and there may have been factors at work we don't know about."

Sam was very still beside Laura, listening intently. Laura looked from him to Ted impatiently. But then Ted went on. "To make a long story short, the boy did live past adolescence, and he bred with his own sister — maybe rape, maybe not, nobody will ever know. His sister, Jess, was what the local folks used to call 'not right in the head,' so you can see there wasn't a very strong gene pool there to start with. She had a child, a girl, and according to the reports, it bore the same genetic deficiencies as its father. The girl was ten years old when the secret finally got out. The townspeople found out. They came to the house with torches. Jess Cobb and her mother died in the flames. Hal Cobb was shot trying to defend his family. But the children — the monsters they had come there to kill — escaped. The townspeople hunted them down for days, but they never found them."

The echo of Ted's voice lingered, and finally faded. Into the silence Sam said softly, in a choked, muffled tone, "Jesus Christ."

Ted looked at him. "Why so surprised, Sheriff? This is your place, right? You know these people. It probably wasn't the first time something like that had happened. It could happen again." And then he dropped his eyes. "In a way, it's not that much different from what we've been doing and thinking these

278

last few weeks ourselves. From what we're doing now."

Sam's voice was hoarse and filled with denial. "I never heard anything about it. I've been living here most of my life and—"

"No, you probably haven't," Ted agreed. "Nobody ever talked about it. Even Dr. Clausen wouldn't allow his book to be published until after his death. There was a lot of guilt between the lines, a lot of horror." He released a breath. "This mountain is full of stories about monsters and Indian legends and Nighteaters . . . but not one word about the night a whole settlement joined together to burn down a house, kill three innocent people, and drive two children into the woods to die."

The silence was long and suffocating. Water dripping. The sound of breathing. And Laura felt as though she had been pummeled over the head repeatedly with some soft, muffled object. She couldn't think. She couldn't take it in. None of it made sense.

Then Ted went on. "It's only speculation from there. They survived, obviously. Scared, they hid during the day and came out at night. They took to the caves for shelter and warmth. They may have been medical idiots, but they weren't unintelligent— they knew how to hunt and kill, use rudimentary tools even. . . ." He stopped himself from glancing over his shoulder, toward what he had so aptly dubbed the food locker. "Preserve their food, to an extent. I suppose they must have had some grasp of language at first, but that probably deteriorated over the years, just as all the elements of civilization do when survival consumes every waking moment. Gradually, they evolved backwards, as it were, into the animal state that's the basis of us all."

"Tarzan," Sam murmured.

Ted looked at him.

Sam seemed a little embarrassed as he explained, "Like Tarzan. Raised in the jungle, by animals—you can only become what you know."

"Something like that," Ted agreed.

Laura couldn't stand it anymore. She looked from Sam to Ted, and her voice was a little wild as she cried, "What are you saying? Do you know what you're saying? That those things are—human, just like us? It's crazy! You *saw* one of them!" she shouted at Ted. "I saw one! I *smelled* it. It wasn't human, you know it wasn't!"

"Yes, I saw it," Ted agreed quietly. "And my reaction, just like yours—just like that of everyone who's ever seen a double amputee or a severely retarded adult or a child born without arms or legs—was to recoil in horror and to think, in whatever secret part of your mind you can't control, *monster*. Because in our species only the strong survive. We push out the weak and deformed because we can't afford to acknowledge them. We're scared of them."

Laura saw the muscles of Sam's jaw tighten, and she felt the ice grip the back of her spine again. Swiftly, with all the clarity of a remembered nightmare, she saw the face of that thing, she heard its cry, she smelled its scent—and just as swiftly, she blocked it out. She didn't want to know. That was the answer. *She didn't want to know.*

Her voice was tight as she insisted, "The smell—"

"When the white man first came to America," Sam said slowly, "they used to complain about the way the Indians smelled. And the Indians had a lot more complaining to do about the way the white men

280

smelled. It was something about their diets being different."

He glanced at Ted as though for confirmation, and Ted nodded.

Laura began to shake her head, adamantly, back and forth. "No. It can't be—they can't be—they're not human! They're killers—"

"And we're not?"

"They're monsters!" she cried. "They—" And she made an inarticulate sound and gestured toward the cave behind them, where Cathy Sykes' mutilated body lay.

Ted looked at her gravely. "They kill out of anger, of hunger . . . and they eat what they kill. That doesn't make them less than human. We invaded their territory, we pushed the game out, so they had to turn to other sources of food. Maybe they don't even recognize us as the same species anymore. Maybe it doesn't matter. Why," he asked softly, as much of himself as anyone else, "is it so much easier to believe they're monsters than that they're a part of us?"

But Laura knew the answer to that. Because nothing was more cruel, more determined or ruthless than man, because human beings were the true master of evil, because sometimes it was better to believe in what you didn't know than to face what you did. Because *they had Christy.* . . .

Her voice was shaking as she tried to push back the desperation. "But—it can't be the same two people. They couldn't have lived that long."

"Hunger and procreation are the two most immutable human drives," Ted said. "Survival."

"And they kept interbreeding," Sam said. "This thing—this cephalonia thing. It's hereditary?"

For the first time, Ted looked uncertain. "It must have been, in this case. How, I don't know. But that's another reason I got out of medicine. Too many things I couldn't explain."

It all sounded so facile, so logical and right . . . yet there was something wrong. Something that did not make sense, something that didn't quite fit . . . or maybe she just didn't want to believe it. Because Ted was right, and there was something in everyone that instinctively recoiled from seeing a part of themselves mirrored in deformity and abnormality. And because it was easier to believe in monsters than the limitless capacity for human aberration.

Ted inhaled deeply, straightening out his shoulders. "One thing I do know," he said. "They're strong, they're fast—they're human. The best hunters in the forest. I don't think we can afford to underestimate them."

For a long moment no one spoke, and the implications sank in slowly, unavoidably. Then Sam got to his feet, and slung the shotgun over his shoulder. "Maybe," he said. "But nobody's ever hunted them before."

He extended his hand to Laura, and they started moving forward again.

Minnie Sykes was not afraid to be in the woods at night. Maybe she was blessed, maybe she was cursed. But her destiny was not to meet her end at the hands of those creatures that prowled the night forest and drank the blood of the unwary. She knew that, and she was unafraid.

She did not know much about explosives, that was true. But her third husband had been in construction, and when he needed to blast out a stump or a rock from a field he was clearing, he'd bring home dynamite. She'd helped him once or twice. She knew how to tie bundles and splice fuses.

And she knew their hiding place, their secret hovels, the holes in the ground that led to the network of caverns where they lived. She knew from her childhood, and from the legends, knowledge passed down from generation to generation that she had never imagined to use.

She trudged through the wet night with the bundles of dynamite shrouded in a plastic garbage bag, and she was tired, Lord, she was tired, and soaked to the bone, and numb with misery. The cave entrances were hard to find in the dark, and sometimes her memory failed her, causing her to retrace her steps. The helicopters with their bright searchlights proved an added annoyance, forcing her to waste time hiding from them.

But she did not give up, not once did she think of turning back. She had until daybreak, when those things returned to their nests. Then she would light the fuses, and nothing would ever come out of the caves again.

They had come to a dead end. Laura couldn't believe it. Frantically she cast her light back and forth. The corridor they had been following ended abruptly on a ledge overlooking a stream, fast-flowing and swollen, that rushed through the channel it had carved for itself in the opposite wall. To her right was nothing but solid rock; to her left more rock, but this time in the form of rubble, crushed granite, and scattered boulders piled to the ceiling.

"No," she said. And then, more loudly, "No! It's not possible! They had to have come this way, there was no place else to go! The cave can't just stop, it can't just disappear. There has to be a way through!"

Ted looked at Sam worriedly. "Could we have missed a turn?"

Sam shook his head and walked over to the rubble pile. "She's right. This is the only way down and we followed it all the way."

He shone his light over the tumbled rocks, and brushed a few of the smaller ones away. They hit the stone floor with a popping sound. "Cave-in," he said. "Probably the same one that . . . the one that happened this afternoon."

Laura stared at him. "How is that possible? We're on the opposite side of the mountain."

Sam checked his compass again. "No. We've been moving more or less steadily southwest. We should be pretty close to the site of the cave-in now, if not right on top of it."

"It doesn't matter," Ted pointed out. "If the tunnel goes on behind there, it's been closed since this afternoon. Christy's kidnapper couldn't have gotten through there, anymore than we can."

That was a strange way to put it: *Christy's kidnapper.* Laura suppressed a shudder. Easier to believe in monsters . . .

Sam said, "Not necessarily. The blasting caused the first cave-in, I'd bet my life on that. But there could have been aftershocks, a delayed effect on weaker parts of the cave. Maybe this happened recently."

Laura looked at them both in despair. To turn back now . . . They *couldn't* turn back now!

Echoing her thoughts, Sam said, "At any rate, we don't have any choice. Let's see how much of this we

284

can move."

Laura did not know how long they worked. Hours. A lifetime. Several lifetimes. There was no measurement of time in Hell. This was eternity.

She was numb, exhausted beyond caring. Her hands, as well as her feet, were bleeding now, and her fingers had been crushed and pinched so many times she could no longer distinguish the separate bruises. Her shoulder muscles, her arms, her back were stripped, and her eyes felt like they were lined with sandpaper; she tasted grit in her mouth and her nose was clogged with dirt. And then they felt that first faint puff of air that indicated the other side of the breach was, indeed, hollow. They had broken through.

Sam shone his flashlight through the spool-sized hole, but could see nothing. They kept on working, prying away the small rocks with their fingers, pushing the big ones down with their feet and their shoulders.

Once Sam inquired, "Christy?"

Laura shook her head. "It's been so long. I don't know—how badly she was hurt. Maybe . . . what if she goes into a coma or something?"

Ted glanced at her, but said nothing.

Sam's voice was gentle. "It's late for a little girl. Probably she's just sleeping."

Then Ted did speak up, pausing in his work. "I didn't want to ask before, but—are you saying your little girl is some kind of telepath?"

Laura shook her head. "No. Just—sometimes we know what each other's thinking, and—those creatures . . ."

285

"She was in communication with them?" Ted's voice was quick with interest.

Laura bent her back to another boulder.

"It's possible, I suppose," Ted murmured, half to himself, "that the same genetic defect that caused the deformity could have reactivated a sixth sense . . . the kind anthropologists say we all used to have, until we outgrew the need for it. Telepathy, ESP—instinct, really. And when they found they could communicate with your little girl . . ."

He turned back to his work, his voice strained with the force of the rock he was trying to lift. "Do you think that's why they took her?"

Laura drew her arm across her face, biting her lip with the pain that shot through her back as she tried to straighten up. "I don't know," she managed after a breath. "Christy understood them. Somehow . . . I don't know. But it must have meant something."

"Animals," Sam said thoughtfully, almost to himself. "She always seemed to have a—thing with animals."

Laura paused, turning that over in her mind. "Remember . . . you said once all children are savages at heart?" Reaching back toward that day, with sunshine bouncing off the sidewalk and Christy skipping beside her in her Big Bird overalls, was like straining toward another lifetime. Merely remembering made Laura's chest hurt. "Maybe . . ." Her throat was thick and she had to try again. "Maybe they understand things that we're too sophisticated to see."

"Or that we don't want to see," Ted put in quietly.

Laura tightened her lips and put more effort into the rock she was trying to shift. It moved a few inches, but she stumbled and almost lost her balance as she bent over again.

"Why don't you take a break?" Sam suggested. "We've still got a long way to go."

"No. We've got to keep working. All of us." But as she tried to move a rock that was lodged at the base of the pile, her legs gave way completely and she fell to her knees. She beat her fists against the rock once, biting back tears of rage and frustration.

Sam said, "All right. But first, bring me the canteen. Have a drink for yourself too."

Laura did not even have the strength to nod. She got up and pushed herself away from the wall, toward the supplies.

It happened in an instant. Sam shouted, "Look out!" And Laura turned to see that the rock Ted had dislodged had disturbed a small avalanches of others. Sam leapt toward Ted, shoving him out of the way, and they both fell to the ground beneath a shower of rubble.

Laura fought her way to them through a fog of dust that spiraled and floated like a flock of blackbirds in the light from the flashlights. Both men were coughing, struggling to get up. "Are you all right?" Ted demanded.

"Yeah." But Sam grimaced as he sat up, his hand automatically going to his right leg. "Make that maybe. My foot is stuck."

Laura joined Ted in clearing away some of the debris, and saw that the large stone that had trapped Sam's foot was partially wedged against two others, offering a handhold. Laura lent her efforts to Ted's, and they managed to lift the stone enough for Sam to wriggle free. But the effort it cost him was evident in the look of excruciation on his face when he moved.

"Is it broken?"

"Only in about five places, from the feel of it."

Sam's voice was tight, and the muscles of his jaw stiffened as he reached down to massage the area just above the top of his boot. "Well," he managed in a moment, "at least it's not fatal."

Laura brought the canteen to him and he took a sip. His face was ash-white.

"It should be splinted," Ted said.

"Splints I forgot to bring." Sam took another sip from the canteen. "I'll test my weight on it in a minute. Maybe it's not too bad." Using his hands, he slid backwards until he could rest his head against the wall. He closed his eyes.

Ted went to examine the contents of the first-aid kit.

Laura sat close to Sam, and in a moment slipped her arm beneath his head, bringing it to rest on her shoulder. She said, "It's bad, isn't it?"

He looked up at her and managed a crooked smile. "With this kind of treatment, I could have a miraculous recovery in no time."

Exhaustion defeated her; even coherent thought seemed beyond her reach. Without Sam, they had no chance. Ted might be smart, and physically capable, but he was as lost in these caverns as she was. He shouldn't even have been here. It was Sam they had counted on to guide them, to defend them, to make the decisions. Without doing anything at all, he was their strength. And now Laura could not see beyond the next minute.

Laura leaned her head back against the wall. "You know," she said quietly, "at the time, I thought being attacked by that man with the knife was the worst thing that could ever happen to me. All these years, I've let that one pathetic little bastard run my life, telling me where I could live, where I could go,

288

whether I could sleep at night . . . and now it all seems so small. So unimportant. Like it happened to someone else."

"Maybe," Sam said, and winced a little at an involuntary movement of his leg, "if you'd had a chance to fight back then, he wouldn't have had a hold on you for so long."

Laura entwined her fingers through his. "I don't ever want to be that helpless again."

Sam's fingers tightened on hers. "You've never been helpless," he said.

In that moment she believed him. She had to.

Ted came back over and knelt beside them. "Aspirin," he said, and shook out four of the pills into the bottle cap. "It's all I could find. Better take them; I'm going to have to try to immobilize that foot, and it's going to get worse before it gets better."

Sam took the pills with water, and Laura helped Ted form a rough immobilizing bandage out of the flannel linings from their jackets and tightly wound adhesive tape. Ted elected to leave Sam's boot on for extra support, and wrapped it from the outside, cutting a narrow slit through the top of the leather to allow for the swelling that had already begun. Sam suffered through their somewhat clumsy ministrations stoically, and when they were finished they all knew the job was less than worthless. Laura saw the frustration and helplessness in Ted's eyes and the exhaustion of agony in Sam's, and she suddenly wasn't sure how much more she could stand. How much more any of them could stand.

She sat back against the wall, smoothing Sam's damp hair away from his forehead. Ted's eyes followed the gesture and recognized the intimacy, but she didn't care. She said, "You know what this is

289

like?" Her voice had an eerie, echoing quality above the sound of rushing water. "Like that game we used to play in college. Dungeons and Dragons. You keep going deeper and deeper and every corner you turn there's some new horror, something else to worry about, something that's going to get you if you don't think fast. You never get a chance to just rest, and think. You just keep going on and on, racking up the points for survival. But you never win."

Ted's voice was thoughtful. "I used to kill off my character. It made me feel like I had won."

Laura glanced at him. "That's against the rules."

He just smiled, and shrugged.

Sam said, with an effort, "I never went to college. I'm beginning to think I didn't miss anything."

Laura stood abruptly. "Maybe the fall opened the hole a little more," she said. "I'll go check."

When she was gone, Ted sat back on his heels and said quietly, "I already checked. The hole's a little wider, but the crawl space is less than sixteen inches deep on the other side. I think we both know an animal of the size we're talking about couldn't have gotten through there, much less carrying somebody else."

"Shit," Sam said wearily.

"We've been wasting our time," Ted agreed. "There's no way through."

Sam's eyes moved to the stream. "There's got to be a way through. *It* came through."

"I don't understand."

Sam followed the movement of the stream as it rushed through the cave wall. "It was raining just before we started down. The first good rain we've had in weeks. This streambed could have been dry a few hours ago."

Ted was silent for a long time. Then he started to push to his feet. "Well. I guess somebody ought to check it out."

Sam grabbed his arm. "What do you think you're going to do?"

Ted informed him mildly, "I'm going to swim underwater and see where that passage comes out."

"And if it doesn't?"

He barely hesitated. "Then it doesn't."

Sam gritted his teeth against the pain as he pushed himself up straighter. "Damn it, Jacobs, what are you trying to prove? Is this some kind of personal quest for you or something? Are you trying to get yourself killed, is that what you want?"

Ted smiled, and for the first time almost seemed to relax. "No, I don't particularly want to die. And if it's a quest—well, no more for me than for you. For any of us."

He looked away for a moment, and back again. Then he said seriously, "I'll tell you something, Sheriff. I was never meant to be a surgeon. I could never accept the fact that the best approach to any problem was to attack it with a weapon. I kept thinking there should be more we could do—and when I found out there wasn't, I stopped practicing medicine. Every time I took a patient I had to face the fact that I might lose him, and I couldn't stand up to that. So I quit."

Laura had returned, but Ted did not notice. His tone had fallen, and his expression was very far away. "One day, some years later, I was out with a friend, and there was a street accident. A little girl was hit by a car. There was massive bleeding from the mouth and nose, crushed ribs. She was alive, but barely. My—friend kept pleading with me to do something, he kept shouting, 'But you're a doctor!' It didn't matter that I wasn't licensed to practice, that I hadn't practiced in years. Everyone in the crowd turned to stare, and I walked away. I knew there was nothing I could do for her. I left her to die. It was easier, somehow," he finished softly, "than trying and failing. It's always been easier to just walk away from the important things."

The silence was heavy, choking, as black as the depths of the earth in which they were buried. And then Ted went on, in a slightly stronger voice. "This thing is important. Maybe I can help. Maybe all I can do is look it in the face. But that'll be enough."

Laura spoke quietly, her voice tense with challenge and anxiety. "What do you think you're going to find? Is this some kind of scientific mission for you? Do you think you're going to be able to bring back one of those monsters on a slab and have a university named after you, is that it?"

Ted shook his head, and the reflected light of a low-burning flashlight showed the faint, sad curve of his lips. "No," he said. "I don't want to bring anything back. As for what I expect to find . . ." He picked up a handful of gravel and let it scatter, then got to his feet. "Maybe it's nothing more than the dark part of myself. The part we're all afraid to look at in the light of day."

"Don't be a fool, Jacobs," Sam said roughly. He braced his hands against the wall and set his teeth against the pain as he pushed to his feet. "This is no time to be spouting your goddamn philosophical drivel, and we don't need any false heroes. That thing is real out there! It's not going to stop at ripping your guts out anymore than it did with Kellerman or with Cathy Sykes. This is not the place to work out your personal problems."

"Oh, no?" Ted turned a look on him that was slightly quizzical. "But isn't that just what you're doing? You may think you came down here hunting a killer, but what you're really stalking is the thing you're most afraid of. The only difference between you and me is that your solution is to kill it with a gun."

"And you can cut out the left-wing bullshit too," Sam said sharply, but even Laura could tell he wasn't really angry. He was in too much pain to feel such an emotion, and even if he did, he wouldn't waste time arguing about it. He was stalling, trying to give Ted a chance to recover his good sense before he committed himself to something he would regret. "The thing we're up against has teeth and claws," Sam went on tightly, "and it's not going to be impressed by your smooth talking ways. We all kill to survive, Jacobs."

Ted looked almost amused. "Yes," he agreed softly. "We do, don't we?"

He walked over and picked up the rope. His movements were easy, his tone normal. "Don't worry," he said, "I'm not suffering from cave fever or whatever madness overtakes people who've been locked in the dark too long. I know what I'm getting into, and all that philosophical drivel and left-wing bullshit was just a little something for you to remember me by." He came back over to where Sam was standing, unwinding the rope. "Do you think you're steady enough to hold this end secure?"

"You're crazy, Jacobs. You don't know how wide the opening is or how long the stream is or if it ever breaks ground. You could drown."

"That's what the rope's for. If I get into trouble,

293

you pull me back. At least we'll know."

Laura looked at the stream that rushed into nowhere. The thought of going into that black place was inconceivable to her. "You've got to be out of your mind," she said. "No one can get through there! The opening in the wall is bigger, if we keep working at it we can get through—"

Ted glanced at her briefly. "Maybe. And if this doesn't work, that's what we'll have to do. But it's worth a shot."

"Wait for the water to go down," Sam said.

Ted was busy tying another harness. "Do we really have that kind of time?"

Neither of them had an answer for that.

Sam and Laura worked to tie off the rope to one of the heavy rocks while Ted secured the harness around his waist. He sat down on the ledge to remove his shoes and socks.

Using the stock of his rifle for balance, Sam hobbled over to him. "Here," he said, reaching into the pocket of his jacket. "Use this flashlight. It's supposed to be waterproof. Button it inside your shirt."

Ted took it with a brief glance of acknowledgment.

"And this." Sam held out the buck knife.

For a moment the two men's eyes met and Laura, from her position behind them, could not guess what message passed between them. Then Ted said, "Thanks," and accepted the knife.

"You've got a little over a hundred yards of rope," Sam said. "Any longer than that and—"

"Yeah, I know." Ted snapped the knife onto his belt and rechecked the harness. "Three sharp tugs and you pull me back."

He looked at them for a moment as though he were trying to think of something else to say. And

294

then, with a small smile and a shake of his head, he said only, "What do you know? No famous last words."

Then he walked to the edge of the ledge and jumped feetfirst into the water.

Cold. He hadn't counted on the white-ice cold that burst through him in a flash of pain that seemed to turn his cells inside out. Precious bubbles of air were lost with the shock, and only by a miracle did he retain the presence of mind to keep from inhaling water. The black current swept him along and he was helpless to fight it. He was thrown against a sharp protrusion in the wall, but his body was so numb he didn't even feel the impact. Move. He had to move. His arms were like lead weights and he couldn't feel his feet. He concentrated fiercely on kicking out, on pushing his arms into swimming strokes.

He opened his eyes but saw nothing; felt nothing but the pressure of icy water against them. Dark and silent, a roar of heaviness against his ears. His lungs were burning. He twisted and writhed, angling himself upwards, clumsily seeking the surface. He flung his arm over his head, seeking the top . . . and his palm met solid rock. There was no top.

Lungs bursting now, he caught the rhythm of the current, swimming forward. He tried not to think about how much longer he could hold his breath. He did not think once about tugging for assistance. It couldn't be much further.

The current seemed faster. He could feel backlashes slapping at his hands and face. That could indicate a change in course, approaching shallows, the end. He struggled forward. And suddenly he stopped moving.

He twisted around, feeling for the rope. It was taut, caught on something, or having reached its end. His chest was on fire, sparks burst before his eyes. He grasped the rope in both hands and pulled. A rush of carbon dioxide bubbles escaped his mouth. Desperately, he tugged sharply three times. Nothing happened. He started to retrace the rope, pulling himself backwards. To die like this, for nothing, without ever having seen the face of what he sought . . . There was a strange sort of justice in that. He almost should have known.

The rope was stuck, wedged between a narrow outcropping and the inner wall. Gray waves rushed and receded behind his closed eyes. He couldn't feel his fingers. He struggled futilely for a moment to free the rope, but couldn't get a grip on it. In a moment he would lose consciousness. He had no choice.

He fumbled for the knife at his belt; he cut the rope. The current caught him and jerked him free, and Ted tumbled forward into the blackest night he had ever known.

Chapter Sixteen

"It's been too long," Laura said hoarsely.

Frantically, they started pulling the rope in, but knew they were too late the moment they felt the slack. When Sam held the severed end of the rope in his hand, the only sound was Laura's stifled sob.

The whispery roar of the stream was the sound of silence, thick, black, and endless. It rushed and sighed and swept on and on, and left only emptiness in its wake.

"How many more?" Laura said shakily. "How many more have to die?"

Sam looked up at the rope a moment longer, then let it drop. His face was set with pain and his tone was grim as he pivoted back toward the cave-in. "Let's get back to work," he said.

The opening they had broken through was about midway up the wall. Laura had to climb on the rock pile, wriggling her body through the opening and prying away loose dirt and stones with her fingers while Sam cleared the debris from the outside. His face was white and beaded with perspiration, and he had to stop more and more frequently to rest.

Finally Laura slid down and said, "I think it's wide enough to crawl through. It looks like there's a downslope about twenty feet or so ahead, more room. Can you make it?"

Sam's expression was a fair imitation of a brave smile. "Easier to crawl than to walk."

Laura took one of the flashlights and Sam's shotgun and pushed them along in front of her. The opening was so narrow that she could hear Sam's shoulders scrape against the top; several times he had to pause and shift position to free himself. So far they had been lucky. The cave-in on this side had consisted mostly of earth and loose rock. But if they came up against an impediment of the sort that had kept rescuers working for five hours trying to free Cathy Sykes, if, in fact, this tunnel led nowhere except to that blocked-up cave entrance . . .

But it didn't. There was a downward slope, just as Laura had expected, a gradual decline of broken stone that led into another chamber, which was almost tall enough to stand up in. That this chamber had once been even larger was evident by the tumbled rocks and fallen earth that lined the floor. Remnants of the broken ceiling crunched beneath Laura's hands and feet as she tried to stand up.

But it was not the evidence of recent destruction that made her freeze in position, every sense prickling into alertness with a wash of hot fear. "Sam!" she whispered.

"I know." His voice was quiet and steady behind her. He got into a semi-crouch position and extended his hand for the shotgun. "I smell it too."

It was a sour, old, faintly sulfurous odor: ancient earth and decaying meat underlined with the faint oily scent of old blood. Repugnant. Cloying. And horribly familiar.

Laura passed him the weapon and gripped the

298

flashlight with both hands. She didn't dare to breathe as she moved the unsteady beam slowly, carefully, across the chamber. Dusty walls. There, a dark patch, indicating another corridor. She turned the beam to the floor, and picked up the glint of something white.

Hesitantly, almost paralyzed with fear, she moved the light along the object. The curve of clinched fingers, an outstretched arm. The arch of a shoulder and part of a back. A small round head. Half-buried beneath a pile of broken rock, it was still. Dead.

Sam lowered the rifle cautiously. Dragging his right foot behind him and clenching his teeth against the pain, he made his way over to the small form. He knelt down and began to move away some of the rocks.

"My God," whispered Laura. The flashlight shook in her hand. "It's no bigger than Christy. It's one of them, but it's—"

"A child," Sam said lowly.

He straightened up, his expression stunned and disbelieving. Slowly he began to move his flashlight around.

There was another body crumpled against the wall, its head crushed and its limbs mangled. There were four in all, some smaller, some a little larger. They were all dead.

Sam propped himself against the wall, his shoulders sagging. Strangely, he remembered Deeanne Keller-man, striding into his office with her eyes on fire . . . then the memory got all jumbled up with the vision of Laura, laughing as she tickled Christy on the staircase, and his chest ached; his head ached.

"Children," he said. His voice was heavy, numb with shock. "We killed their children."

And Laura remembered. That sick, debilitating

299

sense of loss, the awful sorrow . . . *The babies are dead, Mommy!* She had to turn away, shaking. All dead . . .

Sam reached for her and she came into his arms. They held each other, silently seeking strength neither of them had to offer. The warmth of another human being, the sound of another's breathing, the beating of a similar heart. They held on to one another.

After a long time, Laura said dully, "You were the only one. The only one who knew, who kept believing they were human. Just like us."

"No." Sam's voice was weary. "After I saw it—it was too easy to believe in legends. If I'd ever really believed that what I was dealing with was real, I would've done something sooner. I was no different from anybody else. Scared."

Laura looked around in quiet, heavy despair at the tomb of infants. "Oh, Sam," she said softly, "I don't know who the monsters are anymore."

They did not speak for a long time. Then Laura said, "What time do you think it is?"

Sam had neither the energy or the inclination to remove his arm from around her to look at his watch. "Not long before dawn, I guess."

Laura turned her head on his shoulder, gazing without interest toward the opposite wall, and the dark opening that was yet another tunnel. She wanted to stay like this, wrapped in his arms, forever. She wanted to close her eyes and let time spin away, thinking nothing, feeling nothing except the comfort of his warmth, and drift into sleep and never wake up again.

"Morning," she said. "I can't even remember what it looks like. What it feels like." It seemed to her in that moment that she would never see morning again, and the worst was that she didn't even care.

She said softly, "I don't know if I can go on."

For a moment Sam didn't respond. And then, slowly, his arms tightened about her. "You'll go on," he said. "Because if you don't, I can't. And Christy needs us. She needs us both."

The words were spoken with an effort, and they sounded hollow at first, unconvincing. But an effort was all it took.

She would go on, because she had to. And because she didn't have to go alone.

She said, very softly, "Someday, if we get out of here, maybe you'll ask me to make love with you. And I'll say yes."

He bent his head, and she felt the touch of his lips upon her hair. "We'll get out of here," he said. "And I'll ask you."

After a very long time, they moved away from each other. Sam pushed away from the wall and directed his beam toward the corridor. Without another word, they started moving again.

When Ted broke the surface of the water, it took all the strength remaining in his limbs to catch the ledge and pull himself upward. There he lay, stunned and only half-conscious, for an interminable amount of time.

It was a distant, distinct rumbling sound that roused him. A faint but definite shifting of the earth. Fading, as his consciousness was fading. But then again, closer now. A few pebbles scattered across his face. He made himself sit up.

His body was such a mass of sharp aches and dull agony that it was hard to distinguish one pain from the other. He knew he had some broken ribs. Blood had matted his face on one side from a cut on the head. And he was cold. So cold. Hypothermia was imminent, and he retained enough reason to know that the only way he could fight it was to keep moving.

He remembered the flashlight in his shirt. He hadn't lost it, and though it took two tries with his jerky fingers to push the switch, it was still working. He dragged himself to his feet and stumbled down the corridor blindly, following the course of the diminishing stream.

And the earth rumbled again.

Laura shrank back against the wall as a shower of loose dirt was shaken from overhead. She tried to keep the panic out of her voice. "Earthquake?"

Sam shook his head. He was breathing hard, but trying to disguise it; his face was marble-white and shiny with sweat. "Not likely. Anyway, it's too regular. Like explosions."

"They wouldn't be blasting again, not after what happened!"

Again Sam shook his head, checking the luminous dial of his watch. "It's not even six a.m. Barely light out." He braced his hand against her back. His voice was tight, though whether it was from pain or anxiety she could not tell. "Laura, we'd better keep moving. I don't know what's going on, but I don't like the sound of it. We may not have much more time."

He stumbled and let out a sharp cry of pain; Laura caught him with both arms around his waist. She could feel then that he was shivering, though his skin against hers felt hot. "You've got a fever," she said urgently. "Sam, you can't—"

"What?" he demanded sharply, bracing his hand against the wall. "Go on?" His eyes were ferocious in the shadows of her flashlight beam and his breath was choppy. But there was no sign of defeat. "Seems to me we've had this conversation, Laura."

After a moment she nodded, biting her lip. She slipped her arm around his waist. "Lean on me," she said.

He did.

Ted thought at first he was hallucinating, that the gently weaving dot of light at the far end of the corridor must be a reflection off the water . . . except that the stream had dried to a trickle that seeped underground long ago. The rocks beneath his feet were dry, and he had been walking in shadows for so long, with nothing but the frail circle of his own light for company, that it at first did not occur to him that the other light might belong to another human being.

He stopped moving. The other light did not. It dipped and swayed, held steady for a moment, then started moving again . . . away from him.

"Laura?" he said hesitantly. "Sheriff?"

The owner of the light did not appear to hear.

He called, more loudly, "Hello! Who's there?"

The light stopped, and spun around.

The voice that answered did not sound like Laura's, or the sheriff's. "Stop right there, you son of a bitch, or I'll blow you to pieces where you stand!"

"Wait a minute! Who are you?" Ted took two running steps forward, and went sprawling.

Pain jarred through his body and the flashlight rolled from his splayed fingers. A splintered rib gouged his right lung and he clutched his chest, writhing in pain, struggling for breath.

His head cleared slowly and he got to his knees,

inching forward for the flashlight. "Don't—go away!" He tried to shout, but didn't have enough breath. "Wait . . ."

He got the flashlight, and the beam caught something on the floor. He stared at it, disbelieving.

It was a bundle of dynamite.

"What the hell . . ." He stood up, and the stabbing in his lungs eased somewhat. He swung the flashlight forward, seeking out the other beam. "What are you doing?" he shouted. "Are you crazy? There are people in here!"

"Don't try to stop me! I got matches!"

The flashlight arced then, as though its owner had shifted its position, and illuminated a face clearly. It was Minnie Sykes.

Ted started moving toward her.

"Stop where you are, by God! I'll throw it, I swear I will!"

At first he didn't understand what the small red flare signified, and then he didn't believe it. She had a stick of dynamite in her hand, and she had lit the fuse.

He drew a breath to shout something to her; he never knew what he might have said. He was certain, until the last possible second he was certain, she did not intend to throw it. But something went wrong, something in the unpredictable mix of volatile chemicals she had not counted on. One second she was standing there like an avenging angel, silhouetted in the faint orange glow of the fuse; the next instant there was a flash, an explosion, and Minnie Sykes was consumed in a roar of flame.

He screamed, "Noooo!" but his voice was lost in thunder. The walls of the cave creaked and shuddered, reverberating with the explosion. A huge chunk of rock freed itself and tumbled to the floor before him. And through the waves of dust he saw something else: a small spark traveling at an incredible rate along the cave floor.

She had ignited the other fuse.

Ted swung around, stumbling back the way he had come. The beam of his flashlight bobbed off the floor of the cave, bounced off the walls, and he couldn't see it. He couldn't find the bundle of dynamite, he couldn't stop the spark. He had passed it. He swung around, frantically retracing his steps. He saw it. He flung himself to the floor and grabbed the fuse, jerking it free of its detonation point. He sank back against the wall.

And a billowing explosion threw him forward.

He thought he was dead. He stared dumbly at the bundle of explosives still clenched in his hand and he thought, *This is what it feels like.* . . . But then he heard the rocks crack overhead, his face was stung by the pelting of a thousand needlelike pebbles, and he suddenly understood. Sequential charges. The old woman had outsmarted him, had outsmarted them all in the end. Not one fuse, but a network of them, all connected to interlocking fuses. Not one explosion, but several, perhaps dozens, winding through the caves, each one bringing down more rock, closing up more avenues.

He didn't know what else to do. He turned and ran, deeper into the cavern.

And the second explosion hit.

"Laura, look!" Shielding his face with his forearm from the incessant shower of grit and stones, Sam turned his flashlight toward the left. Even through the fine fog of dust there seemed to be a faint difference in the quality of the dark; it was grainier, less cohesive. "It might be a way out."

Laura coughed, wiping her watering eyes with her sleeve. "I can't—leave Christy. She'll be buried alive!"

In that brief instant she knew what he was thinking, for it was what she was thinking: She might already be. But Sam's fingers clamped down hard on her arm and he replied, "We're not going to leave her. But remember this way back."

The icy fingers of panic clawed at her stomach again. "You remember it. You'll get us out."

She started to turn away, but he grabbed both her arms and made her look at him. The lines of pain on his face were so deep they looked like scars, streaked with mud and perspiration. His eyes were dull and there was no color left in his lips. He seemed to be breathing very shallowly. "Laura, listen. I might not make it back."

"No!" She tried to twist away, but he held firm.

"Stop it! Just listen." He tried to take a deep breath. "If I pass out, or . . . you've got to leave me behind. Don't waste any time. The way this place is breaking up—"

Almost as though his words had conjured it, another explosion rocked the chamber. Laura cried out as something struck her shoulder, and Sam jerked her forward, pressing her flat against the wall.

"Mommy, mommy, the sky is falling! Help me!"

"Christy!" Laura cried. "I heard her!"

Sam stared at her. For a moment he didn't seem to be able to speak. Then he whispered, "So did I."

He grabbed her arm, pushing her forward. "Hurry!"

Logic. Intelligence. The ability to reason. Man above the beast. Even in the icy throes of panic, even as his body failed him and the world shattered into bits of dust and debris around him, Ted made himself think. Minnie Sykes had planned on escaping. The heaviest charges would have been set deep within the cavern. He had to turn back the way he had come. He had to go back toward the place he had first seen her, for she had been on her way out.

The destruction was enormous and still increasing as he turned to retrace his steps. There were places where his flashlight beam wouldn't penetrate the dust for more than a few inches, and every cough sent a slice of white-hot agony through his chest. He plunged headlong into boulders that had not been there before, and had to press himself flat against the wall in several places to inch by blockages. He came to a place where the rubble was piled taller than his head; it was almost a complete cave-in. He didn't think he could scale that pile, not in his condition, and for a moment he leaned against the wall, clutching at the pain in his chest and gasping for breath. But he didn't have a choice. *Better,* he thought, *to die trying.* It sounded like something the sheriff would say.

The rock pile was unsteady and offered few handholds. Twice he slipped all the way to the bottom and had to start over again. As he neared the top he had to crawl on his belly, pushing the broken rib deep into soft tissues. His lip was bleeding from the force of biting into it. With an enormous effort he pushed himself over the top and slid down the other side amidst a battering of rocks and broken clods of earth.

The force of the landing was hard, and it took a moment for his head to clear. He got stiffly to his feet, and as he did he thought he saw something—he was *sure* he saw something—coming from the left. It was a flash of light, just beyond the curve of the corridor. A flashlight.

And at the same time he heard something.

It was deep and horrible, a half growl, half moan. It was the sound of an animal in pain, very close, alive. Ted felt ice grip the pit of his stomach, slide up his spine, prickle his scalp, while visions lurked in the shadows just out of reach. Monsters in the dark. A nameless little girl, dying in the street. Craig's face. *Run. Move away. Don't look.*

There was safety just ahead. The flash of a light, other human beings. If he lingered they would be gone.

God, don't make me look.

Slowly he turned around, directing the beam of his flashlight toward the sound.

It was lying on its side, its huge body pinned to the ground by a boulder that had crushed its legs and most of its torso. A dark pool of blood glistened in Ted's light, and as he watched one enormous hand stretched and flexed, grasping at air.

Ted took a horrified step backwards, and stopped. He looked over his shoulder, toward the direction in which he had seen the flashlight. And he looked back at the beast. He could hear the hiss of its breath, that low wet sound of agony.

He moved toward it.

He dropped to his knees beside it, and let the flashlight slip from his fingers. He knew it was hopeless, he knew it was futile, but he grasped the edge of the boulder and tried to shift its weight. His arms shook with strain and bright spots danced before his eyes, but it wouldn't budge. He gave up, gasping.

308

Hesitantly, he moved forward, closer to the creature. He touched its soft, supple skin. It was warm, just like his. And then the creature turned its head.

Ted looked into the face of the man, and watched him die.

The voice was getting closer, and it wasn't just in Laura's head. A child sobbing, shrieking with fear, calling out.

"Mommy, Mommy! Where are you? Come now, Mommy! Come *now!*"

"I'm coming, baby, I am! Just hold on, Christy!"

"Over here!" Sam turned her sharply to the right. "It sounds like it's coming from over here!"

The earth rumbled again and a rock struck Laura's upswung arm, sending a burst of pain all the way to her shoulder. She kept moving. She almost stumbled into the cavity in the floor; Sam pulled her back.

It was a ragged chimney leading to a lower chamber, much like the one through which they had first entered the caverns. "It's coming from down there!" she cried. "I hear her!"

She got down on her stomach and leaned into the hole, shining her flashlight down. "Christy!"

"Mommy! Mommy, please, I'm scared!"

"It's okay, baby, I'm coming!"

She swung around. "She's down there—I can't see her but her voice is close. It's not very deep—six or seven feet."

Sam's face was grim, his voice sober. "Laura, I can't make that jump. Even with the rope, I doubt I could get back up."

Laura swallowed hard, and nodded.

"Here, take this flashlight. It clips on to your belt."

She did as she was told, then sat on the edge of the opening, swinging her feet over. He caught her hand.

"Laura, before you go. I wanted to tell you. . . ."

She turned to him. The pain and uncertainty on his face were more than physical. She leaned forward, cupping her hand behind his neck, and kissed his lips. "I know," she said huskily. "And I'm not leaving you behind."

Then she turned, caught the opposite end of the ledge, and lowered herself down into the darkness. When her body was fully extended she flexed her knees to absorb the impact, and let go.

She was standing on a ledge that was about four feet wide. Dividing it from the opposite ledge was a three-foot chasm; she could have crossed it easily. But the diffused beam of her flashlight showed that the other ledge was very narrow, and most of it was taken up by a huge white creature. It was holding Christy in its arms.

Laura's heart seemed to stop, and at the same time burst. The tears that she had been fighting back for so long suddenly washed her eyes in an acid flood, clogging up her throat, stopping her breathing. Terror. Hopelessness. Relief. Her baby, alive. And held captive by that thing.

But not a thing. A woman. A woman with pale, sun-starved skin and a large, malformed head to which a few thin strands of hair clung. A woman, naked and afraid, holding a child in the dark. A woman who had never been anything else.

She had wedged herself into a slight hollow in the wall as protection against the sporadic showers of stones caused by the rumbling of the earth. Her head was lowered and she held Christy with both arms, like a mother would cradle a child. There was a big, ugly wound on her shoulder. A bullet wound.

Laura moved toward the edge. She extended a shaking arm toward her daughter. Somehow she made her voice work. "Christy," she said unsteadily. "I'm here. Mommy's here."

Christy twisted around. Her face, her beautiful little face, streaked with mud and tears, and those frightened eyes . . . There was a dark bruise on her forehead and a patch of her hair was dark with blood. But she was alive. And so close. An agony of joy and helplessness exploded inside Laura.

"Mommy!" Christy cried, and reached for her. "Mommy!"

The female raised her head and bared her teeth at Laura in a low, fierce growl.

"Christy, no!" Laura stepped quickly away from the edge. "Don't move, honey, don't fall! Don't—don't make her angry!"

There was another explosion, a deep reverberation, and loose rocks began to splatter from overhead. And what Laura saw then was incredible. The woman let out a roar and sank deeper into the hollow, pressing Christy's head against her breast. Protecting her, shielding the child with her own body, taking the pelting of rocks that would have struck Christy. Just like Laura would have done.

Laura's hand went slowly to her lips. She could feel the short, stifled puffs of her breath. She thought, *My God . . . my dear God . . .*

Laura moved toward the edge again, stretching out both arms. "Christy," she said softly. Her voice was thick with tears, almost indecipherable. "Carefully. Try, honey. See if you can reach my hands."

Christy wriggled around, but the female caught her

311

close, pressing her against her breast. Christy started to cry.

"Please!" Laura cried. "She's my child! Please give her to me!"

The female raised her head. Laura looked into those small deep-set eyes and she did not flinch away. She saw fear there, and confusion, and a trapped desperation. And determination. The ferocity to protect her own.

She stood up, cradling Christy tightly in her arms. Carefully she started to edge away, further down the ledge.

"No!" Laura gasped. She swung forward, reaching for her. "No, please! She's my baby!"

Laura followed the steps of the other woman as she moved slowly away, but the fissure between the ledges had begun to widen. Soon she would not be able to reach Christy at all. She could hear Christy's smothered whimpers and hot tears sting her own face. "Please." Desperately she stretched out her arms. "Please . . ."

Suddenly there was a cracking sound and the ledge on which the woman was standing shifted and abruptly dropped three inches. Only an incredible sense of balance kept her from tumbling into the abyss.

Laura screamed. Christy twisted around, flinging out her arm, sobbing. "Mommy!"

"Please!" Laura cried. "Give her to me! Now!"

The ledge fell another inch, scattering up puffs of dust. The woman looked around wildly. Another moment and they both would fall, swallowed up by the darkness. There was another rending, cracking sound.

"Please!" Laura screamed hoarsely. She stretched forward as far as she could, opening her arms.

Far away another earth rumble. A shower of pebbles. The ledge shifted. The female hesitated, then bent forward, Christy held in her outstretched arms.

Laura's hands brushed those of the other woman, and then grasped Christy. She swung Christy over the gap and fell back against the wall, hugging her, sobbing, drinking in the smell of her, the warmth, the small arms locked around her neck. "Christy! Oh, my baby, oh, my darling . . ."

With a howl of the purest sorrow Laura had ever heard, the female turned and ran away. She had only gone a few steps before there was another tremendous cracking sound, and she fell into the blackness below.

Laura buried her face in Christy's hair, and wept.

"Okay, honey, give me your hands. Stretch up as far as you can."

Sam leaned over the chimney until he felt his hands close around two small wrists, and the emotion that went through him was so intense it left him weak. He had to close his eyes for a moment, and take a deep breath, before he could speak.

"Okay," he called to Laura. "I've got her."

There was a sound behind him. He could have imagined it; it could have been the dropping of another rock as the earth shifted. He started to turn his head, but then he stopped, seized by a premonitory awareness, a swift horrible certainty; suddenly he *knew* that if he looked around he would never see Christy again, that there were moments, only seconds, to get her to safety. His heart thundered in his chest, and he gripped her wrists and started to haul her upwards, and then he caught the movement out of the corner of his eye. It was more than a movement: a scuffle, a rush of breath, the dull scrape of feet on rock, and the smell. . . .

"Laura!" he shouted, and released Christy's wrists.

He rolled over, flinging out his arm for his shotgun, and it burst into sight less than ten feet in front of him, a reflection out of a nightmare: massive, bone-white, and charging straight for him.

Distantly he heard Laura's scream. His mouth was dry and his muscles were frozen. His flashlight was on the ground and all he could see was what his night vision told him, what his senses shouted at him. His hand closed on the barrel of the shotgun and he swung it forward, but he couldn't get his balance; shards of red-white fire exploded through his foot as he tried to maneuver himself into a crouching position. He jammed the stock against his shoulder and his finger found the trigger. He could hear it, he could smell it, and panic was the metallic taste of sweat on his lips as he searched the dark but saw nothing.

Then he got it in his sights, a blur of movement that was not running toward him, after all, but parallel to him, toward the exit. . . .

Someone swung a flashlight beam and pinned the killer directly in the light. There was an instant when the running form paused, startled by the light, and swung around. Sam had a clear shot. And then it looked at him. The expression on the flat, malformed face was confused and terrified and . . . human.

"No!" Ted lunged at Sam, grabbing the shotgun by the barrel and knocking Sam off balance.

Sam sank back against the wall and the fugitive ran, toward the lighter part of the dark that heralded the exit, toward freedom, toward safety. And Sam watched him go.

314

Sam pulled Christy over the edge and into his arms, hugging her hard. She was shuddering with hiccuping sobs and crying for her mother, and he brushed a kiss across her hair before turning her over to Ted's keeping. "It's okay, honey," he said breathlessly. "Everything's okay now. Here comes your mom."

He leaned over again, stretching further out, to reach Laura's hand. Until he saw her, until he actually got his hands beneath her arms and pulled her over the edge, he didn't dare believe that it was over. Christy flung herself into her mother's arms and Sam embraced both of them, and for a long silent moment they simply held each other. The three of them, together at last. And safe.

Then Sam happened to look at Ted. He was examining Sam's shotgun with a sober expression. When he looked up, Sam wouldn't meet his eyes. It was over. He couldn't think about it anymore. It was over.

Christy wriggled a little bit way, and reached up to wipe her mother's tears. "It wasn't so bad, Mommy," she said. "I wasn't all *that* scared."

Laura laughed, and hugged Christy harder, and Sam smiled. He didn't want to let them go. He didn't want to stop touching them. Sometimes miracles happened. Sometimes there were happy endings.

Laura stretched out her hand and grasped Ted's, smiling. They didn't say anything, just squeezed each other's hands for a moment. Sam stroked Laura's hair, and then Christy's. But another shower of debris from overhead reminded him that it wasn't over yet. "Come on," he said huskily. "Let's see if we can find our way out of here."

Chapter Seventeen

The dawn was gentle and diffuse, smelling of clean clear air and deep forest secrets. A low mist clung to the ground, scattering patches of sunlight across the forest floor. The trees stretched upward, tall and straight, like giant palace guards. The quiet was a rich, deep, palpable thing, and for a long moment the three adults simply stood there, drinking it in.

Ted was still holding Sam's gun. Almost hesitantly, he offered it back to him. "The safety was still on," he said quietly. "But I guess you knew that, didn't you?"

Sam took the shotgun, looking at it without seeming to see it. After a long moment he nodded. His voice was subdued, weary. "Maybe," he said. "That's the only thing that separates the monsters from the good guys. The luxury of making a choice."

Ted's voice sounded heavy. "And is that what we are? The good guys?"

"I don't know." Sam looked back toward the cave. "I guess we all just do what we have to, to survive."

Ted touched a low-hanging, leafy branch, wiping off the dew. He looked off into the distance, where the mist line rose. "Three hundred thousand years ago," he said, "we weren't so different from them. Something—some genetic accident plunged them back down the evolutionary scale. But they were the best hunters in the forest, and they survived."

Then his voice fell, and he added, "Who knows? Maybe they weren't the accident. Maybe we were."

Laura said softly, as though from far away, "We were afraid of them. But they were really more afraid of us, weren't they? Because we're really the best hunters in the forest."

For a long time no one spoke. Christy wrapped her arms around her mother's leg and leaned her head against her thigh.

Ted had told them about Minnie Sykes. Laura kept turning it over and over in her head, pieces of the puzzle that wouldn't quite fit. "Minnie Sykes must have known about the Cobbs," she said. "Her parents were probably there when it happened. But she kept telling all those stories. . . ."

And then she remembered. *The earliest mention of the creature comes from the journal of Lever Foulks . . . in 1640.*

She looked at Ted slowly. "Stories," she said, "that started a long time before the Cobbs came here, or ever had any children."

Ted's face remained unmoved.

Sam looked at him, a curious frown drawing at his brows. "That recessive gene you keep talking about, it had to come from somewhere."

"And," Laura said unsteadily, "if it kept recurring, generation after generation, it wasn't really recessive was it?"

Ted met their eyes evenly, and his voice was calm. "It's over now. They're gone."

For a moment they were silent. It was over, best

317

forgotten. Best not to question too closely what you don't understand . . .

And then Sam said quietly, "All but one."

Laura looked back at the cave, the gaping dark hole that led to nowhere. An empty graveyard now. The earth would keep its secrets for another millennium.

Then Christy said in a small voice. "More than one, Mommy. Not here, but other places. Lots of them."

A shiver caught the back of Laura's neck, and her hand tightened on Christy's shoulder. Her eyes met those of the two men.

No one asked how Christy knew that. No one wanted to know.

The heavy beating sound of helicopter blades broke the silence. It was such an alien, inappropriate sound in this pristine place that each of them started, and looked skyward as though, for a moment, they couldn't identify what the sound might signify.

Then Christy tugged at her mother's jeans. "I'm tired," she said. "Can we go home now?"

Laura bent down and lifted Christy to her hip, smiling, holding her tightly for a moment. "Yes," she said softly. "Home. That's just where we're going."

Sam lifted a hand and touched Laura's hair lightly, then let it drop. "Home," he repeated, and tried to keep his tone expressionless. "Back to Philadelphia?"

She looked at him for a moment, then moved her eyes back over the forest, through the mist, down the slope of the hill. Morning had never been so sweet, and the forest was just a forest. They were still out there, the monsters that weren't monsters at all, the things that had the power to kill and maim and terrorize in the dark. Perhaps they always would be.

318

She looked at Sam. "No," she answered. "I like it here. This is my place now. This is where I'm staying."

He smiled, and rested his hand on her shoulder. Together, they moved down the mountain.

ED MCBAIN'S MYSTERIES

JACK AND THE BEANSTALK   (17-083, $3.95)
Jack's dead, stabbed fourteen times. And thirty-six thousand's missing in cash. Matthew's questions are turning up some long-buried pasts, a second dead body, and some beautiful suspects. Like Sunny, Jack's sister, a surfer boy's fantasy, a delicious girl with some unsavory secrets.

BEAUTY AND THE BEAST   (17-134, $3.95)
She was spectacular—an unforgettable beauty with exquisite features. On Monday, the same woman appeared in Hope's law office to file a complaint. She had been badly beaten—a mass of purple bruises with one eye swollen completely shut. And she wanted her husband put away before something worse happened. Her body was discovered on Tuesday, bound with wire coat hangers and burned to a crisp. But her husband—big, and monstrously ugly—denies the charge.